A-HUNTIN

His own addiction was ma
him not
found g
became

He i
experie
despite
he hadn
him the

The
to the e
those around him, confident that they could no more stop
him than arrest the sunrise, he indulged himself at will. If
that was arrogance, so be it.

Who was there to challenge him?

Titles by Lyle Brandt

THE GUN
JUSTICE GUN
VENGEANCE GUN
REBEL GUN
BOUNTY GUN

THE LAWMAN
SALDE'S LAW
HELLTOWN
MASSACRE TRAIL
HANGING JUDGE
MANHUNT
AVENGING ANGELS
BLOOD TRAILS

BLOOD TRAILS

— THE LAWMAN —

LYLE BRANDT

BERKLEY BOOKS, NEW YORK

THE BERKLEY PUBLISHING GROUP
Published by the Penguin Group
Penguin Group (USA) Inc.
375 Hudson Street, New York, New York 10014, USA
Penguin Group (Canada), 90 Eglinton Avenue East, Suite 700, Toronto, Ontario M4P 2Y3, Canada
(a division of Pearson Penguin Canada Inc.)
Penguin Books Ltd., 80 Strand, London WC2R 0RL, England
Penguin Group Ireland, 25 St. Stephen's Green, Dublin 2, Ireland (a division of Penguin Books Ltd.)
Penguin Group (Australia), 250 Camberwell Road, Camberwell, Victoria 3124, Australia
(a division of Pearson Australia Group Pty. Ltd.)
Penguin Books India Pvt. Ltd., 11 Community Centre, Panchsheel Park, New Delhi—110 017, India
Penguin Group (NZ), 67 Apollo Drive, Rosedale, Auckland 0632, New Zealand
(a division of Pearson New Zealand Ltd.)
Penguin Books (South Africa) (Pty.) Ltd., 24 Sturdee Avenue, Rosebank, Johannesburg 2196,
South Africa

Penguin Books Ltd., Registered Offices: 80 Strand, London WC2R 0RL, England

This is a work of fiction. Names, characters, places, and incidents either are the product of the author's imagination or are used fictitiously, and any resemblance to actual persons, living or dead, business establishments, events, or locales is entirely coincidental. The publisher does not have any control over and does not assume any responsibility for author or third-party websites or their content.

BLOOD TRAILS

A Berkley Book / published by arrangement with the author

PRINTING HISTORY
Berkley edition / August 2011

Copyright © 2011 by Mike Newton.
Cover illustration by Bruce Emmett.
Cover design by Steve Ferlauto.

ISBN: 978-0-425-24265-0

BERKLEY®
Berkley Books are published by The Berkley Publishing Group,
a division of Penguin Group (USA) Inc.,
375 Hudson Street, New York, New York 10014.
BERKLEY® is a registered trademark of Penguin Group (USA) Inc.
The "B" design is a trademark of Penguin Group (USA) Inc.

PRINTED IN THE UNITED STATES OF AMERICA

10 9 8 7 6 5 4 3 2 1

For Jared Maddox

Liz Stoudenmire was drunk. Not an unusual condition, given that she worked and lived in a saloon, especially considering the kind of work that was her specialty. She was an entertainer in the broadest sense, paid—and poorly—to amuse the patrons of her employer's establishment.

Liz sang a little, danced with an approximation of finesse, could tell a joke, and laughed at anything a paying customer might say. When she and any given customer retired upstairs, another set of skills came into play.

Some might describe Liz as a soiled dove.

Mostly, people knew her as a whore.

It hadn't always been that way, of course. No one she'd ever met was born to whoring, though the daughters of a brothel madam Liz had known in Little Rock came close, their sorry futures planned out in advance. In Liz's case, like most, it was a downward spiral ending in a two-bit crib where anyone could rent her time, her body, and her feigned enthusiasm.

It was safe to say that Liz's parents wouldn't recognize her, if their paths should cross by chance. Not that the Reverend Denver Anniston would ever set foot in a joint where liquor, sex, and gambling were the stock in trade. He might stand on the street outside, railing from scripture while his rigid, straitlaced wife sang hymns beside him to the passersby, but those inside the den of Satan had surrendered their humanity. They were as bits of dead wood, gathered for the fire.

And Liz's former husband damn sure wouldn't recognize her, if he was alive today. He'd been a good man, not as rigid as her father, but with strict ideas about a woman's place in Nature and the home. After her childhood, Liz had found him almost liberal, had followed him with something close to pleasure from St. Louis westward, into Kansas and a golden new tomorrow.

How could she have known their spread would be a blighted patch of rocks and clay, misrepresented by the agent who'd relieved them of their money prior to vanishing for parts unknown? How could she know that stubborn Howard Stoudenmire would try to make a go of it, regardless? That the grueling work would rupture something in his brain and leave her widowed and all alone?

The rest of it was something from a third-rate farce. Liz saw the humor in it now, when she was drinking, though she'd missed its funny side when it was happening. There'd been a man, of course, who'd offered shelter in return for certain favors. She'd been shocked at first, but fear and hunger had a way of undermining principles. Her hints at marriage were ignored, then answered with abuse.

She'd fled that bastard's home with looks intact but nothing much remaining of her reputation. No one wanted her behind the counter of a shop, much less watching their children. Even scrubbing floors was out, unless she gave the master of the house a little extra polish on the side, when wifey and the children weren't around. Liz finally decided that if whoring was her lot in life—and so it seemed to be— she might as well go on and make the most of it.

Which wasn't much, as it turned out.

Liquor definitely helped.

But sometimes it could get her into trouble.

Laughing at the earnest, sweating cowboy wasn't the best move she'd made all day. Of course, she hadn't *planned* it. Truth be told, Liz didn't spend much effort planning anything. She let life take her where it would, safe in the knowledge that it wouldn't draw her far from the saloon.

But, honestly! How could she *not* laugh at his huffing, puffing, gimme-just-another-minute style of screwing, with his face all twisted up like he was sitting on a cactus. And his tiny tool . . . well, it was just too much.

Liz felt the laughter welling out of her and tried to swallow it, knowing he wouldn't take it well, but she was three sheets to the wind and didn't give a damn.

At first, when she was only chuckling to herself, he didn't notice. Then, a chafing minute later, his dull eyes popped open, focused on her face, and he demanded, "What'n hell's so funny?"

"Nothin', lover," Liz assured him. "Gimme ever'thing you've got!"

And naturally, that set her off again. No hiding it this time, and no excuses would suffice. He slapped her with an open hand, and had a clenched fist ready for the follow-up, when Liz exploded from the mattress, cursing him into the middle of next week and clawing at his eyes.

Mills Vandiver was working on his third beer when the ruckus started. Noise was what he normally expected from the Klondike or from any other good saloon: laughter, good-natured arguments—some with heat behind them—jangling music from a slightly out-of-tune piano played by someone with more stamina than skill.

But when the racket started overhead, he knew it wasn't right. And damn it, beer or no, it was his job to intervene.

Vandiver was a lawman by default. He'd been a mediocre cattleman, until the foot-and-mouth disease killed off his herd and took his meager savings with it. That was in McLennan County, Texas, and he'd looked around for some job that would feed him without any kind of capital investment. Being fairly large and handy with his fists, he'd wound up as a bouncer at the Paradise Saloon in Waco before getting hired on as a marshal's deputy.

There'd been unpleasantness in Waco, later on an accusation, never proven, that Vandiver used his badge to line his pockets and procure favors from working girls. It had been time for him to go, and after sundry misadventures he'd washed up in Jubilee, a growing Oklahoma town in need of someone who'd enforce the law without making a mess of things.

Which meant he had to keep the louder drunks in line, prevent or punish damage to the property of decent folk, and generally keep them safe without stepping on any tender toes. The job seemed perfect when he took it, but of late, Vandiver thought he might be overmatched.

And now this.

The best part of his job, Vandiver thought, was being forced to hang around saloons, where nearly all of the disturbances in town occurred. He drifted back and forth between the Klondike and its rival, the American, taking his time with beer and conversation, soothing ruffled feelings when he had to. Keeping everybody settled.

Three years, and he'd only fired his pistol at a mad dog that had wandered in from nowhere, last July, snapping and frothing at the mouth along Main Street. One shot had done the job, and Vandiver had been a hero for about an hour and a half.

They had a different kind of mad dog now in Jubilee, but running him to ground had proved impossible, so far. Vandiver knew that if he couldn't solve the problem soon, his easy life would be in jeopardy.

But while he worked on that, thinking it through and washing down the bitter taste of failure with his beer, he had a screaming whore to deal with, not to mention her raging customer.

Vandiver took the stairs two at a time. Al Loving met him on the second-story landing, looking just perturbed enough to make him seem civilized.

"Glad you're here," he said, as Vandiver swept past him, toward the third door on the balcony above the barroom.

And he didn't bother knocking but barged in on them without warning, shouting, "What the hell is going on in here?"

He recognized the girl, of course. Long Liz, they called her, for her legs. The cowboy looked familiar, too, behind the rage and bloody furrows on his cheeks.

Before he had a chance to land his punch, Vandiver grabbed the cowboy's arm and hauled him backward off the sagging bed. No dignity about it, everybody naked but the constable, and Long Liz bleeding from the nose where she'd already felt the sting of knuckles.

She was coming back for more, cursing a blue streak, when Vandiver straight-armed her between her breasts and slammed her back against the wall, then turned his full attention to the cowboy, dragging him well back in the direction of the doorway, standing over him ready with the Colt, to brain him with it if he couldn't manage to control himself.

Vandiver wasn't getting busted up for any row between a hooker and a randy cowpoke, not when he had so many other problems on his plate.

"Goddamn it, settle down, the two of you!" he snapped. "The first one swings on me is gonna spend the weekend in the calaboose."

The cowboy—Chris Something, Vandiver thought—spat back at him, "I'll teach that bitch to laugh at me!"

"How 'bout I drag your ass downstairs and let 'em all laugh," Vandiver suggested. "How's that suit you?"

Sullen silence. Vandiver faced Long Liz, asking her, "Has he paid you, yet?"

"Not for my nose," she hissed.

"Another dollar," said Vandiver.

"For a nosebleed?" asked the cowboy, squirming at his feet.

"Another dollar, or walk to jail dressed like you are."

"Well, shit! It's in my pants."

"Next time," Vandiver said, "you oughta keep it there."

The huntsman stood in darkness, hidden in the alleyway between two buildings, sweeping Main Street with his eyes. The shops were closed, of course. There was nowhere for anyone to go in Jubilee at this time of night—make that morning—except to one of the saloons. And even they were winding down, the brash piano music stammering, the forced hilarity of drunkards starting to unravel.

Soon the most determined drinkers would go lurching off toward bed, wherever that might be. Those who'd come into town from some outlying ranch or farm might trust their horses to deliver them back home. Failing that, they might sleep at the livery and turn up late tomorrow, offering a Sunday prayer for leniency from their employers.

It amused the huntsman to observe such human frailty. He had sampled many versions of debauchery before discovering the one that suited him and, having settled on it, now eschewed any activity that jeopardized his self-control. The pleasure to be found in alcohol and opium was fleeting, with a list of penalties attached. The headaches, nausea, blurred vision, all the rest of it, sapped energy and muddled thinking.

They could put his life at risk.

His own addiction was magnificent, exhilarating, and it cost him nothing. Each time he indulged himself, the huntsman found greater enjoyment in the act. Each time, the memories became more vivid and seductive.

He imagined that his senses were enhanced by every new experience. Tonight, the smell of blood enchanted him, despite his distance from the open second-story window. If he hadn't known who occupied that room, what waited for him there, the huntsman fancied that he could have guessed.

The game excited him on many levels, from the visceral to the exalted intellectual. Convinced of his superiority to those around him, confident that they could no more stop him than arrest the sunrise, he indulged himself at will. If that was arrogance, so be it.

Who was there to challenge him?

The huntsman drew his knife, a skinner with a five-inch blade, and teased his thumb along the razor edge before resheathing it. He walked back to the fire escape and stared up at the window twenty feet above his head.

So near and yet so far.

His prey might be asleep, but could he count on that? If she was still awake, he knew there was a good chance she might scream, perhaps even defend herself. Some slatterns carried knives or razors for protection from their rougher clients, and he'd known one who preferred a derringer. It hadn't saved her, in the end, but each time was a new experience, pregnant with possibilities.

What did it matter, in the last analysis?

The huntsman, in his darkest heart, believed he was invincible. No woman could resist him. No man hunter's eye could penetrate his simple yet brilliant disguise.

How long had they been trying now to stop him? All in vain. He was a ghost, a whisper in the darkness, there and gone. A nightmare haunting those who'd hunted him and gone home empty-handed.

Tired of waiting, he began to climb the fire escape, testing each step in case it creaked beneath his weight. A slow, steady ascent. Anticipation surging through his bloodstream like a drug.

He thought, *I'm coming, dearest. Almost there.*

Jimmy Yung came to work at the Klondike after the round-eyes went home or else upstairs to bed. By then, the whole place smelled of sweat and alcohol, tobacco smoke and desperation. On the second floor, it also smelled of sex—a scent that made the cleaner nervous.

Jimmy knew the girls who lived at the Klondike were *chāngjì*—whores—but even round-eyed girls who sold themselves were off-limits to him. There was a line he could not cross and hope to still live in Jubilee.

Or live at all.

His name was not Jimmy, of course. He'd been born Yung Chang-li—Chinese surnames preceded a child's given name—in the teeming anthill of Shanghai, in the Year of the Dog. His father was a craftsman, skilled in metal work, who scrimped and saved despite the taxes levied by the Empress Dowager Cixi and continual extortion by the Triad gangs to guarantee "protection" of his modest shop. Six months after Chang-li's birth, in April 1875, the family had sailed from China to a new world far away.

They wound up in Seattle, Washington, where craftsmanship took second place to brute survival. Chang-li's parents worked alternating twelve-hour shifts in a laundry that looked, smelled, and sounded like Hell in a medieval painting. When not at work, they cared for little Chang-li's needs and stayed among their own, already sure that if the fabled streets of gold existed in America, they did not run through Chinatown.

Chang-li was seven years old when Congress passed the Chinese Exclusion Act, barring further immigration from China, in May 1882. He was ten when round-eye nativists rioted in Seattle, driving hundreds of Chinese from their homes. The Yungs settled next in Wyoming Territory, where Chang-li's father went to work in a copper mine at Rock Springs. Tension between round-eye miners and Chinese newcomers exploded in September 1885, leaving both of Chang-li's parents among the twenty-eight victims slain by rioters in a savage frenzy.

Chang-li had escaped from Rock Springs with his life and little else. He'd drifted eastward, then veered to the south when cold weather set in. By the time he reached Jubilee in Oklahoma Territory and discovered its insular Chinese community, he was approaching his seventeenth birthday.

A man in all ways but one.

The grim example of his parents and their friends had taught Yung Chang-li that America was white man's country, no matter what the newspapers or Constitution said. He'd seen Chinese—as well as Mexicans and Africans—shot dead or hanged for arguing with whites, competing with them for a miserable job, or even looking at them the wrong way.

Whatever that meant.

In the round-eyed white man's world, *any* look could be wrong. Any word or gesture might be construed as a mortal insult, imposing a blood debt for honor's sake. Meanwhile, as far as Yung Chang-li could tell, the whites were free to cheat, rob, rape, and kill anyone whose skin was darker than theirs or whose eyes were a different shape.

In Tucson, when a round-eye laundry manager with only six teeth in his head could not pronounce Yung's name, he shortened it to "Jimmy." Chang-li did not argue. In a sense, he welcomed it. The separation from his old life made him more American somehow, though he would never truly fit the mold.

So Yung Chang-li had become Jimmy Yung. His former people made him welcome in Jubilee; the round-eyes never would. He had a job in their world, though, cleaning up at the Klondike Saloon after hours. One dollar nightly for a top-to-bottom sweep and taking out the trash.

The best part of his night was cleaning on the second floor. He worked as quietly as possible to keep from bothering the girls or Mr. Loving in his private quarters at the far end of the hall. Each night—or early morning—Jimmy lingered at the doors of different rooms in turn, imagining the supple bodies almost close enough to touch, enthralled by his imagination of the acts performed with strangers in those rooms, for cash.

This morning, dark and early on a Sunday, Jimmy pushed his broom along the balcony that overlooked the barroom, bedroom doors immediately to his left, a railing and a long drop to his right. His broom had smeared the blood before he noticed it.

Blood?

Yes. A small amount had trickled out beneath the door marked with a number 3. Not much compared to some spills that he'd seen around the Klondike. Still . . .

Holding his breath, taking his life in trembling hands, he knocked.

No answer.

He should leave now, write it off to white man's business, but a kind of fever gripped him, made him knock again, more forcefully this time.

Still nothing.

Almost palsied now, he crossed the final line, reached for the doorknob. Finding the door unlocked, he opened it a crack, enough to peer inside.

A lamp was burning, and it showed him everything.

His shriek reverberated through the Klondike as he turned and bolted, shouting, "Mr. Loving! Mr. Loving! You come quick!"

The last thing Mills Vandiver needed in the cold, dark hours prior to sunrise was a Chinaman to wake him, jabbering about big trouble at the Klondike. When he tried to make out what the trouble was, the boy dissolved into a quaking fit and said something about "too much blood alla time."

That made Vandiver's stomach roil with expectations of catastrophe. Too much blood was exactly what they'd had in Jubilee of late. He didn't want to see another drop of it, but something told him that his earnest wish counted for nothing in the scheme of things.

Too much to hope that he'd catch someone in the act, but Vandiver still took the time to buckle on his gunbelt. Just in case. Seemed like the time a lawman needed iron the most was when he didn't have it on his hip.

"You're Jimmy, right?" Vandiver asked, more for something to say than any desire to collect information.

The Chinaman bobbed his head. "Yes, sir. I all the same Jimmy."

"Well, Jimmy, let's go have a look."

"No lookee me," Jimmy replied, shaking his head in an emphatic negative. "I see enough!"

"We all have, boy. But someone has to do the looking, anyhow."

It seemed a long walk to the Klondike, but they got there. Jimmy stayed at the bottom of the stairs and pointed toward the balcony. Al Loving and the other girls were clustered there, around an open door.

Vandiver reached the landing, greeted by the Klondike's lord and master. "Christ," said Loving, "what a mess. I can't believe this bastard's nerve."

"Same as before?" Vandiver asked.

"See for yourself."

The hookers stepped aside as he approached, clearing the way. Vandiver hesitated on the threshold and glanced back toward Al Loving. Loving made a little shooing gesture, urging him along.

Turning to face the room, he registered a stream or trail of blood that stretched between the threshold and the bed. Beyond that, everything was crimson—sheets and blankets, pillows, walls, even some speckles on the ceiling if he could believe his eyes.

Nor was it only blood.

With stomach churning, brain reeling, Vandiver struggled to identify the various components of a human being. Some were obvious, while others—never meant to see the light of day—confounded him. At last, dizzy, he turned away and scanned the other women, matching names to frightened faces.

"That's Long Liz?" he asked, at last.

A couple of them nodded. Others simply wept.

"What are the odds?" Loving inquired.

"You'd know better than me," Vandiver said.

"Seems pretty clear."

"Before you get a rope," Vandiver said, "I need to fetch the mayor."

"He won't thank you for that," said Loving.

"No. I don't expect he will."

Al sent the Chinaman, after confirming that he knew the mayor by sight and could locate his house. Before returning, he was also told to fetch the undertaker, Silas Guidry.

There was work for everyone tonight.

Roland Johansson turned up fifteen minutes later, looking sleepy, flustered, and uneasy at the close proximity of six young women dressed in next to nothing.

"Well?" he said.

"You need to see it," Vandiver informed him.

"Can't you—"

"No."

"All right for God's sake! But I still don't—"

Stepping to the open door, Johansson staggered, caught himself with one hand on the jamb, then lurched away, face ashen.

"It's the same," he gasped.

"No, Mayor," Vandiver said. "It's worse."

2

"I do . . . I *do* . . . I do . . ."

No matter how he rolled the words around inside his mouth, they still felt strange and awkward to Jack Slade. Which was a problem, since they might turn out to be the most important words he'd ever say.

The wedding had been his idea, of course. That's how it worked. He'd popped the question willingly, with no manipulation whatsoever on the other side. Likewise, he had no doubts about being in love. He recognized the feeling—his first time for something more than simple heat—and he exulted in it.

If anyone had asked Slade whether he was having second thoughts, he would've answered in the negative.

Still . . .

Part of what he felt now had to do with his intended. When they'd met, Faith Connover was newly widowed, more or less. Which is to say she'd been engaged to marry, and her fiancé had been murdered. Now the twist: her groom-to-be had been Slade's brother, Jim. More than brothers, however, they'd been identical twins.

Faith later said that the first time she met Jack, she felt as if she'd seen a ghost. It didn't help that Jack was only passing through to find his brother's murderers and put them under ground. Judge Isaac Dennison had managed to convince him that the law should take its course, had even talked Slade into putting on a U.S. marshal's badge, but nothing ever seemed to work out quite as planned.

Jim's killers had abducted Faith, still angling for a land grab. Slade had rescued her from death—or worse—and taken down her kidnappers the hard way, under circumstances that displeased the judge but left him no room to file charges.

Quite the opposite, in fact, as he'd persuaded Jack to keep his badge and try another side of life, beyond the gambling and drifting that had been his style for years on end. It seemed to fit all right, though Slade couldn't imagine how or why. And as he'd grown into the new job, his new life, he'd stayed in touch with Faith.

At first, he was just checking in—or so Slade told himself. In fact, however, he'd already known that Faith was fully competent as both a rancher and a businesswoman who could hold her own against rustlers, Indian raiders, and pushy male neighbors who coveted her *and* her land. Over time, Slade grudgingly acknowledged his attraction to his dead twin's fiancée, and just about the time he got his guilt in check, he realized that Faith liked him, as well.

Which raised more problems than it solved.

First, he didn't know—and couldn't bring himself to ask—if Faith was drawn to him for his own sake or just because he was the mirror-image of his brother. Was she trying to recapture what she'd lost when Jim was killed? Just using him to salvage broken dreams?

Although Slade knew he'd never answer that question with iron-clad certainty, their long and loving acquaintance had convinced him that the best answer was, *probably not.* Faith would never forget his brother—how could she, when she saw Jim's face each time she looked at Jack? But Slade and Faith had built their own storehouse of memories, and they were adding to it every day.

His second problem: some of those memories were very grim indeed.

His job would always be a problem for the two of them. Slade's last time out, a gang of fanatical gunmen had followed him back to Faith's spread and wreaked havoc there, killing some of her hired men and trying to burn down her home. Granted, that wasn't the routine for his man-hunting expeditions, but the threat of violence lingered over every move a lawman made. Slade knew it worried Faith, that she'd be happier if he was riding herd on cattle—or just loitering around the spread—than chasing felons all to hell and gone around the territory.

But would Slade be happier?

He didn't relish killing, didn't like the time away from Faith now that he'd found her, but he'd never truly been a *settled* man. A runaway from home when he was barely in his teens, he'd made his way through life by wit and wile, learning that poker could support him, more or less. It kept him moving, too, since no one liked a winner all the time, and there were always those who'd say his skill came from the bottom of the deck.

Jim's slayers weren't the first men he had killed, but now, to some extent at least, it seemed to Slade that he was in the killing business. Granted, it was legal—all done by the book, under Judge Dennison's watchful and unforgiving eye—but it got old.

And someday, Slade was confident, he'd meet a faster gun.

He had to look beyond himself, now. Had to think about how Faith would feel, the day some shooter left him face-down on a dusty street or laid out on the prairie, with coyotes fighting one another for his bones. It wasn't just his life—or wouldn't be, after he took the vows.

"I do . . . *I* do . . . I *do* . . ."

Slade paced his small hotel room, feeling foolish. It was just two words, for heaven's sake.

But they would change his life, and Faith's. Change everything.

Until those words were spoken, either one of them could call it quits for any reason—or, hell, for no reason at all. Slade knew he'd never tire of Faith, but if she tired of him, his job, his moods, she simply had to aim him toward the door. He'd hit the highway, and regardless of the pain it caused him, there would be no looking back.

If they were married, though, it all got tangled up in law, the Bible, and society's demands. Slade wasn't sure if he could fit into the "husband" mold and pass inspection from the people who'd be judging him.

Alone, he wouldn't give a damn.

With Faith, he had to care.

For her sake, he could try. For Faith . . .

"I do . . . I—"

Sudden rapping on his door distracted Slade. He answered it without his Colt, a luxury he only had at home in Enid or on nights he spent with Faith.

Noah Pratt stood on the threshold, looking spiffy in his three-piece suit and bow tie. "Judge is asking for you, Marshal Slade," he said.

Pratt was Judge Dennison's new clerk. His predecessor had been murdered in the courthouse by a stalker who was gunning for the judge. The shooter's friends had nearly finished Dennison, as well, but they were all gone now.

Another day, another bloodbath.

Maybe ranching wouldn't be so bad, at that.

"I'll be along in just a minute," he told Pratt.

"Yes, sir." Still, Pratt lingered. Said, "You know, it's more in what you feel than how you say it. The I-dos."

"I'll keep that in mind," Slade replied, closing the door on Noah's helpful smile.

And now, he felt a perfect fool. Who else had listened to him as they passed along the hall outside his door?

Forget it, Slade chided himself.

Judge Dennison was waiting for him, maybe with congratulations or a small gift for the wedding. Maybe . . .

Only one way to find out.

Slade cinched his gunbelt snug around his hips, put on his hat, and left the room behind.

For a time, after the shooting that had nearly claimed his life, Judge Dennison had moved his chambers to the ground floor of the federal courthouse in Enid, Oklahoma. Being hip-shot, he'd had trouble climbing stairs. Today, he managed nicely with a silver-headed cane and hardly any limp at all. His rooms were now back on the second floor.

Slade found him there and knocked, although the office door was standing open. Dennison turned from his window overlooking a courtyard and gallows built to accommodate six men at once, facing Slade with a frown.

"Come in, Jack. We'll want the door closed."

Slade did as he'd been asked, no apprehension yet, as he watched Dennison circle his desk and sit. He waited for the judge's nod, then pulled one of the extra chairs across to plant himself before the desk.

A silent moment stretched between them, then the judge said, "I'm afraid I have bad news."

"What's that, sir?"

"I know that you're supposed to tie the knot on Saturday."

"Yes, sir."

"Which is the day after tomorrow . . ."

"Right."

"But I'm afraid you'll have to ask the lovely Faith for a continuance, on my behalf."

"Why's that, sir?"

"Something's happened—I should say that it's *been* happening—which now demands attention, urgently. We weren't informed in a timely fashion, and I'll be investigating that myself, but in the meantime . . ."

"Sir, one of the other deputies—"

"If there was anybody else available, I'd send them, Jack. Believe it. Eddie Hanrahan is out in Durham, looking for that girl who's disappeared. He thinks some renegade Cheyenne may be behind it. Ben Murphy's in Eldorado, helping with the cleanup there. I know you heard about Jeff Graham."

While the other deputies were tracking badmen, Jeff had stopped to use a privy in Camargo, without noticing a fat black widow spider underneath the seat. Their sawbones reckoned he would live, but with the pain and swelling from the venom he could barely walk, much less saddle a horse and ride.

Slade nodded, saying, "Judge, if there's a way this job could wait till Sunday, maybe even Monday . . ."

"Sorry, no," said Dennison. "You'll understand when I've explained it." Without waiting for an answer, he pressed on. "I guess you've never been to Jubilee?"

"Not yet," Slade said.

"It's in the panhandle, up near the Kansas border. Founded back in '86 or thereabouts, and growing fast. They hope to have a railhead, sometime in the next few years, and turn the town into a shipping point for live-stock. As it is, they're working on an image, trying to attract more business and more settlers."

Silently, Slade waited for the part that meant his wedding had to be put off.

"About five weeks ago, they tell me now, somebody killed one of the town's saloon girls. Cut her up like nothing anyone in Jubilee had ever seen. They blamed it on a drifter, ran a posse up and down the countryside, and came back empty-handed. It's an easy thing to blame the victim, say she brought it on herself somehow. The life she led, the men she lay with for a dollar. These things happen."

"Even if they shouldn't," Slade replied.

"So, two weeks pass, and there's a second murder. Same thing, but a little worse, if there's a scale for judging such atrocities."

"Another working girl?" asked Slade.

"Correct. The first one had been left beside the livery. With number two, her killer operated in an alley next door to the church."

"When you say 'operated' . . ."

"I'm informed that he—or they—removed some of the lady's vital organs. Most were found beside the body."

"Most?"

"Not all."

"Sounds like some kind of lunatic," Slade said.

"Barring an actual connection to the moon—which wasn't full on either night, as I've discovered from my *Farmers' Almanac*—I'd say you're absolutely right. Whoever did it must be crazy as a bedbug, though it may not show in his daily life."

Slade waited for the rest of it, thinking, *There must be more.* After another moment, Dennison continued.

"Three days back," he said, "there was a third murder. The worst so far. This time the victim was killed in her room, at one of the town's two saloons. From what I hear, the butcher took his time. It must have been . . . appalling."

"Sir, who'd you hear this from?" asked Slade.

"A messenger arrived from Jubilee last night. Belatedly, he brought a letter from their mayor, describing the events. I'm sending back an order for the mayor to present himself in Enid and explain the long delay, as soon as this business is settled."

Slade knew what that meant, but he sidestepped the question and asked, "Has the messenger gone back, already?"

"Left this morning, first thing after breakfast," Dennison replied.

"I would've liked to question him." Strike one, as baseball players said. He'd missed his chance to question the most likely, and only, suspect.

"He was a youngster," Dennison explained. "The only thing he knew about the crimes is that they've got the whole town up in arms."

"I'm not surprised," said Slade.

"Sadly, they're not unique," the judge went on. "You may have read about the so-called 'Ripper' murders back in '88, in London."

"Rings a bell," Slade said. "They never caught that fellow, did they?"

"Not officially," Judge Dennison replied. "Soon after the last murder, a prime suspect drowned himself. I understand that some detectives treat the case as closed."

"Meaning some don't."

Dennison shrugged. "There was a list of suspects, and the evidence against the one who killed himself was . . . vague."

"You've studied up on this," Slade said.

"I'm fascinated by mankind's capacity for evil," said the judge. "The more we understand such crimes, the easier it should be to arrest and punish those responsible."

Should be, Slade thought, guessing that knowledge of a man who got away with killing whores in London wouldn't help him much in Jubilee.

"The good news," Dennison continued, "is that they already have a suspect for you."

"Oh?"

"It seems the latest victim quarreled with one of her, um, customers on the night she was killed. It got violent, both of them bloodied. The man's face was marked. There's a chance that he tried to get even."

"Wouldn't really help explain the other two," Slade said, "unless he argued with all three of them."

"Something for you to check," said Dennison.

"They have this character in jail?"

"He hadn't been arrested when the mayor prepared his note to me. The suspect lives outside town limits, on a ranch where he's employed. The constable of Jubilee has no authority to bring him in—and, I imagine, he may be afraid to. Meanwhile, the tension's rising. No one from the ranch is safe in town, and there's been vigilante talk."

"It just gets better," Slade remarked.

"Your kind of job, I thought," said Dennison, unsmiling. "It requires a specialist."

"You sure I qualify?"

"Trust me," the judge replied. "You bagged the Benders, Jack, and they'd been on the run for over twenty years. You stopped the Danites. And I'm not forgetting how you scotched the plot against my life."

"Almost too late."

"They would have tried again. I'm sure of it."

Slade forced a smile. "You want to thank me, Judge, I'd much prefer a honeymoon with pay."

"You'll have it. Just as soon as you get back from Jubilee."

Slade nodded stoically. "It's late for me to leave, today. On top of which, I've got an explanation to deliver."

"I can help with that," said Dennison.

"No, thanks, sir," Slade replied. "I'd better handle this myself."

Slade dreaded telling Faith. He knew she wouldn't take it well. The only question now: how angry would she be?

Faith could be fiery in an argument, one of the many traits Slade loved about her, but she wasn't one for lashing out or throwing things. There would be words, no doubt about it, but he didn't think she'd break things off. After the first wave of resentment broke, she'd grant that taking down a man who butchered women was a job Slade couldn't just refuse.

The job again.

How many times could he let something like this come between them, ruining their plans, the disappointment canceling out whatever love she felt for him? How long could Faith stand having horrors like the new job tracked into her home, where any woman was entitled to feel safe?

Slade thought about resigning—not the first time, likely not the last—but one thing that he *couldn't* do was leave a madman running loose when there was no one else on hand to tackle him.

But when he got back, they would have to talk. Either before or after the I-dos.

And sooner, too. Because he had to break the news before he left for Jubilee.

Slade packed up for the road. Spare clothes, spare ammunition. In addition to his Colt Peacemaker, he'd be carrying a pair of Winchesters—a lever-action rifle that used the same .44-40 cartridges as his handgun, and a twelve-gauge Model 1887 lever-action shotgun. Slade favored the Colt, but the rifle gave him more reach, while the shotgun was handy for taking down doors or breaking up mobs.

To sustain him on the trail, he'd carry two canteens of water and a good supply of corn dodgers and jerky, both available for purchase in the local shops. His court per diem covered half the cost of meals when Slade was sent away from home, so that was something.

Other gear: his bowie knife, a compass, a spyglass, and a thirty-foot coil of rope. His horse could graze along the way, so there was no point packing feed.

When Slade had stalled as long as possible at the hotel, he clomped downstairs and told the manager he'd be away for a few days. No problem there. The staff knew that Judge Dennison would cover any rent outstanding if Slade didn't make it back.

That cheery thought in mind, Slade walked down to the livery, carrying saddlebags over his shoulder and a long gun in each hand. No one he passed along the way thought it peculiar. They were used to marshals traipsing in and out of town on errands for the court. Somebody else in trouble, somewhere down the line.

Slade saddled up his five-year-old roan mare, filled his canteens, then doubled back to get provisions for the trail. That killed another half an hour, and he couldn't think of any other reasons to delay his grim errand.

Faith's ranch lay three miles out from Enid. Not a long ride, but it gave Slade time to think. And worry. He'd been slow about proposing, by the standards of some men he knew. Faith hadn't pushed him into it, by any means—she'd seemed surprised, in fact, and possibly relieved.

First thing out of his mouth, he'd have to make her see that the postponement of their wedding wasn't his idea. Assure Faith that he'd make it up to her and they would have their perfect day.

Unless, of course, he wound up getting killed somehow.

Slade wasn't sure how Faith would take that. Oh, he knew she'd grieve for him and all, but what would it really do to a woman, having two fiancés shot out from under her? Two brothers, at that, who aside from their scars looked exactly the same.

It might be enough to break some, Slade supposed, but he knew Faith was tougher than most. Make that tougher than any he'd known, except for a few working girls who would brawl at the drop of an insult, behaving more like vicious men than females.

Faith's toughness, her resiliency, derived from strength of character. Some of the church ladies in town might question that, because she'd shared her bed with Slade and his brother before him, but there was more to spiritual strength than waving a Bible and damning your neighbors.

Slade had been born and raised in that kind of

atmosphere—had put it all behind him at an early age, while Jim stayed on—and he believed that the extreme religious folk were actually weaker than the great majority who took life as it came and dealt with it, trusting their own ability as much or more than any invisible pal in the sky.

Given a choice between a dusty book and a courageous heart, Slade reckoned it was no real choice at all.

He took his time; there was plenty of daylight left for him to reach Faith's spread before they started cooking supper. Maybe she would let him stay and eat after he broke the news. If not, he'd get a start toward Jubilee and camp wherever sunset found him, with his corn dodgers and jerky. Not the first night he'd have spent alone.

And not the last, if Faith disowned him.

What he knew was this: she'd never put him in a corner, never force a choice. She'd tell Slade how she felt, and they would go from there.

He'd never asked Faith how it had been with Jim. Slade's brother was a settler, would have fit precisely with the plans Faith had for sinking roots into the land, building a home—even an empire; hell, why not?—and raising children who would carry on their work.

That dream had been shot down. Now, in some secret corner of her mind, did Faith believe that she was settling for second best? Or would a rootless lawman even rank that high?

Slade crossed onto Faith's land at half past four o'clock. A couple of her riders spotted him five minutes later, recognized him from a distance, and passed on. Ten minutes later, Slade was in the dooryard, reining in his mare. Faith must have seen him coming, for she met him on the porch.

She read his face and lost her smile.

"Oh, Jack," she said. "What now?"

3

Slade told her everything, except a couple of the grisly details that he thought might make things worse. He was already disappointing Faith; there was no need to turn her stomach in the process.

When he'd finished, Faith leaned forward on the sofa, took his hand, and said, "You had me worried for a minute. This is a relief."

"Relief?"

His mind raced, trying to decide how that could be a good thing.

"Absolutely," Faith replied. "I saw the doomsday look that you were wearing when you rode up to the porch. I thought you were about to tell me it was off and you were leaving."

"What?"

Slade wondered if he'd fallen from his saddle on the way to Faith's and cracked his skull. Was this a dying dream of how he wished their conversation might have gone? But he could feel the pressure of her fingers on his gun hand, lightly stroking with her thumb.

"And now you look surprised," she said, half smiling.

"Well . . . um . . . sure. I mean, I had in mind that you'd be . . . what's the word I'm looking for?"

"Heartbroken? Furious? Ready to shoot you on the spot?"

"I pictured all of those," Slade said.

"It's disappointing, Jack, of course," she said. "But honestly, it's just a ceremony. There's some inconvenience—I'll have to speak with Reverend Frick about rescheduling—but otherwise, it's not a tragedy."

"It's not?"

"Jack, think it through. We're getting married here, so there's no problem juggling dates for the church or a reception hall. Nobody's coming in from out of town, which means no hotel bookings have to be revised."

"Well . . . sure. You're right," Slade said. "I guess I sweated all the way out here for nothing."

"Not so fast," Faith said. "This doesn't mean you're off the hook."

"I'm not?"

"Not by a long shot, Marshal."

"Oh. Well—"

"Just because I'm easygoing doesn't mean you haven't hurt my feelings."

"I know. I'm *truly* sorry."

Faith pressed on as if he hadn't spoken.

"I was looking forward to our wedding. And our wedding night."

The lump in Slade's throat made it difficult to answer.

"So was I," he said. "Trust me."

"The way I see it, Jack, you owe me one. No, make that two."

"I'm not sure I—"

She rose and tugged his hand. "Jack, shut up and come with me."

•   •   •

After the second go-round, they talked some more about the job in Jubilee. Slade would've liked to let it go, but didn't have the strength or inclination for an argument.

"I do remember something in the paper, years ago," Faith said, curled into him and covered by a sheet up to her waist. "About the London murders. What was it they called him?"

"Jack the Ripper," Slade replied, wishing he could've left all that outside.

Faith shuddered at the name.

"Don't even tell me how he got that name."

"Okay. Assuming that it was a *he*."

"What do you mean? You can't believe a woman would be capable of anything like that."

"If I recall," Slade said, "one of the theories at the time involved a midwife who was helping women out of trouble with abortions. Now and then, some thought, she'd mess one up, the patient dies, and all the rest of it was meant to cover the illegal operations."

Faith considered it, then said, "I don't believe it. Oh, the first part, absolutely. That goes on, without a doubt. But all the . . . *ripping* . . . No. I can't see that."

"Maybe the midwife had a partner, like the working girls have pimps. Someone to bring her customers and clean up her mistakes."

"All right. A man might do it. And in London, with the slums and overcrowding, I can see it. But out here? I hate to think there'd be another man like that on Earth."

"They never caught the first one," Slade reminded her. "But I can promise you, there's no shortage of evil men, whether you look in Oklahoma Territory or in Timbuktu."

"That's why I hate your job." Faith caught herself too late, hand rising to her lips, then said, "Oh, Jack. I don't mean that. Not really."

"No?"

"I understand that what you do's important. You save

lives, my own included. If you weren't a marshal . . . well . . . I know some of the evil men you mentioned, those you've hunted, would be free right now and victimizing others."

Evil men and women, Slade almost corrected her, remembering Kate Bender, but he didn't want to think about her, much less speak her name while he was lying there, with Faith beside him.

"But I worry," she continued. "You must know that."

"More particularly since I led a pack of crazy killers to your doorstep."

"No!" She pinched him, hard. "I'm not worried about myself, for heaven's sake! You had to help that family, not only for your job but for your soul. It would've been a sin to leave them on their own, when they were being stalked like animals."

The Danites—what their church regarded as "Avenging Angels"—had been scouring the country for apostates. Anyone who left the fold and tried to lead an independent life was marked for death. Slade and Faith had stopped the murderous crew, but it still troubled him to think that other so-called "angels" were pursuing their agenda, spreading death and misery across the land.

"I could've done a better job," said Slade.

"Judge Dennison asked you to leave them here that night," Faith said. "If I was mad at anyone, it would be him, not you."

"Well."

"Never mind. When are you leaving?"

"I could do this today," he said. "Clear weather. Sunset's still an hour off."

"Too late for that," she said and slid a slim leg over his to pin him down. "I thought tomorrow, after breakfast at the crack of dawn."

"Still leaves tonight," Slade said.

Faith rolled on top of him and said, "Let me take care of that."

•   •   •

The huntsman listens. It is a survival skill that he has practiced from an early age. Say less, hear more. His foolish
enemies reveal their plans themselves, without an inkling
that their own lips have betrayed them. Is it any wonder that
he has eluded them despite their frantic efforts to identify
and capture him?

So has it always been. So will it ever be.

"If you could quiet down and give me your attention,
please," the mayor spoke over people jabbering at one another in the Mercy Baptist Church. No other covered space
in town would hold so many souls.

The noise died slowly, some not caring if the mayor was
miffed. Roland Johansson waited until all but four or five of
them were quiet and the straggling talk had faded down to
whispers.

Finally he said, "I called this meeting to inform you all
of what's been done so far."

"Not much!" somebody called out from the back.

The huntsman managed not to smile.

"Now, that's not true!" Johansson said. "And you all
know it. Constable Vandiver has been looking at these awful
crimes and doing everything he can to stop them. Plain fact
is, we're dealing with a crazy man like no one's ever seen
around these parts before."

Not crazy, thought the huntsman, frowning slightly. But he
liked the bit about *these parts.* Some of his favorites were—

"Still," said Johansson, "there's a time to stand back and
admit we've got a problem we can't handle by ourselves."

"Why not?" another voice called out. "We know who
cut Long Liz!"

That sent an angry ripple of a murmur sweeping through
the sanctuary, washing up around Johansson's feet.

"We *don't* know that," the mayor replied. "And there's a
matter of the legal jurisdiction. Which is why—"

"A rope don't have no jurisdiction," said a third voice from the crowd, heavy with righteous indignation.

Pastor Booth stepped up to join the mayor, wearing a face like thunder. "That's enough!" he bellowed. "We'll have no more talk of lynching in the house of God! If you can't mind your manners with the Good Lord looking on, then leave!"

True silence fell over the crowd this time. Johansson picked up where he had been interrupted.

"Which is why, as most of you already know, we sent Rube Barrow off to Enid with a message for the judge there, and he's sending us a U.S. marshal. Should be here by to-morrow or the next day at the latest."

John Horvath, the town's blacksmith, spoke up to say, "We've waited too dam—sorry, Pastor—too durned long, already."

"There's no point in hashing that over until the cows come home," the mayor replied. "What's done is done. The best we can do now is work with whoever they send us to clean up this mess."

More muttering. The huntsman thought Johansson might have trouble in the next election. He enjoyed watching the top dog squirm.

"Now, in the meantime," said Johansson, "Constable Vandiver and myself have asked Al Loving and Ben Tewks-bury to keep an extra close eye on their property and their . . . well, um . . . employees."

"Meaning harlots!" said one of the women in the crowd.

Another spoke up quickly, saying, "You should run them out of town. We'd have no problem, then."

The constable, sidelined with Pastor Booth, stood up and joined Johansson at the lectern.

"Excuse me, but we don't know that to be a fact," he said. "It's true the man we're looking for has only picked on the saloon ladies so far—"

"Ladies!" another of the righteous women snorted.

"—but we can't say what he mighta done if there were

none of them around. It seems to me that he hates *women*, and for all we know, could've gone for wives and mothers just as easy. Still might, if it comes to that."

The huntsman stifled yet another smile as silence gripped the crowd. It was amusing to him for the lawman to suggest that whores performed a public service, acting as a human sacrifice. And he enjoyed the chill of fear that gripped the so-called decent women salted through the crowd.

Decent, my ass, he thought, but kept his face impassive. Watching. Listening.

"Now, when the marshal comes from Enid, I intend to tell him everything we know," Vandiver said. "Whatever moves he makes outside of Jubilee are up to him. With any luck, we'll put this all behind us soon and get on with our lives."

The huntsman made approving noises with the rest of them. *Don't count on it.*

Breakfast was ham and eggs, flapjacks and coffee, dished up before dawn. On nights Slade stayed with Faith, they generally had a later morning, but her thinking was that since he had a hundred miles to ride one way, he ought to get on with it, finish his business, and come back as soon as he could.

Slade couldn't argue with her, under the circumstances. It was still a four-day trip, without allowing for the time he'd have to spend in Jubilee. If the cowboy suspect didn't pan out—or couldn't be connected to the first two killings—Slade would have to hang out for God knew how long in pursuit of a shadow.

He pushed those glum thoughts out of mind, concentrating on Faith and the food. She was all smiles this morning, maybe putting on a brave face with her talk about how pushing back the wedding gave her extra time to plan and make it all just right. Slade knew she was unhappy, worried, but she wouldn't let it show. And he knew that pressing her to air her feelings wouldn't make for fond farewells.

"I'll have more roses blooming by the time you're back," she said.

"Roses are good."

"My favorite," she said.

"I seem to recollect that."

Flowers were a treat that Faith allowed herself amidst the constant chores and drudgery that made up ranching life. She dealt in cattle, with some horses on the side, and Slade thought gardening might help her feel connected to the land, the way he'd heard some farmers talk about their crops.

She'd paid enough to get the spread, and then to keep it—sweat and tears and blood, as well as cash. Slade hoped it wasn't wearing on her, but he'd seen no signs of that so far. Some farmers' wives looked like they'd been forced to run from less rugged climes to the territory, where they'd pitched in working with their husbands and would never stop until they died.

That life held no appeal for Slade—or hadn't, anyway, until he had become involved with Faith Connover. Even now, he couldn't see himself behind a mule and plow, but raising cattle might be different.

Might be.

In a certain light, it looked like sitting on his ass while hired hands did the work and Faith handled the business end of things. Slade knew she'd think of things for him to do, to help around the place and make him think he had a purpose, but the spread had run without him long enough that Slade had no illusions about making any kind of difference.

Glum thoughts again. He steered around them, tried to match Faith smile for smile. He didn't want to spoil things for her over breakfast when she'd been so understanding yesterday, and then so loving all night long. He definitely didn't want to think about the Jubilee investigation dragging on and on. Refused to think about it winding up with him injured or worse.

A man who carved up women didn't frighten Slade. He was disgusted by the thought, but if the butcher tried to tackle Slade, he'd soon learn the folly of bringing a knife to a gunfight. Slade knew he'd sleep the better for it, and Judge Dennison wouldn't be overly upset, as long as there was ample evidence of guilt.

Slade meant to help with washing up, after they finished breakfast, but Faith wouldn't let him. She was more intent than ever, now, on rushing him to leave and do his job, so she could get things back to normal.

Whatver *normal* meant for marshals in the Oklahoma Territory. Slade had worn the federal badge for nearly two years, and he still had no idea. He'd have been lying if he said that there was never a dull moment. On the other hand, he got to travel, meet new people—and arrest some of them for assorted heinous crimes.

Or shoot them, if they wouldn't come along without a fight.

That was the side of Slade's work that he could've done without, but any lawman in the territory—anywhere at all, he guessed—knew some offenders didn't have it in them to surrender peaceably. For some, fighting was bred into them from the cradle up. Others got scared and couldn't bear the thought of jail, much less a rope.

If your future was a noose, why not resist?

Judge Dennison could only hang you once, and being shot was preferable to dangling like a hooked fish on a line.

"You'll hurry back," Faith said when they were on the porch with Slade's mare waiting. It didn't sound like a question, but he responded anyway.

"You know I will."

"And everything will be just fine," she said.

"Already is, except the leaving part."

"But coming home is sweet."

"It is. I love you, Faith."

The Big Words.

"And I love you, Jack. Now go, before I start to cry and ruin everything."

He went, paused once to look back from a hundred yards or so, then set his face toward Jubilee.

The huntsman wasn't worried about any lawman coming in to track him. He'd outwitted others who were no doubt better educated, more experienced, and wiser than the adversary who was on his way from . . . where, again?

Enid.

It amused the huntsman when he heard the names of frontier towns. In his travels he'd seen Comfort, Paradise, Prosperity, Redemption, Bliss, Hope, Haven, and Felicity, before he'd settled for a spell in Jubilee.

What were the yokels thinking?

Did they honestly believe the name selected for a town assured its future—or, by extension, their own? And if so, why were so many towns saddled with names portending ruin?

Tombstone. Deadwood. Desperation. Waterloo. Last Chance.

And what about the settlements whose citizens had literally named them after Hell itself? Gehenna. Abaddon. Tartarus. Hades. Perdition. Purgatory. Brimstone.

No. On balance, he preferred a place like Jubilee where the people still had hope. It made them so much easier to shock and terrorize.

His work, in that respect, was well advanced. Of course, shocking the public did not satisfy the huntsman's basic need. His quest, his mission, was to learn the deepest, darkest secrets of the women whom society insisted on describing as his *victims*.

Of course, that was ridiculous. It didn't take a genius to see that harlots were leeches who preyed on men, first picking their pockets, then draining their vitality and leaving them infested with disease. How many lives and families had been destroyed by women who sold their bodies? How many could the huntsman save by eradicating the species?

Sudden rage flared in his stomach, churning, roiling, but he managed to contain it with an effort. Self-control was paramount, except during the act of delving and exploring, when he could allow himself free rein.

Before he could exterminate his enemies, he had to understand them. Had to see the rotten core of them and find out why corruption lured men from every walk of life to soil themselves beyond redemption. When he'd solved that riddle, through dissection of selected specimens, the huntsman could begin a new campaign imbued with confidence of victory.

But so far, they had frustrated him. Of all the slatterns he'd examined, no two were identical. At first, the huntsman had been puzzled by their great diversity, later infuriated by it, finally driven to distraction. Logic told him that there must be something common to them all, beyond the obvious. Some *secret thing* a man could never see or touch, which nonetheless ensnared him and propelled him toward his doom.

To find that secret thing, excise it, and reveal it to the world at large, had been the huntsman's goal since he picked up his knife.

How long ago?

It seemed forever, but in terms of years the quest had barely spanned a period equivalent to childhood. What would the alienists make of *that* comparison, he wondered? Would they claim that something in his own upbringing had warped and twisted him, setting his feet upon a path that led to butchery and shame?

In fact, the huntsman was ashamed of nothing he had

done so far, although his failure to unmask the filthy secret of the leeches privately embarrassed him. Knowing that he was right, that he would ultimately triumph, made his failed experiments more galling, but the huntsman realized that scientific exploration involved trial and error. Great discoveries were sometimes made by accident, but even then, true scientists were forced to replicate results and standardize procedures.

Nothing could be left to chance.

He felt another operation coming on. A subject was required, but there were still plenty to choose from in the squalid dives of Jubilee. A dozen more, at least, before he would run short of specimens.

And what of the lawman now coming to stop him?

What of him, indeed.

He had yet to meet a policeman whose mind rose above the pedestrian level. Even those who had a modicum of higher education were hobbled by strictly conventional thinking. Official institutions discouraged innovation, penalized imagination.

All the better for the huntsman.

As he labored to complete his studies, striving for illumination, so the men with badges who pursued him failed for lack of understanding. They might label him insane, perverse, or simply evil, but those terms were meaningless, products of childhood brainwashing.

The huntsman stood above such mundane notions, though he was committed to the cleansing of society. Not from a hidebound concept of "morality," but for the very preservation of the human race.

What cause could be more noble or exalted?

He had attempted to communicate his motives in the past, anonymously, but had been met with ridicule, vituperation, and abuse. These days, he simply left the tokens of his study for an audience that was, at once, both awed and terrified.

Which pleased the huntsman greatly.

He deserved awe for the sacrifices he had made in his attempt to save mankind. And terror was appropriate, even though most of those who viewed his work after the fact were frightened of the huntsman, rather than the parasites he had exposed.

So be it.

He would labor on, pursue his quest in solitude. Anticipate the day when he could step out of the shadows and receive his just reward.

Meanwhile, God help whoever tried to stop him.

If there was a God.

If he could match the huntsman's wrath.

4

Riding northwest toward the town of Jubilee, Slade did not follow an established road. Despite its ever-growing population and expansion of the railroad system, despite Governor William Renfrow's push for statehood, Oklahoma Territory still had nothing resembling the network of highways and roads found in long-established jurisdictions of the North and East. That was why Slade traveled with a compass, to keep from going astray as he rode across country between distant towns.

Jubilee lay at the northern extreme of a section known as the Cherokee Outlet, which ran for two hundred and twenty-five miles along the territory's border with Kansas. Before Slade's birth, in 1836, one of Washington's countless treaties had granted the land to the Cherokee tribe as an open hunting area "in perpetuity." That went out the window thirty years later, when other "friendly tribes" were jammed into the strip at gunpoint, squeezing out most of the Cherokees. In 1883 a group of white ranchers, organized as the Cherokee Livestock Association, had leased grazing rights to the land for one hundred thousand dollars per year, and six years later Congress started haggling with tribal leaders to buy back all rights to the land. This very year—1893—the tribes had settled for close to nine million dollars, and a new land rush began to parcel out the strip for farms.

Jubilee had beat that rush by seven years, established as a marshaling point for herds on their way up to Kansas, bound for railheads at Abilene, Wichita, or Dodge City, from which they'd be shipped on to slaughter in Chicago's stockyards. It had grown from there, according to Judge Dennison, and hoped to have its own railhead before much longer, send its own condemned beef north, or maybe build an abattoir right there. Why not?

But in the meantime, Jubilee was troubled by a butcher of another sort. It would be Slade's job to identify him—or, at least, a likely suspect—then arrest or kill him, as the case might be. Ideally, he would find sufficient evidence to make a murder charge stand up in court. Judge Dennison would sentence the accused, and justice would be served on Enid's scaffold.

Good for everyone. Except the women who'd been killed and any family they left behind who might find out about their means of passing months or years from now.

Slade didn't want to think about the women yet. He'd have to, later, when he got to Jubilee and started putting facts together, but there was no point in dwelling on them now. Why give them faces, personalities, or hopes and dreams that had been dashed somewhere along the drab course of their lives? Slade knew that if he thought about them too long, they would all begin to look like Faith, and then he'd have to see the rest of it in waking nightmares, thinking, *There but for the grace of God* . . . .

But that was wrong.

Slade couldn't think of any circumstances that would put Faith on the street or in a crib upstairs from a saloon. He wasn't one of those who thought all working girls were born to sin. In fact, Slade wasn't even sure what qualified as "sin," besides a willful act of harming others without cause. He wasn't prudish, never had been, and he didn't think hookers "deserved" abuse of any kind—although it definitely was a fact of life in their untidy world.

How many acts of brothel violence had he seen since putting on a badge or when he made his living with a deck of cards? Slade didn't like to think about that, either. Didn't want to know how women came to choose that life or found themselves inexorably driven to it like a line of cattle through a slaughter chute.

He'd known a pimp once, who, aside from buying girls or trading them with others of his kind, sometimes abducted them just as sailing captains used to shanghai deckhands from saloons in busy ports. When Slade found out about it, he'd informed the local lawman who, in turn, advised him to consider leaving town and minding his own business. Slade had left, after he paid the pimp one final visit with a crowbar, leaving him in no fit state to walk or make a fist, ever again.

That had been years ago, when he was young and reckless, passing through the southern corner of Nevada and a wide spot in the road they called Las Vegas. Part of Slade rejected what he'd done on that occasion; other portions, not so much. But one thing he was sure of: punishing the pimp had saved no women.

Not a single one.

Whatever drove the working girls to seek their cribs and street corners, he could've clubbed a thousand pimps without relieving the root causes. Hell, Slade couldn't have said exactly what the causes *were*.

He knew—and hated knowing it—that some men took the same path into degradation, but from personal experience he guessed their numbers must be microscopic compared to the thousands, even millions, of women working as hookers worldwide.

How did they come to it?

He'd read that in some countries daughters were considered worse than worthless, mouths to feed who couldn't pull a son's weight on a farm or in a rice paddy. Their so-called parents sold them to the highest bidder, thankful for the pittance they received, without a thought for the ultimate fate of their helpless child.

Elsewhere, including the United States, girls could be cast out for various reasons, including rebellious behavior, unwed pregnancy, or a refusal to cooperate in Daddy's dirty little games. Marriage was no escape, either, since male-dominated legislatures widely considered wives as the property of their husbands. If hubby died or did a disappearing act, the wife was often left with nothing but a chance to earn a meager living with the only tools at her disposal.

Thoroughly depressed, Slade tried to brighten up his thoughts by turning them to Faith and started looking for a decent place to camp.

The huntsman tried to choose his subjects carefully, though time and circumstances sometimes left him frustrated. Stalking a certain girl did not ensure that she would be available on any given day—or, for that matter, that she wouldn't leave town unexpectedly and slip his net entirely.

He'd been interrupted more than once during an operation. Nearly caught a time or two, but he was fleet of foot, ferocious when cornered. The best defense was a cunning disguise, but a blade between the ribs would always serve in a pinch.

Long Liz had failed him, as the others had before her. When he had subdued her, once he got *inside*, the huntsman had experienced that old familiar surge of confidence, a sense that he was bound to find the harlot's secret this time and extract it. Carry it away for study at his leisure, where he would not be disturbed.

But once again, it had evaporated. Vanished, just as he felt sure his blade and fingers were poised to secure it and claim its dark knowledge.

Another disappointment.

Of course, retrieving one whore's secret would not prove his case. As science demanded replication of experiments, so he would be required to prove that *all* loose women shared the same evil power, rooted in flesh and blood. One sample might be aberrant, a fluke or mutation. A dozen or so . . . now, *that* would be proof.

But, Christ, it was taking forever!

No matter. The huntsman was patient enough to press on, find the truth, and reveal it before time ran out for his race. Humanity would thank him in the end, might even recognize his subjects for their grudging contribution to the betterment of all mankind.

But first . . .

He had his eye on Thelma Lou tonight. She was a red-head, working out of the American Saloon. Shorter than Long Liz, as might be expected, but well proportioned. Not compressed, as some short women are, which makes them spread.

At five foot one or two, he reckoned her a living doll.

For now.

Working on smaller women was an extra challenge in itself. The huntsman was of average size, without a giant's awkward hands, but navigating in confined spaces still required special skill. Keen vision was required, as well, since blood made everything inside look more or less the same.

Another mechanism to conceal the secret.

The huntsman did not relish company. He patronized saloons because his subjects congregated there, and because showing up in such places—posing as "one of the boys"—helped cement his disguise. Tonight, he shared a table near the bar with three men who supposed themselves his friends, although in fact he didn't care if any of them lived or died.

The huntsman's dedication to mankind was universal and abstract. It did not focus on a single individual, community, or state that would eventually benefit from his discovery. In truth, he found the company of most humans banal at best, excruciating in the worst case.

Why, then, did he strive to help them all collectively?

Because it was his destiny.

The huntsman had been chosen as a child to save the world. He could no more avoid his fate than could a man propelled before a speeding train. And why would he avoid it when the exploration brought him so much pleasure?

Sometimes, in quiet moments, he was moved to wonder whether there were others like himself, plumbing the secret or pursuing other goals of similar importance. In the cities where he'd operated, the authorities and newspapers seemed to regard him as unique. Although united in condemning him, as ignorant of his intent as they remained of his identity, all granted that he was a new phenomenon.

A new man for a new age.

Thelma Lou moved past his table, smiling at the huntsman and his two companions. One of them reached out for her, making a joke she felt obliged to laugh at, while the huntsman wished that he could slit the pushy bastard's throat and leave him choking on his own blood while they poured another round of drinks.

Not here. Not now.

He'd only killed one man, so far, and that had been an emergency. Male bodies held no secrets worth investigating, as the huntsman saw it—though, he sometimes thought, a woman might feel differently.

Now, there was something to consider. If a woman should be drawn to study men who rented harlots, if she felt a driving need to turn them inside out and find the rotten organ that propelled them, might she be a suitable companion for the huntsman?

When he laughed aloud, the man beside him beamed, thinking the sound was a response to his crude jest at Thelma Lou's expense. If he had known the truth, he would have shriveled in his chair or bolted out of the American Saloon into the night.

The huntsman shook his head and sipped his whiskey.

He would never find a woman like himself, to share his passion for investigation. In his heart, he knew the notion was preposterous. He would continue as he had begun his quest, alone.

Leaving a trail of bodies in his wake.

Slade camped beside a shallow stream that gave his mare a chance to drink throughout the night while grazing on the grass along its bank. There was a single giant oak nearby, with gnarled roots making ridges in the soil like buried serpents, but he pitched his camp some fifty feet away from it, mindful of insects and in no need of a leafy roof when there wasn't a cloud in sight.

Eating jerky and corn dodgers could be thirsty work. Slade settled for water from one of his canteens, planning to refill both before he rode on in the morning. No coffee, since he didn't like to risk a fire in open country if he could avoid it, and the night was warm enough to do without. The mare would warn him if a predator approached, and Slade preferred his night vision unspoiled, if shooting was required.

Inevitably, his thoughts turned again to Faith and Jubilee. Knowing his sleep would be disturbed—or lost entirely—if he pictured Faith as they had been the night before, together, he focused instead on the task he'd been sent to accomplish.

There was a certain protocol for marshals entering a

town they'd never visited before. He'd have to touch base with the constable, maybe palaver with some other bigwigs, hearing their official version of the crimes. He wasn't their subordinate to boss around, and couldn't let them think he was, but neither was it wise to irritate them if he could avoid it.

Early on, he'd need full information on their suspect, still unnamed to Slade, the cowboy who had fought with victim number three. Going to see him on the spread he worked could be a problem, if the owner and his other hands were all defensive, but Slade couldn't let him slide without at least examining his alibi.

If he had one. If there was any reason not to haul him in.

And that could be another problem, if the cowboy's friends were up in arms. He couldn't fight a group of trigger-happy men and hope to ride away from it unscathed—but, once again, the badge prevented him from simply throwing up his hands and calling it a day.

If circumstances called for an arrest, he'd have to try.

Which left another problem on his plate. Suppose the cowboy hadn't murdered number three. Or *had* cut her but didn't kill the other two. What then?

It left a mystery.

As a child he had loved unsolved riddles. The money pit on Oak Island. The vanished colony of Roanoke. Tales of the Jersey Devil. Spooks and goblins.

As a lawman, though, Slade *hated* mysteries. At least the ones where laws were broken and lives lost. He wanted every criminal accounted for, locked up, and doing time. To Slade, these days, a mystery was simply an unfinished job. A failure he had yet to rectify.

And Jubilee might well turn out to be just that sort of mysterious.

When Slade turned in, he kept his weapons handy, pistol more or less in hand and resting on his stomach, under his light blanket. Rifle on his left, the lever-action shotgun on his right. Unless somebody sniped him from a distance, aiming by starlight, he'd have a decent chance to come up shooting at intruders in his simple camp.

What were the odds?

Slade made it sixty-forty that he'd sleep the night through, undisturbed, and hoped that might be too conservative. The point was that a solitary traveler could never be too careful.

Given half a chance, Slade would've flown a banner reading U.S. MARSHAL while he slept, but that could cut both ways. Some wicked drifters would avoid a lawman like the plague, but others might feel more inclined to seek him out, settle old grudges with the law by punishing the first random cop they encountered.

Instead of dwelling on the darkest possibilities, Slade started counting stars. He'd never been much good at spotting constellations, but the number and immense variety of skylights fascinated him. Another holdover from childhood, this one still untainted by his job.

Sometimes, when he went out to spend a night with Faith, they'd walk out some fair distance from her house and hired hands in their quarters, gazing at the heavens with a sense of awe. From time to time they'd see a shooting star and Faith would make a secret wish while urging Slade to do the same. He'd fake it, just to please her, but the truth was that he had nothing to wish for.

In Faith's company, Slade felt the most contentment that he'd ever known.

And looking at the stars now, he had no doubt whatsoever that there must be something greater than himself or all mankind. What that might be eluded him, and Slade still knew with perfect certainty it couldn't be the raging Old Man of the Bible, hedged around with fairy tales and contradictions.

But there must be *something*. Maybe even *someone*.

With all the stars and planets in the sky to choose from, would he—or she—know or care what happened on Earth?

And if knowing or caring, could someone actually intervene?

Again, Slade doubted it.

From childhood to the tale of Jubilee, he'd seen too many cases where good people suffered needlessly and evil went unpunished. It would never be enough, for him, to simply shrug and say that God moved in mysterious ways.

Tired out by hours on the trail and thoughts of things he couldn't fix, Slade pulled his blanket up, hiding the Colt, and went to sleep.

Going on one o'clock, when Jubilee's good citizens were fast asleep and most of the shady ones were running out of steam, the huntsman made his second visit of the evening to the American Saloon. He walked with purpose and avoided Main Street, keeping to the shadows, navigating alleys quite as much by feel as sight or sound.

He'd need a different means of entry, this time, with the second-story windows shut. The huntsman was considering the risks—and thrills—of entering the ground floor, going up the stairs as bold as brass, when he saw someone else approach the rear of the saloon.

A man. A face he recognized by starlight.

Well, now.

While the huntsman watched, the new arrival looked around, then bent to pick up something from the ground and toss it at a window overhead. He heard the pebbles tap on glass, then rattle back to earth.

The window opened seconds later to reveal a smiling Thelma Lou. She waved her caller up, but he responded with a head shake, gesturing for her to join him down below. After a pouty moment, she ducked back inside, lowering the window.

While the huntsman waited, he considered possibilities. If Thelma Lou refused her late-night suitor, he would have to kill more time, waiting for her to fall asleep, then make his way inside to breach her room. If she went off with her admirer for the night, his fourth experiment in Jubilee would have to be postponed.

Already rigid with excitement, now he felt the nagging ache of raw frustration shudder through him. He would not—*could not*—delay the operation, come what may. But with a grown man in her company . . .

Why not?

He had the blackjack that he carried, to subdue his subjects, and his operating tools. It would be dangerous, of course, but if he took them by surprise . . .

Two sudden blows, instead of one, and if he cracked the randy bastard's skull, what difference did it make? Convesely, if the backdoor Romeo survived, it could be entertaining and could assist the huntsman in preserving his anonymity.

He felt a cold, delicious thrill of fear as Thelma Lou emerged from the saloon's rear entrance, rising up on tiptoes for a kiss. She pressed against her secret lover, ground her hips against him till the huntsman thought they might complete their dealings where they stood, with Thelma Lou pinned to the wall. At last they stepped apart, though, and proceeded arm-in-arm into the night, eastbound.

The huntsman followed.

Two quick swings, forward and backhand, ought to do the job. The one thing he could not afford to do was miss his first strike, at the man. He had to drop the horny fraud with one blow, never giving him a chance to see the huntsman's face. If he was seen and recognized, there'd be no question of the man surviving.

Only death would guarantee his silence.

Would a surplus murder spoil his mood? Prevent him from completing his experiment? Once in the past, he'd claimed two subjects in a single night, but only when the first had been denied to him by unexpected passersby after he'd cut her throat. The second operation was complete—but once again, the harlot's secret had eluded him.

As he pursued his quarry, taking care to let his footsteps make no sound, the huntsman drew his blackjack. It was simply made, a knob of lead with an embedded metal spring, surrounded by a sheath of braided leather. Even with its striking force, he'd have to put his weight behind the first swing, since his rival of the moment wore a stylish bowler hat.

When it appeared the happy couple were about to end their journey at the back door of a single-story house, the huntsman knew that if he didn't move at once, his opportunity would slip away.

A rush of sudden footsteps from behind them, he swung the blackjack overhand, slashing it down atop the Casanova's head. The blow propelled his target's face into the door jamb and the double impact dropped him, properly insensate, to the ground.

Before his swift attack could wring a cry from Thelma Lou, the huntsman clipped her with a backhand swing, his bludgeon thunking solidly against her temple. With a huffing little whimper, she collapsed.

The huntsman looked both ways, drawing a ragged breath, then knelt beside her prostrate form and drew his knife.

5

An hour short of sundown, day two on the trail, Slade got his first clear glimpse of Jubilee. The town had been a speck and then a smudge on the horizon for the past two hours. Now it sprouted shapes he recognized as buildings of different shapes and sizes, some with plumes of smoke rising to stain the sky.

Tired as he was of riding, Slade still didn't hurry. Why wear out his roan with a dramatic burst of speed across the finish line when there was no one to impress? They'd called for help and he was getting there, without breaking the mare's neck or his own.

Viewed from a distance, Jubilee seemed like a decent town. Still growing, the older buildings had been well maintained. He knew already that it had the basics: two saloons, one church and one hotel, a livery, a restaurant, assorted shops and stores. No bank yet, but they'd get around to it if Jubilee survived a little longer.

And the town had secrets. That was guaranteed.

Not just a killer preying on its working girls. There would

be other hidden sins Slade might encounter while he beat the bushes for a maniac. In each new town, it seemed, he stumbled over crooked businessmen and straying spouses, crazy preachers, local lawmen who were cowards, thieves, or worse. All human beings caught up in the petty dramas that comprised real life.

Slade's problem here, as always, would be separating wheat from chaff. Sifting through the lies and secrets, focusing on those that mattered to his job and putting all the others out of his mind.

Main Street was more or less what he'd expected. Everything seemed tidy at a glance. He got the normal stares any stranger could expect from dwellers in a frontier town. Expressions changed with notice of his badge, but whether that was good or bad in some cases, Slade couldn't tell.

Instead of looking for the constable first thing, he rode directly to the Jubilee Hotel. Someone's idea of an imaginative name. The clerk was in his early thirties, smiley, acting happy to meet Slade. The town was waiting for a knight in dusty armor, and he'd finally arrived.

But they would have to wait a little longer.

After signing for a room and carrying his things upstairs and washing his face and hands, Slade rode his mare down to the livery, beside the blacksmith's shop. A solemn red-haired youth assured him that his horse would be well cared for and his tack secure.

Still putting off his visit with the constable, Slade walked back to the restaurant—MacDonald's, thankfully, not Jubilee—and let a freckled waitress lead him to a table by the window. Tired of bite-sized food prepared to last for weeks, he ordered steak with beans and fried potatoes, biscuits, and a mug of coffee.

The restaurant had half a dozen other customers for early supper, and he felt them watching him. It was completely normal, something he'd grown used to since he started working for Judge Dennison. The badge evoked a broad range of emotions: curiosity, suspicion, fear, hostility, sometimes even relief.

The citizens of Jubilee would know why he was there. In most towns, Slade's arrival came as a surprise to the majority of residents—and not always a pleasant one. He'd never had a whole town turn against him, yet, but there'd been some whose people wouldn't lift a finger to assist him when he needed it. Slade kept a mental list of those and mused on ways to pay them back sometime.

In Jubilee, his fellow diners—and the passersby who saw him in the window, slowing down to gawk before they caught themselves and moved along—knew he was there to rid them of a murderer. The fact that one of them might *be* the murderer did not escape Slade. He had come to Jubilee devoid of expectations, preconceptions, of the vaguest of ideas on how he'd solve the case.

Unless the nameless cowboy was responsible, he'd have to start from scratch. And what he knew about the kind of man who slaughtered women for the hell of it could fit inside a thimble, with some room left over.

Learn as you go, he thought and dug into the food his waitress had delivered with a smile. It was delicious—or perhaps he'd simply had too many corn dodgers to tell the difference.

When Slade was halfway through his meal, he saw a portly man striding along the south side of Main Street, opposite the restaurant. He wore a pistol, which seemed rare in Jubilee, and as he veered to cross the street, Slade saw his badge.

The constable.

Slade didn't rush on his account. The lawman might be testy, irritated that his office hadn't been Slade's first stop on arrival, but he'd have to live with it. The men in charge of Jubilee had kept the murders to themselves for five whole weeks. Another hour wouldn't matter.

Slade was ready when the constable approached his

table. Said, "You must be Vandiver. Sit down, if you've a mind to."

Thrown off stride, the constable said, "No, thanks. Marshal . . . ?"

"Slade. Jack Slade."

"I thought you might've checked in at my office, when you got to town."

"It was my next stop," Slade assured him.

"How much longer do you think you'll be?" Vandiver asked.

"Not long. You in a rush?"

"Sort of. Marshal, I thought you'd want to know we caught the killer."

Slade settled up his tab and followed Vandiver onto the wooden sidewalk. People passing by steered wide around them. Too much law in one place for the average citizen.

"When you say 'caught,' you mean he's in your jail?" Slade asked.

"Safe under lock and key," Vandiver said. "That is, if no one gets it in their head to take him out and hang him."

Slade swept Main Street with his eyes, seeing nothing that resembled the inception of a lynch mob.

"Do you think that's likely, Constable?"

"Not *likely*, but I wouldn't rule it out, feelings the way they are. And you can call me Mills."

Ignoring that, Slade said, "All right. Let's see your prisoner."

"Before we get to that," Vandiver said, "the mayor would like to have a word with you. If that's okay."

Damned politics, Slade thought but nodded, saying, "Lead the way."

They wound up at a house halfway between the hotel and the end of Main Street, with the prairie stretching on beyond it to infinity. The house was painted blue with white trim, and it had lace curtains in the windows. Vandiver led him to the front door, used the brass knocker discreetly, and stood waiting, hat in hand.

The man who answered after half a minute was a few years older than Vandiver, call it forty, with a blond mustache and thinning hair to match. Vandiver solemnly performed the introductions.

"Mayor Johansson, U.S. Marshal Slade."

"Deputy marshal," Slade corrected him.

The mayor's handshake was firm but didn't test Slade's strength or try to grind his knuckle bones. Johansson beckoned them inside and introduced Slade to his wife, Emmeline. She was what people had begun to call a looker—trim and shapely, creamy skin, long hair as dark as her husband's was fair.

She offered coffee. Slade declined, then felt an obligation to explain. "I'm sure your coffee's good, ma'am, but I'm fresh out of the restaurant."

"I found him having supper," said the constable, as if he'd caught Slade smoking opium.

"Well, please sit down," Johansson said. "We have the sofa, or—"

Slade found a chair and settled into it, before the mayor could list each piece of furniture located in the parlor. While the others blinked at him, he said, "Your constable tells me you've caught the killer."

"It appears so," said Johansson. "Yes, indeed."

The mayor and constable sat down together on the sofa, while Mrs. Johansson quietly excused herself, leaving a hint of perfume on the air. When she was gone, Vandiver spoke.

"Early this morning, on his way to work, the blacksmith found them."

"Them?" asked Slade. "There's more than one?"

"Well, no," the mayor put in. "What Mills means is, the blacksmith found our killer and his latest victim."

"Thelma Lou, from the American," Vandiver said.

"That's the American *Saloon*," Johansson amplified.

"And she was dead?" asked Slade.

"Oh, my, yes," said Johansson. "It was horrible."

"I'd say Long Liz was worse," the constable replied.

Slade nipped their budding argument.

"Before we get to that," he said, "you're telling me your blacksmith caught the killer in the act?"

"Um . . . well . . . that's not exactly right," Johansson said.

"I guess you'd better clear that up," said Slade.

"You see, he was *unconscious*."

"What?"

"It's strange, I grant you," said the mayor. "But we surmise there was a struggle. Thelma Lou was strong and not afraid of scrapping. Oh, my, no. It's evident she struck him on the head somehow—the injury is plain to see—before he finished her and did the rest of it. Then, he . . . um . . . finally passed out."

Slade looked from one man to the other, trying to decide if they were serious. Their faces reassured him that they were.

"I'd say that would be quite . . . unusual," he told them.

"I imagine so," the mayor replied. "But he *was* found beside the body—what was left of it—and there's the knife."

"You have the knife?"

Johansson and Vandiver nodded simultaneously.

Said the mayor, "When he lost consciousness, the butcher failed to . . . um . . . I mean to say, he left the knife *inside* her."

"Well, I'll need to meet this character," Slade said. "Who is he? Do you know him?"

"Oh, my, yes!" the mayor replied. "And that's another thing. He actually *is* a butcher."

"Otto Heidegger," Vandiver says. "He's got a shop right here in Jubilee."

"Oh, my Lord!" Johansson blurted out. "I hadn't thought!

You don't suppose . . . I mean to say . . . the missing parts. . . ."

"For Christ's sake, Mayor!" Vandiver had gone pale. "Don't even think it!"

"No. Of course, you're right."

"Before we start upsetting anybody's stomach," Slade suggested, "let's go see your butcher."

Thinking to himself, *And find out how someone who's grown accustomed to it passes out while cutting up a woman on the street.*

Otto Heidegger looked like a butcher. He was heavyset, red-faced, and stocky, with a thick walrus mustache. He occupied one of the two jail cells available in Jubilee, the other being empty for the moment. Seated on the low-slung cot when Slade arrived, wringing his hands and muttering, he rose and stepped up to the bars to greet his visitors.

"You know me, Mayor," he said, in a pronounced Germanic accent. "Mills, ve haff ze drinks togedder. I am innocent!"

Instead of arguing, the constable said, "Otto, this is Marshal Slade. You recollect the meeting after Liz . . . well, after . . . where the mayor told everyone a marshal would be coming out from Enid? This is him."

"Marshal." The butcher stuck a hand out through the bars, as if to shake, but Slade ignored it. Looking almost pained, Heidegger said, "You let me out now, yes?"

"We need to have a talk about what happened," Slade replied.

"Of course! I wish to catch ze man who does zese tings as much as you. More, even!"

"That's good to know," Slade said. "Now, you've just said you're innocent. By which I take it you're denying that you killed this Thelma Lou, last night?"

"I haff kilt no one, Marshal! Never in my life! Only

the animals I butcher for my shop, as did my *vater* and my *grossvater* before me."

Slade took that to mean his father and grandfather. So, the butchering ran in his family. But did he only work on animals of the four-legged variety?

"I hear you," Slade replied. "But here's my problem. You were found this morning with a mutilated woman's body and a bloody knife."

"Und I vas *unbewusste,* eh? How do you say . . . ? Unconscious!"

"Some would say you struggled with the lady, hit your head somehow, then went about your business with her and blacked out when you were done."

A sidelong glance at Mayor Johansson and the constable caught both of them frowning. Slade hadn't seen the woman Heidegger was charged with killing, but she would've had to be a powerhouse to take the butcher down—much less deliver any kind of blow that struck with a delayed reaction.

"Iss a lie!" the butcher said, gripping the iron bars with both large hands. "I vould not harm a hair of Zelma Lou. I vas . . . ve vere . . . in love."

Slade blinked at that.

"You were in love with her."

"And she vit me. If only you could ask her!"

Right, Slade thought. *If only.*

"Since we can't," he said, "some other kind of proof would be a help. If there were letters, for example . . ."

"Zelma Lou, she couldn't write," Heidegger said.

"Someone she might have talked to," Slade suggested. "Told them how she felt about you."

"*Nein.* It vas our secret, till she quit from ze saloon."

"Last night," Slade said, "you went to see her after closing time. Was that a normal thing between you?"

"*Ja.* She vas afrait of Herr Tewksbury, vat he say if he find out she doesn't charge me."

Slade half turned to face the constable. "Tewksbury?"

"He owns the American Saloon," Vandiver said. "Al Loving has the Klondike."

"Mr. Heidegger, how did you feel about the lady you're in love with seeing other men at the saloon?"

"It doesn't make me *glücklich*—you say happy," Heidegger admitted. "But she quit soon. Vas a promise zat she make."

"I see. And how long were the two of you . . . in love?" Slade asked.

Heidegger thought about it, then replied, "Six months, I tink. Since Christmastime it vas."

"One last thing for tonight," Slade said. "If you could turn around and let me see your head . . ."

"Ja, ja."

The butcher turned his back to Slade and hunched his shoulders, giving Slade a clear view of his balding, battered scalp. Someone had obviously slugged him from behind, a blow descending on his head, not coming from the side or straight in from behind.

"All right, then," Slade told Heidegger, "I'll likely see you here again, sometime tomorrow."

"I must stay anudder night?" the butcher asked.

"At least," Slade said, trailing Vandiver and Johansson as they left the jail.

When they were on the sidewalk, Mayor Johansson said, "You see, Marshal? His story makes no sense."

"Here's what I see," Slade told them both. "Somebody taller than your butcher hit him from behind. Unless this Thelma Lou was a six-footer and she had some kind of club, I doubt she could've done it. And I'll bet you twenty dollars, here and now, she couldn't do it even *with* a club, if he was facing her."

"What are you saying, Marshal?" asked the mayor.

"I've said it," Slade replied. "Heidegger took a hit that dropped him while his back was turned. The way his scalp looks, I don't think he knew what hit him. As for carving up his lady friend after he took the hit, I'd guess it was impossible."

"Hold on, now," said Johansson. "That's another thing. This nonsense about Heidegger and Thelma Lou having some great romance."

Slade shrugged and said, "I've known men who fell in love with working girls. One time, there was a girl who claimed she loved the fella back. One night, they up and ran away together, out of Wichita. I can't say how it all worked out, but they were trying."

"Or, maybe Otto has a jealous streak he doesn't like to talk about," said Vandiver. "Maybe he kills the others cuz he's mad at Thelma Lou but can't work up the nerve to hurt her."

"Right," Slade said. "But then he kills her? And knocks himself out while he's at it?"

"What about the knife?" Johansson asked.

"Was it a butcher's knife?"

"Um . . . no."

"Well, then."

"Okay," Vandiver said. "Who did it then?"

"Beats me," Slade said. "I'll sleep on it, then go and see your cowboy in the morning."

"Cowboy?"

"The one you thought killed number three," Slade said, reminding them.

"Oh, Chris."

"I'll get his details and direction to his spread before I leave," Slade said. "Meanwhile, keep a close eye on Heidegger. If someone harms him in the jail, it's down to you."

Slade had a lot to think about before he turned in for the night. The butcher didn't strike him as a criminal mastermind.

Was he clever enough to put himself in a frame so awkward it screamed innocence—and reckless enough to face the consequences if it got him hanged?

Slade answered no to both questions, while granting that he might be wrong. Playing the odds, he guessed that Jubilee still had a maniac at large. Based on the butcher's height, call him a man who stood six feet or better, with a strong right arm. A man who hated women, or who loved them in some twisted way Slade couldn't hope to understand.

With any luck, he never would.

There were two ways that he could take last night's event. One version, Otto Heidegger was stepping out with Thelma Lou, behind her boss's back, when Jubilee's other butcher happened along by chance and couldn't resist. Maybe he even saw the opportunity to lay his crimes on Heidegger—but that could only work if he stopped killing.

Or he moved on to slay more women somewhere else, where no one ever heard of Jubilee.

The other way to see it: he was stalking Thelma Lou specifically and maybe was surprised when Heidegger came by to see her after business hours. From there, he either hatched the plan to set up Heidegger—maybe as punishment for spending time with Thelma Lou—or else, simply decided that he couldn't put off killing for another night and rushed ahead, heedless of any risk.

One way, he was a planning man. The other way, he might be on the edge of losing all control.

Not good, in either case.

Slade thought about the cowboy, Chris Something. If he'd killed number three the week before, was it a crime of rage or part of an ongoing series? Did he sneak back into town for number four, and maybe seize an opportunity of shifting the suspicion from himself?

And if he'd killed all four women in Jubilee, what had the first two hookers done to set him off? Was it a word, a laugh, a look? Or had it been enough for him that they were female and available?

Slade dropped that line of thought. He didn't want to prejudice himself against the cowboy when they hadn't even met. He'd get more details from Vandiver in the morning, then ride out and try to find his man. If Chris Whoever was in hiding, it was bound to count against him. Whether it made sense or not, most people viewed running away as proof of guilt.

And if he *did* find Cowboy Chris, defended by a gang of comrades angry at the town in general and lawmen in particular . . . well, Slade would wait until he faced that obstacle and see what happened on the day.

For now, he'd have to take it one step at a time. Might have to question everyone in town, although he dreaded that prospect. He could spend days—or weeks—in Jubilee and still not spot a killer who was lying to his face.

As long as Slade's quarry hung back and managed not to slaughter anybody new, controlled the urge to cut and run, there was a fair chance he could get away with what he'd done so far. Slade fancied that he had a knack for spotting liars, but a man this sick might even manage to convince part of himself that he was innocent. If he could play that part in public, with his neighbors, day in and day out, deceiving Slade shouldn't be any drastic challenge.

And before Slade fell asleep, he knew where that process of thought was leading him. He didn't like it, but the path was plain to see.

If Otto Heidegger and Cowboy Chris were innocent, the best way for Slade to catch Jubilee's madman would be redhanded. He'd have to wait and hope for another attack, be Johnny-on-the-spot when it occurred, and hope like hell he was in time to stop another grisly murder.

If he failed . . .

Slade figured it was even money, whether his presence in Jubilee frightened the killer off or pushed him into trying for another victim prematurely. Never schooled in the science of the mind, he'd learned enough at poker tables to know that some players would always rise to a bluff, while others folded. Some would raise with lousy hands, while others were conservative to a fault.

His problem, now, was sitting down to play against a man he'd never met, when lives were riding on the line.

Dozing at last, Slade hoped he wouldn't dream.

6

Slade was the second customer in line for breakfast at MacDonald's restaurant the next morning, ordering the eggs and bacon, thick-sliced toast with jam, and coffee. Thinking of the ride he faced, he passed on beans.

Vandiver found him just as Slade was being served, a habit Slade decided he would love to break. The constable had coffee, looking like he needed it.

"You're going out for Chris this morning, then?" he asked.

"Soon as you tell me what I need to know, and I get finished here," Slade said.

"I'm not so sure about him now," Vandiver said.

"It doesn't matter. I'm the one needs to be sure."

"He's got some friends out there."

"That's nice for him," Slade said. "I still can't let a murder suspect wander off."

"Because you'll have no one to back you up."

"Yeah. We've established that."

"It ain't my fault, you know. There's rules," Vandiver said.

"I ain't the county sheriff. And we haven't got a county, even if I was."

Slade honed his voice down to a cutting edge. "You have some information for me, or is this a whining session?"

Coloring around the cheeks, Vandiver said, "You're looking for a cowhand, Chris Christofides. I heard somebody say he was a Greek or something."

"And?"

"And you can find him at the Bar-B. Ride out six miles east of town. He works for Mr. Gallagher."

"The place easy to find?" asked Slade.

"Don't worry about that," Vandiver said. "Gallagher's men should find you quick enough. They keep a sharp eye out."

Vandiver flagged the waitress with his empty coffee mug and she refilled it. Slade, still working on his meal, got an impression that the constable had more to say.

"You're backing off the cowboy as a suspect in the third death. Why is that?" Slade asked.

Vandiver stared into his coffee for a moment, then leaned back and peered around the room. Looked everywhere, in fact, except at Slade.

"We may have jumped to a conclusion there," he said, at last. "Chris had a fight with Liz the night she died, okay. It looked bad. But she had a fight with someone every couple weeks. None of the others doubled back to carve her up."

"It only takes one," Slade reminded him.

"But Chris had no connection to the first two, that I know of. And with Thelma Lou . . ."

"You still think Heidegger's the killer?"

"Otto's who we've got. I understand your argument against it, but unless you pin this thing on someone else—"

Slade interrupted him, saying, "The only thing I pin on anybody is my own badge, in the morning. Short of a confession, evidence is what Judge Dennison will want to see."

"We're back to Otto, then," said Vandiver. "Lying beside the body with a bloody knife."

"You said the knife was in the body, not the butcher's hand."

"Okay. So, what?"

"You have a doctor here in town?"

"O' course. Doc Wheatley."

"And an undertaker?"

"Silas Guidry."

"One or both of them could give me some idea about the women's injuries, I take it?"

"Injuries!" Vandiver scowled. "Shit fire, man! They were *gutted.*"

Slade pushed back his plate and said, "Last night your mayor mentioned some missing parts."

Vandiver's sour look turned positively grim. "That's right," he said. "Some female parts, is all I know. You'd have to see Doc Wheatley about that. You think it matters?"

"A case like this," Slade told him, "everything matters."

"But Otto—"

"Was found at the scene, knocked out cold. If anything was missing from the lady . . . where'd he hide it?"

"Oh." Vandiver swallowed hard, then said, "That wouldn't put him in the clear on any of the others, though."

It was a struggle not to roll his eyes as Slade replied, "Let's think about it for a second. If he didn't do the fourth one, what is there to nail him on the other three?"

"Well, I don't—"

"Nothing," Slade supplied the answer to his own question.

"So, then we're back to Chris?"

"Not necessarily. I'll talk to him, see if he's got an alibi and whether it holds water. If he wasn't here in town the night before last, though . . ."

Slade left the statement hanging. Let Vandiver draw his

own conclusions. From the constable's expression, they were dour.

"Jesus! So, you think it's *neither* of them?"

Slade replied, "I don't play guessing games. Ask questions first. Study the evidence, then see what theories fit."

"Aw, hell!" Vandiver rose, left money on the table, turning toward the doorway as he said, "I'd better go and break this to the mayor."

The huntsman was an early riser, and he saw the marshal was as well. Examining the lawman, he saw average intelligence or better, coupled with determination and self-confidence. A killer with the pistol that he carried and remorseless when he deemed it necessary.

Perfect.

It had been five years or more, the huntsman calculated, since he'd faced an adversary who was worthy of him. This one might not qualify in all respects, but he was infinitely better than the plodding peasants normally collected to pursue him.

This one might be interesting.

He might pose a challenge.

In his gut, the huntsman knew his wisest course of action would consist of doing nothing. Watch and wait until the marshal tired of wasting time with hicks whose knowledge of the crimes he'd come to solve was nil. How long that wait might be, the huntsman could not estimate.

And when the marshal left, then what?

If he resumed his operations, there would be another cry for help. Another visit from the lawman, or some other figure of authority. What would it profit him to play that seesaw game?

Two choices, then.

One was to stall the marshal, wait until he left, then slip away from Jubilee. Make some excuse, rather than fleeing in the night, and thereby keep the rumors to a minimum. No reason anyone should name him as a suspect, if his reason for departing sounded plausible. And later, if authorities were moved to check on his itinerary, they would find . . . nothing.

The other course involved a game of cat-and-mouse. Both players would be predator *and* prey, although the lawman wouldn't know that he was playing.

Not, with any luck, until it was too late.

First, bait, to keep the marshal chasing his own tail. It could upset the frame he'd built around the kraut, but any fresh confusion worked to the huntsman's advantage. Two suspects and counting gave him room to breathe.

Room to select another subject.

Should he take it seriously or toss out a sacrifice solely for the imported lawman's sake? On one hand, it would be a shame to waste his time and energy with no hope of advancing his search for a solution to the harlot's mystery.

But on the other . . .

He could change the game completely with a polar shift in choice of subjects. Never in the past had he selected anyone from the "respectable" community. Such women did not interest him, because he understood their purpose in society—as ornaments and tools of procreation. Without mothers, obviously, there would be no human race. The urge to reproduce was paramount, and in the culture he was born to, that required the so-called sacrament of marriage to legitimize offspring.

Should he deviate from his established norm, as a diversion?

No.

The huntsman was concerned with whores, but he could work within that framework to defeat the man hunter. The town was already on edge. If it was seen that he could kill beneath the lawman's very nose and get away with it, the tension might reach crisis level.

Who knew what could happen, then?

The prospect made him smile. Passing along the sidewalk, nodding to his neighbors, he felt perfectly secure. No one suspected him of anything. Why should they? He presented to the world a bland façade of mediocrity. A cog in the community machine. There was no reason for a solitary soul in Jubilee to look beyond his mask.

For all intents and purposes, the huntsman was invisible.

Which didn't mean the lawman might not speak to him at some point, in the hours or days ahead. He welcomed it. Looked forward to the test, when he could pit his skill against another guardian of public safety and emerge victorious.

So let it be.

Meanwhile, he had a business to conduct. A life to lead.

The huntsman was enjoying every moment of it.

It was nearly eight o'clock when Slade rode out of Jubilee, already warm beneath a blue sky marked by tufts of cloud like floating cotton balls. He checked his compass when he was a hundred yards beyond the eastern end of Main Street, kept it handy as he gave the mare her head, and watched the road play out after a quarter mile.

He felt a certain apprehension about running down Vandiver's sort-of suspect. First, because the Greek cowhand apparently had friends at the Bar-B who might feel obligated to resist his being carried off. It was a situation Slade had faced before, with variations, and he'd managed to survive it.

Still, first time for everything.

Most people only got killed once.

He'd double-checked his Colt, rifle, and shotgun at the livery, making the hostler cock an eyebrow as he watched. The guns were ready, not that Slade would have a chance to use all three of them if anything went wrong.

Do what you can, and let it go, he thought.

Picturing Faith.

The way to play it: he was duty-bound to question Chris Christofides, and anyone who didn't like it had a problem with the law—which ultimately meant Judge Dennison. That wouldn't help Slade in a showdown at the ranch this morning, but his adversaries had to know that killing one marshal meant facing others, somewhere down the line.

If they were thinking clearly.

If they stopped to think at all.

Two lookouts met him ninety minutes out from Jubilee. There'd been no marker for his passage onto Bar-B land, and for a second Slade thought maybe they were drifters, border trash, but they were too well groomed for that. Too clean.

Approaching at a gallop from the north-northeast, they slowed at fifty yards, hands on their pistols as they cantered up to Slade. He sat the roan and waited for them, easing off his holster's hammer thong.

"Lawman," the taller of them said.

It could've been a greeting or a statement of objective fact. Slade didn't bother to respond.

"This here is private property," the shorter cowboy said.

"It's part of Oklahoma Territory," Slade replied, "in the United States."

"So, what?"

"Lean closer, and you'll see the 'U.S.' on my badge."

"You got some kind of business here?" The taller one.

"I'll take that up with Mr. Gallagher," Slade said. "Or Chris Christofides."

Hoping that he'd pronounced the Greek name properly.

The riders looked at one another, then turned back to Slade.

"Supposin' they don't feel like talkin' to you?" asked the shorter one.

"They tell me that in person, I'll be on my way," Slade said. Adding: "To fetch however many men it takes."

"Hard case," the taller one observed. "What if we stop you here?"

"Your funeral," said Slade. "Let's get it done."

"A *real* hard case," the shorter one decided.

"Shit." The taller one. "You may's well come on up to the house."

"You first," Slade said and followed them, not letting either one circle around behind him. Ten or fifteen minutes later they were in the dooryard of a spacious ranch house, flanked by barns and other outbuildings.

If someone opened up on Slade from hiding, he'd be cut to ribbons. But he was determined not to go alone. His escorts, first. And after that . . .

A tall man with a craggy face came through the front door of the house and stopped in shade, on the front porch. After a fruitless, momentary staring contest he announced, "I'm Thomas Gallagher. This is my spread. What do you want?"

"A word with one of your employees," Slade replied.

"Concerning?"

"Murder in the town of Jubilee."

"You're after Chris," said Gallagher.

"Not to arrest him, yet," Slade said. "But there's a need for talk."

"Just talk?"

"So far."

"Some of those Jubilunks have got it in for him," said Gallagher.

"That's possible," Slade granted. "I still need to sort it out."

After another moment, Gallagher nodded to one of Slade's escorts—the shorter one—and said, "Fetch Chris and bring him to the house."

"Now, Mr. G.—"

"Do like I tell you, Blake," said Gallagher. "And be damn quick about it."

• • •

The Greek cowboy was five feet nine or ten inches tall without his high-crowned Stetson, dusty from his work, and could have used a shave. He wore a gun that hadn't seen much use, and ducked his head a bit whenever Thomas Gallagher addressed him. Even though some time had passed, the healing marks of fingernails were visible across both cheeks.

Gallaher led them to a spacious dining room and indicated two chairs near the table's head, facing one another. When Slade and the cowboy were seated, Gallagher sat in the tall chair between them.

"I'm staying," he told Slade. "My place."

Slade ignored him and spoke to the cowboy. "Mr. Christofides . . . is that how you pronounce it?"

"Yep."

"You have a fair idea of why I'm here?"

"About the whore who clawed my face. The one they call Long Liz."

"Past tense," Slade said, correcting him. "You know she's dead, right?"

"Sure."

"Somebody carved her seven ways from Sunday, the same night she marked your face."

Making the point.

"I know it." Warming up a little. "Wasn't me."

"You say."

The cowboy shrugged, failed in his bid to conjure up a grin. "I oughta know," he said.

"See? We agree on something," Slade replied.

"Man's innocent until he's proved guilty, the way I hear," said Gallagher.

Slade froze him out, locked eyes with Chris Christofides.

"My problem is that you had motive—getting even for your face, there—and the opportunity."

"What opportunity?" the cowboy asked.

"No one saw you leave Jubilee that night," Slade said. "A jury might suspect you hung around and made her pay for marking up your hide. Maybe for laughing at your little problem."

"I ain't got no *little* problem!" Angry color in the cowboy's marred and bristled face.

"That temper's hot enough to get you hanged, all by itself," Slade said. "They get you on the witness stand and prod you just a bit, you'll go off like a string of firecrackers. Our prosecutor's just the man to do it, too."

"The hell you want from me?" Christofides demanded.

"Just the plain and simple truth."

"Okay. I had too much to drink that night. The fight with Liz was stupid, but she made me mad."

"Had that effect on lots of people, what I hear," said Gallagher.

"All right," Slade said. "A stupid fight. What, then?"

"The bouncer come up first, then Mr. Loving. Liz is screamin' at all three of us, till Mr. Loving pasted her and shut her up."

"He hit her?"

"Sure."

"How many times?" asked Slade.

"The one time did it."

"So, what then?"

"Then, Mr. Loving and the bouncer walked me back downstairs and out of the saloon. Told me to stay out of the Klondike till I learned to mind my manners."

"And then, you left?"

"Before that come the constable," Christofides replied. "He hangs around at the saloons most of the night, one or the other place."

"And what did he say?" Slade inquired.

"Told me to get my ass back to the spread and thank my lucky stars I wouldn't haveta spend the night locked up."

"He watch you leave?"

"Can't say. I did, though. Leave."

"And got back here about what time?" Slade asked.

A shrug. "Ain't got no watch. Still dark. I went to sleep. It was a while before the breakfast call."

"Did anybody see you, coming in? Night riders? Someone in the bunkhouse?"

"Not that I recall. You heard me mention I'd been drinkin'."

"He was here for breakfast," Gallagher told Slade. "Chris hasn't missed a day of work since he hired on, if that's of any help to you."

"Just means he made it back before you started serving," Slade replied. "How long has he worked for you?"

"It's comin' up on eighteen months," said Gallagher.

"And you keep records of the times he goes in town?"

"Don't write it down or anything," said Gallagher. "But I can tell you that I let my hands go in on Saturdays, after they finish work. On Sunday mornings, if they ain't in church, they sleep it off."

Meaning Christofides should be exonerated of the first two killings if they fell on any other nights. Unless he broke the rules and snuck away. Unless Tom Gallagher was lying for him.

"Okay, then," Slade said. "That's all the questions that I have, for now."

The rancher stood, saying, "I understand you've got someone arrested for these killings, since the one you're asking Chris about."

"We've talked to someone about one of them," Slade said, then climbed out on a limb. "Smart money says he's innocent."

"Well, so's Chris," Gallagher replied. "He may get hot under the collar, like the rest of us, but I can't see him cuttin' up no whores."

Instead of asking whom he thought the younger man

might cut, Slade simply said, "I'll let you all get back to work. Thanks for your time."

He had the whole ride back to think about Christofides, already more than half convinced that while he might turn out to be a nasty drunk, he hadn't slaughtered any working girls in Jubilee.

"So, you believe the cowboy's innocent?"

Slade studied Mayor Johansson's anxious face before replying. Clearly, it was critical for him to see these murders solved. Already, Slade supposed, there was a chance they'd cost him reelection to another term, if he had planned to seek it. And he seemed to like the office, with its trappings of authority. Enjoyed being respected by his fellow citizens or, at the very least, having them fake it to his face.

"I doubt he killed the one you call Long Liz," Slade said. "On the first two jobs, he's got an alibi of sorts, depending on the nights they happened."

"Becky Hatcher was a Tuesday," Constable Vandiver said. "Sunday for Mary Vaughn."

"Would that be Sunday night or early morning after Saturday?" asked Slade.

"The night going to Monday," Vandiver replied.

"Well, Gallagher's prepared to testify his people only come in town to drink on Saturdays. Can't really prove it, but he claims it's ironclad."

"That sounds right," Vandiver said. "I couldn't swear to it, myself, but thinking back, I don't remember seeing any Bar-B hands around on any other night. Some wind up sleeping over into Sunday, but he works 'em long and hard."

"That still leaves Otto Heidegger," Johansson said.

"I gave you both my reasons why I don't believe he's guilty," Slade replied. "I don't plan on repeating them, unless it goes to trial."

"You'd testify on *his* side?" Mayor Johansson was appalled.

"I have no first-hand knowledge of the crime," Slade told them. "But I'd give the court my personal opinion, citing evidence to back it up. You need to understand there's more to marshaling than locking people up. First thing, you need to find the *right* people."

Johansson launched into his litany. "I'd say that when he's found beside the victim's body with a bloody knife—"

"We've been all over that," Slade cut him off. "No point rehashing it."

"So, you think I should turn him loose?" Vandiver asked.

"Explain his options to him."

"Which are . . . ?"

"No one's tried to lynch him yet," Slade said, "but that's no guarantee he's safe outside the lockup. On the other hand, he's got a shop to run, and you need charges to confine a man against his will."

"I reckon he can kiss the butcher shop good-bye," Vandiver said. "Who's gonna trust his sausage now, for God's sake?"

"Everyone except a few odd yahoos, if we catch the man behind these killings," Slade replied.

"So, how's that going?" asked the constable. It did him credit that he didn't smirk.

"So far, you know as much as I do," Slade admitted. "But there's one thing in our favor."

"What is that?" Johansson asked him.

"Pressure."

"Come again?" Vandiver said.

"Inside the killer. Building up and pushing him to find another victim. When it redlines on the boiler, he'll do something, even if he knows it's dangerous. Maybe *because* he knows that. It's the way these characters are made."

"You speaking from experience?" Vandiver asked.

"I've met my share," Slade told him, thinking of the Benders.

More than anybody's rightful share.

"So, we just sit and wait until he kills again?" The mayor looked stricken as he spoke.

"Until he *tries* again," Slade said. "We know he hunts saloon girls, so we keep a good, close watch. Not being obvious about it, but we need to be there when he makes his move."

"There's only two of us," Vandiver said.

"And two saloons," Slade answered.

"Right. Okay. No days off, then."

"Unless you have a deputy."

"Not lately."

"Then you knuckle down," Slade said. "We're lawmen, right? It's what we do."

7

Slade found the local doctor's office down an alley and behind the general store. A shingle at the alley's mouth read simply DOCTOR, with an arrow pointing north. Slade hadn't known physicians to be bashful in the past, about their trade, but he supposed some small-town residents might not want everyone in town to know they had been visiting the doctor.

Feeling well enough himself, at least in body, Slade approached the office door, which bore a small sign at eye level, reading DENTON WHEATLEY, M.D. The office appeared dark inside through the small windows, with no way to determine from outside if anyone was home, so Slade rapped on the door.

The best part of a minute passed before it opened to reveal a man of middle years, about Slade's height, well built, with a full head of iron-gray hair. He wore a pair of wire-rimmed spectacles that had a way of sliding down his nose, so that he peered across, rather then through, their round lenses. He looked at Slade's face first, then at his badge.

"Good afternoon, Marshal . . . ?"

His British accent came as a surprise.

"Jack Slade. You're Dr. Wheatley?"

"Guilty." Spoken with a smile. "Are you unwell?"

"Fit as a fiddle," Slade replied.

"So, good for one of us."

Sladed nodded. Said, "You've likely heard that I'm in town to see about the recent murders."

"Word does travel in a town the size of Jubilee."

"And Constable Vandiver tells me you performed examinations on the victims' bodies."

"That's correct. A ghastly business. Ghastly."

"Doctor, if you have the time to share some information . . ."

"But of course. Where are my manners? It's provincial life I blame. Come in, by all means. Please."

Slade stepped into a small reception room, waited while Wheatley closed the door, then trailed the doctor to a smallish office farther back. Along the way, they passed the open door of what Slade took to be an operating room. There was a raised table covered in white linen. Diagrams of human organs hung on the walls. Bright instruments lay out, ready to go.

When they were seated in the doctor's office, separated by a simple wooden desk, Slade said, "I'll take a guess that you're from England."

"So I am," Wheatley agreed. "No grudge against John Bull, I hope?"

"I never met an Englishman I didn't like," Slade said.

Before that afternoon, he'd met exactly one, a cheerful rogue who'd wound up dealing cards in the Dakota Territory. He'd been nice enough, but he was dead, shot through his left eye in an argument about a missing ace.

"To business, then," said Wheatley. "What is it you wish to know?"

"Your mayor and constable were late reporting on these crimes," Slade said, "so I'm still catching up. I understand the women killed were more or less . . ."

"Eviscerated," Wheatley said. "Or disemboweled, if you prefer."

"Uh-huh. And would you say that it required any degree of special skill or knowledge, Doctor?"

"Special knowledge or skill," Wheatley echoed, then paused to consider. "Clearly, any medical student could do it if he—or *she,* these days—was so inclined. Physicians can't be squeamish, if they hope to serve and prosper, eh?"

"I guess not," Slade replied.

"Of course, you don't need medical instruction to evacuate a body cavity. An hour spent with *Gray's Anatomy* will tell you where the organs are. Beyond that, hunters do the same thing, more or less, each time they bag a deer. And butchers . . . Oh. Poor Otto. Do you really think that he . . ."

"It's still under investigation, Doctor."

"Certainly. I understand completely."

"In these four cases, now, I understand that certain organs were removed," Slade said.

"That is correct. A kidney from the first poor woman, more specifically the left. From the other three, the murderer removed the womb."

"Womb?"

"Uterus," Wheatley explained. "And from the one they called Long Liz, both ovaries."

"So Thelma Lou, the latest victim, had the same . . . thing missing?"

"Worse," Wheatley replied. "She was pregnant."

"Pregnant?" Slade was confused. "But if he took . . . I mean . . . how can you tell?"

"He failed to excise the placenta," Wheatley said. "There's no mistaking it."

Jesus.

Slade played a wild card.

"Some years back," he said, "your people had a character like this in London, I recall."

Wheatley looked grim. "Red Jack. The Ripper. Yes, what of it?"

"Who was never caught," Slade said.

"One hears so many different stories," Wheatley said. "A suicide. Commitment to a lunatic asylum by a wealthy family. A sailor passing through with time to kill. I really couldn't say."

"Some people thought he might've been a doctor."

"Or a Hebrew knackerman, a pimp, a sodomite, a dope fiend, someone driven mad by syphilis, a Satanist. Some thought it must have been a copper, to escape detection. Take your pick."

"Did you have any favorites?" asked Slade.

"A poor lost soul, I'd say. Beyond the reach of human mercy."

"Sounds right," Slade said, "except the 'poor' part. Thank you for your time, Doctor. If you think of something else that might help sort this out, I'm staying at—"

"The Jubilee Hotel?"

"Where else?"

"Good luck, Marshal. I fear that you may need it."

Slade's next stop was the only church in town. He wasn't in a praying mood, but knew some pastors had a knack for gleaning secrets from their flocks. Most kept them safe and tried to give the best advice they could, within the stricture of their faith, but some were prone to go another way. He'd known some so-called men of God who wouldn't shy from blackmail or seduction, given half a chance.

Slade had no reason to suspect the local preacher was a predatory sort. In fact, he hoped the opposite. A wise man's observations of his neighbors could be useful. Any word on secret sins might point Slade in a new direction with his manhunt.

Jubilee's church was predictably white, with a twenty-foot belfry. Slade supposed its bell was on order from somewhere back East, or perhaps had been canceled entirely, depending on cost. There was no sign outside identifying a denomination. Slade took off his hat and held it in his left hand as he passed through the open doors into the shady nave. He was still waiting for his vision to adjust when someone called out to him from the general direction of the chancel.

"Welcome to God's house."

At first glance, coming from the shadows, the approaching figure seemed rectangular. Broad, squared-off shoulders in a black, unbuttoned frock coat that eliminated any hint of narrowed waist or hips. Beneath the coat, a white shirt with a black string tie. The head atop those shoulders was a squarish shape, as well, with dark brown curly hair and bristling eyebrows on a somber face.

The preacher didn't offer Slade his hand, but said, "You need no weapons here."

"Maybe we ought to talk outside," Slade said.

"As you prefer."

Clear of the nave's restrictive atmosphere, Slade introduced himself and learned the preacher's name was Isaac Booth.

"You've come about the harlot slaughter," Booth declared.

"Four murdered women, that would be," Slade said.

"Some call them fallen angels or soiled doves," said Booth. "I've never held with sugarcoating God's own truth."

"It seems to me I recollect a story about Jesus and a woman who had sinned. The way I heard it, he left judgment to whoever had a clean slate of his own and couldn't find one in the crowd."

"John 7:53 through 8:11," Booth replied. "Of course, the

sin in question was adultery. Ephesians 5:5 tells us that no whoremonger will share Christ's heavenly reward."

"Whoremongers being men who pay for favors," Slade observed. "Another time, I think he told some temple bigwigs that the whores and bartenders would beat them into heaven."

"Matthew 21. You've had religious training, sir."

"Long time ago," Slade said. "Right now, I'm more concerned with what's been going on in Jubilee these past few weeks."

"Of course. And what brings you to me?" asked Booth.

"In my experience," Slade said, "a small-town pastor generally knows what's going on among his people, even if they aren't all strict observers. Maybe more so, in that case."

"I would agree."

"And I was hoping you might know if someone was inclined a certain way. Whoremongering, for instance. Maybe with a nasty side."

"Is there a *good* side to it, Marshal?"

"I believe you understand me, Pastor."

"Certainly. And if I knew of any person such as you describe, I would be duty-bound to tell our constable."

"Meaning that since you haven't . . ."

"I cannot contribute to your knowledge of the crimes in that regard."

"All right, then. Sorry to have bothered you."

"Which doesn't mean that I'm without ideas," Booth said.

"I'm listening."

"You may wish to discuss the matter with our dry-goods merchant, Marshal. He's a Jew, you know."

"And that's significant because . . . ?"

"You know your Bible. Who killed Christ our Savior, Marshal?"

"I believe it was the Romans."

"But at whose insistence? The Sanhedrin!"

"Interesting, but it doesn't fall within my jurisdiction," Slade told Booth.

Booth leaned in close enough for Slade to smell his breath and said, "My point is that the killing never stopped. Ritual murder has persisted to the present day among these so-called *Chosen People*. Martin Luther warned us of it in the sixteenth century. Have you read his classic work, *On the Jews and Their Lies*?"

"Must've missed it," Slade said.

"He damned their synagogue as an *incorrigible whore and an evil slut*," said Booth, apparently quoting from memory. "He said they're *full of devil's feces, which they wallow in like swine*."

"Sounds like he had some problems," Slade remarked.

"A holy man of God, sir!"

"And you've passed this theory on to Constable Vandiver?"

Stiffening, the pastor said, "He lacks the education to appreciate it."

"Ah."

"And if the presence of a heathen Jew amongst us isn't bad enough," said Booth, "consider the celestials!"

"The which?"

"Chinese barbarians! They're well-known peddlers of opium and cannibals!"

"How do you peddle cannibals?" asked Slade.

"You mock me, sir?"

"I wouldn't dream of it," said Slade, anxious to disengage. "Thanks for your time."

"Look to the heathens, Marshal!" Booth called after him. "They bear close watching, sir!"

Slade thought, *And so do you.*

The huntsman followed Marshal Slade on his appointed rounds. He was unobtrusive about it, and didn't tread on the lawman's heels or draw attention to himself in any way. He started on the north side of the street, while Slade patrolled the south, then switched midway along, between the livery and the hotel. His neighbors greeted him with smiles, but most of them had little time or energy for pleasantries today.

Small wonder, with the latest shock and Otto Heidegger in jail. The huntsman had enjoyed a conversation earlier that morning with a merchant's wife who literally shuddered at the thought of buying meat from Heidegger. It tickled him, but he could not afford to laugh over the so-called tragedy in public. How would that look to the townsfolk in their hour of tribulation?

With his somber face composed, he paused at one shop, then another, making minor purchases. He dawdled past a third and fourth, tracking the man hunter's reflection in their windowpanes. It was a warm, but not oppressive, afternoon. Nothing unusual about his presence on the street, communing with the citizens of his adopted home.

The huntsman was well traveled. He had literally been around the world and back again, a four-year journey filled with opportunities to sample new delights and horrors, ply his trade and blade in settings most men of his age and background could scarcely imagine.

His mission to reveal the darkest secret of the harlot species had begun before he sailed, but circling the globe confirmed that they were all the same in every way that counted. Never mind the race, supposed religion, or the patois spilling from their painted lips.

A whore was a whore.

His goal was not simply removing them, of course. That would require concerted effort by a global army and could only happen once their deadly secret was exposed. Disarmed. Made impotent. When *that* had been accomplished, then the purge could run its course.

And he would he a hero for the ages.

It amused the huntsman to imagine monuments erected in his honor, in the very cities where he had been hunted through the streets and vilified in print. Brilliant Paris. Rainy London. Cold Saint Petersburg. Calcutta, where the dead were scarcely noticed. Bangkok, in Siam, where he had very nearly been arrested. Rio de Janeiro, where a fever interrupted his crusade but could not halt it.

In the States, he'd carved a long swath through the Land of Opportunity, finding no streets of gold but leaving pavements stained where harlots gathered in Savannah, Richmond, New York City, in the shadow of Chicago's slaughterhouses, Denver, San Francisco, and the busy former pueblo of Los Angeles.

Some might regard his presence in a town like Jubilee as evidence of cowardice, or even failure. Nothing could be further from the truth. The huntsman understood that whores were all the same at heart, no matter where you stalked them. He was just as likely to unmask their secret in a tiny frontier burg as in a great metropolis. More so, perhaps, if they felt safer there. Let down their guard.

So far, that had not been the case, but he was hopeful.

Now, the lawman complicated things, of course. He was an obstacle, but not a fatal one. Outwitting him would do the huntsman good on many levels. Boost his confidence, which had begun to flag a bit of late. Renew his energy for the ongoing quest. Strike fear into the locals, well beyond the *angst* occasioned by another harlot sacrifice.

And afterward, when he had proved himself superior, would it be safe to stay and work in Jubilee?

Most likely not.

He would be cautious, offer up a sound and simple reason for departing. Leave no trail for anyone to follow north, south, east, or west. A coach ride to the next railhead, or should he strike off by himself, on horseback? It would be a new experience, and fraught with danger if the tales of border outlaws could be credited.

The huntsman wasn't worried.

He would meet no one on city streets or open prairie half as dangerous as himself.

But leaving Jubilee could wait.

He felt a chess game coming on.

Slade felt ridiculous even considering the accusations spewed by Pastor Booth, but chasing wild geese and false trails was a part of his job. He didn't buy the preacher's crazy rant on Jewish human sacrifice any more than he thought the working girls of Jubilee were killed by rogue Comanches. And yet, something itched at the back of his mind.

What was it?

Something Dr. Wheatley had said, about London's Ripper. One of the suspects he'd mentioned was *a Hebrew knackerman*—or butcher, to the Brits. Since no one had been charged with Red Jack's crimes in England, Slade assumed the case against that suspect wasn't strong enough to fly in court. Still, he was paid to study every angle of a case, pursue each lead.

Including trips down dead-end alleys strewn with garbage.

As for the Chinese . . .

Slade found the dry-goods store between a barber's shop and lawyer's office. From the slightly weathered sign, he figured that the owner's name must be Shapiro. Swallowing a hard knot of embarrassment, Slade tried the door. It opened, and he went inside.

Dry goods normally included fabric, finished clothing, knitting yarn, and "notions"—a broad range of small household items that fell short of qualifying as hardware. The shelves surrounding Slade as he entered the shop held sewing items, candlesticks, bedding, a range of plates and silverware. The walls were hung with tapestries and empty picture frames.

A small bell set above the door summoned the shop's proprietor from somewhere in the back. Slade put him somewhere in his thirties, smartly dressed, with gleaming hair combed straight back, flat against his skull. A tidy beard fleshed out a face that might have seemed too long without it. His engaging smile seemed out of place with wary eyes.

"You must be Marshal Slade."

"Small town," Slade said.

"It is. Amos Shapiro." The shopkeeper's grip was strong, and yet reserved. "May I assume you're not in need of fabric or flatware?"

"Just meeting folks in town," Slade told him. "Doing what I can to get a feel for Jubilee."

"And pick out suspects, eh?" Shapiro kept his smile, but it was showing signs of strain. "Such dreadful things, these murders."

"I'm a stranger here, Mr. Shapiro. I don't know your town, its people. Anything that I can learn may point me toward the killer, somehow, even if it's trivial."

"And would it be presumptuous of me to think you've spoken with our self-appointed voice of God?"

"I've had a word with Pastor Booth," Slade granted.

"Pastor." Now Shapiro lost his smile. "It's from the Latin *pastorem*, meaning a shepherd. One who tends a flock, stands guard, and keeps it safe. This one, I think, would drive his sheep over a cliff to satisfy his prejudice."

"You two don't get along, I take it," Slade replied.

"*He* doesn't get along with 'children of the Devil.' Did he quote from Luther for you?"

Slade couldn't help but smile. Said, "I believe he did."

"Someone should tell him it's the nineteenth century," Shapiro said. "Alas, it's not my place. And if I tried, he'd only say that Satan put me up to it."

"You get a lot of that?" Slade asked.

"Less than you might expect," replied Shapiro. "Personally, I have never been attacked. Insulted, yes. Of course. I am, as you can no doubt see, a 'Christ killer' with all the money in the world at my disposal."

"Say this for you," Slade replied. "You hide it pretty well."

Shapiro laughed at that. "It's difficult to dominate the planet from a shop in Jubilee, I grant you. But I have high hopes."

"Well, let me know how that works out for you," Slade answered. "In the meantime, any thoughts you have about the killings, I'd be glad to hear them."

"These are crimes of hatred," said Shapiro. "Hatred for the women of a certain class. Or, I suspect, for females as a whole. I've made no special study of psychiatry—"

"Sigh what?" Slade interrupted him.

"Psychiatry. The healing of disordered minds," Shapiro said. "Today's alienists were once called 'mad doctors,' which has it all backward."

"Okay. You were saying . . . ?"

"Without any specialized training myself," said Shapiro, "it takes no great genius to guess that our killer hates women. The way he attacks them, their . . . well, it seems obvious, eh? No great lover, this one. All the failure, rejection, and anger builds up over time. He explodes, but the tension remains, like steam in a geyser. He can never rid himself of hatred or the shame attached to it."

Slade thought about it. Asked Shapiro, "You know anyone who might fit that description?"

The merchant smiled, a hint of sadness to it.

"If I were spiteful," he replied, "I might suggest our Pastor Booth. You may have gathered that he has no truck with harlots. Also, he's a bachelor by choice, although his creed has no objection to the marriage of its holy men."

"So, you think Booth could be the killer?"

"Honestly? I doubt it. He's been too outspoken on the subject. Anxious to be heard and recognized as an authority on all things that pertain to sexual morality. Your killer, I expect, will be a creature of the shadows. A chameleon, disguised to blend with his surroundings."

"Could be anyone," Slade said.

"Indeed."

"Well, thanks for that."

Another laugh, but rueful.

"Thanks for nothing, eh? I've been no help to you at all."

"I wouldn't go that far," Slade said.

"What will you do with this man, Marshal, if you find him?"

If, not *when*.

"My job is to arrest him," Slade replied, stating the obvious. "Take him to Enid, for Judge Dennison."

"Who, I presume, will hang him?"

"More than likely."

"And if he won't consent to be arrested?"

"I've met some like that," Slade said.

"You'd kill him, then."

"Whatever's necessary, for the end result."

"He may insist on it," Shapiro said. "He might even regard it as a favor."

"He could always do that part himself," Slade said.

"Perhaps. But if he lacks the courage . . ."

"Not the squeamish sort," said Slade.

"It's not the same at all. A man can wade in blood and still fear death," Shapiro said. "Or life."

"Well, when we meet," Slade said, "he'll have a choice to make. Right then and there."

"Always assuming that you recognize him, Marshal," said Shapiro. "Bear in mind, you may have met your man already. And be careful, please, for your own sake. For all of us."

8

Amos Shapiro told Slade where to find the tiny group of Chinese who had come to Jubilee for reasons still unclear and had stayed to serve the town in different ways. They ran a small laundry, some of them worked as handymen or janitors, and the children ran errands for pennies. Despite the warnings brayed by Pastor Booth, there'd been no sign of opium or fan-tan games. The solitary Chinese girl who'd turned to whoring had been disowned by her family and lived full-time at the Klondike saloon.

Another stop Slade had to make, along with the American. He'd need to speak with both proprietors, find out if the strain of competition might have prompted one or both to kill the other's working girls and stage the crimes to blame a phantom lunatic.

Not likely, Slade acknowledged to himself. But possible.

The Chinese camp in Jubilee—no standard Chinatown, by any means—consisted of three little bungalows, a shed where laundry could be boiled and starched, and several sheds for tools or other odds and ends, all tucked away behind the livery, well out of sight and close to where the first victim was found. There were three families, Shapiro had explained, interrelated in some way the merchant didn't fully understand.

Which meant nothing to Slade, as long as none of them were killers.

He'd been told to ask for Hoop Wong, elder spokesman of the group, but never had a chance to ask for Wong or call him out. The man himself appeared as Slade approached the little town-within-a-town, flanked by two younger men who stood like stone-faced bookends.

None of them had any weapons Slade could see, but he kept a respectful distance, stopping ten feet short of where the trio stood. Behind them, other Asian faces peered through windows, waiting for the show to start.

Slade touched his hat brim as a courtesy and introduced himself, adding, "I'm here to see Hoop Wong."

"Nobody here by that name," said the old man in the middle.

"Oh? That's funny. I was told—"

"My name is *Huping* Wong," the old man interrupted. "Round-eyes can't pronounce, so shorten it to please themselves."

"Huping," Slade said. "It's not that hard."

"For someone of intelligence," Wong answered.

"Hmm. I'll take that as a compliment," said Slade.

"The choice is yours," Wong said.

"Now that we've got the names all sorted out," Slade said, "I've got a couple questions for you about what's been going on in town."

"Murders of round-eye women."

"That's it, in a nutshell," Slade agreed.

"We have no business with the saloons," Wong said, "except to wash their sheets and sweep their floors. Sometimes a small repair. Yung Chang-li discovered the third woman. He was not responsible for her condition."

"No, sir. No one's saying that."

"Some round-eyes maybe think it. Say we're cannibals and cook their babies in *tsap sui*, even when no babies missing. Is a strange thing, yes?"

"I'd say so," Slade agreed.

"We are not criminals. We have no tong."

Slade thought of fireplace implements and knew he'd better ask. "Did you say *tong*?"

"Secret society from China," Wong explained. "Sometimes involved in crime. Have many members in your San Francisco, New York City, other places. Fight sometimes, for power."

"I'd just as soon avoid them, if I can," Slade said.

"Wise man. My family left your Seattle when the tong say we must pay them tax for business. Move to your Wyoming Territory, dig in ground for copper, until round-eyes have enough and kill Chinese. Meantime, other round-eyes drive all Chinese from Seattle, tong or no. Is funny, yes?"

"That's not the word I'd choose," said Slade.

"None of my family kill women," Wong declared, "although one of our own—my granddaughter, Yung-hu Miao—disgraces us with round-eyes in employ of Mr. Loving. Is a joke, perhaps, that name?"

"I doubt it," Slade replied. "But, then again, you never know."

"The Klondike and American saloons sell *hai*, not love," Wong said. "I think your Mr. Loving is a great *nan yeung*."

Slade didn't ask for a translation that time, figuring that he could work it out himself. Instead, he thanked Wong for his time and turned away, the flesh between his shoulder blades itching until he reached the nearest corner, rounded it, and put the little Chinese neighborhood behind him.

Slade knew he couldn't write them off entirely, thought one of the younger men might be upset enough about Yung-hu Miao's defection to the seamy side of life that he'd take out his rage on other working girls.

Unlikely, Slade decided, but he'd file it all the same.

His stomach growled, reminding him that he was hungry, and he struck off toward MacDonald's with new purpose in his stride.

The restaurant was pushing steak and chicken, both with beans or roasted vegetables and fresh-baked bread. Slade chose the bird, ordered a cup of coffee with it, and was savoring aromas from the kitchen when he saw Mills Vandiver outside, shading his eyes with one hand, peering past the window's glare.

Terrific.

Slade supposed he'd have to give up on the prospect of a quiet, solitary meal in Jubilee. He had himself composed, a poker face, before the constable entered and beelined toward his table.

"Mind if I sit down?" Vandiver asked.

Slade nodded to an empty chair without replying. Vandiver removed his hat and dropped into the seat.

"You making any progress?" he inquired, as Slade received his coffee.

"Well—"

The red-haired waitress had distracted him. Vandiver ordered steak and beans, then turned to Slade again. "Sorry."

"None to speak of," Slade replied. "Progress, I mean. This afternoon I've seen the doctor, preacher, and a couple others. Some of them have notions, but I'm not sure what to do with them."

"Know what you mean," Vandiver said. "The reverend, land's sakes. He carries on, you know?"

"I got a sampling," Slade replied.

"You ought to hear him of a Sunday, raising Cain. No disrespect intended, mind. But some of his ideas about the Jews and the celestials—"

"What's that about?" Slade interrupted him. "Celestials."

"I heard two diff'rent stories," Vandiver replied. "One says the Chinese call their country some kind of celestial kingdom, meaning that God picked their emperor. Crazy. Some other folk claim they aren't human at all, but come down from another planet out in space somewhere. I'd call that *double* crazy."

"Right."

"I mean, because they breathe the same air we do, yeah?"

"Seems so," Slade granted.

"There you go. It's good enough for me."

Their meals arrived to save the day, and Slade dug in, fending off questions while he ate. Before he'd finished, rushing it and losing much of the enjoyment from his meal, Vandiver had explained that he was holding Otto Heidegger in jail for one more night, for his own safety. There had been no open lynching talk, but Vandiver was worried someone still might take a shot at Heidegger when he was freed.

"Maybe someone who liked one of the girls particularly," said the constable. "They got no families in town, o' course, or anywhere I know about. No way for word to reach kin, anyhow. Been planting them in Potter's field."

"You know best about the butcher," Slade allowed. "You say your town's under control, I'll take your word for it until you're proven wrong."

"You understand I can't guard Otto once he's out."

Something to think about. If it appeared that Heidegger was in the clear, was there a chance the killer might attempt to silence him? The butcher hadn't seen whoever knocked him out, but if the murderer suspected that he might remember something, watching Heidegger might still pay dividends.

Or simply waste Slade's time.

"Do what you think is best," he told the constable. "I need to get some sleep. See how it looks tomorrow."

"Right. Sure thing," Vandiver said. "I'll go ahead and meet you here for breakfast, then?"

"Your wife might want to cook a meal for you herself," Slade said.

"Might, if I had one. Never took the altar walk," said Vandiver.

Defeated, Slade replied, "I guess I'll see you then, if nothing else comes up."

"You think he'll keep on killin', with you here in town?" Vandiver asked.

"Just have to wait and see," Slade answered.

Knowing that if Jubilee's madman had sense or discipline enough to stop, he'd likely get away with it.

Hoping he *wouldn't* stop, Slade walked back to his room with guilt dogging his tracks.

The work around God's house was never done. It seemed to Isaac Booth that Providence should lend a hand with fixing shingles, painting and the like, but there was truth in the old saying that the Lord helped those who helped themselves.

That didn't come from scripture, though most people Booth had met believed it was a Bible quote. They often looked bemused when he told them Ben Franklin had coined the phrase, in his *Poor Richard's Almanack*, a quarter century before there was a United States of America. It still amazed Booth now and then, the things some people didn't know.

And the things they refused to believe.

He'd seen the U.S. marshal peering at him in confusion and disdain, as Booth tried to explain the Jewish menace and the threat of Chinese cannibals among them. Slade was another of the countless unbelievers who would learn the mortal error of their ways on Judgment Day.

When that day came, would Booth be able to contain himself? Would he collapse in laughter at his Savior's side, watching the sinners and the heathens cast into a roiling lake of fire? Could Booth restrain himself from crowing out, "I told you so!" to his detractors, all engulfed by flame?

Maybe.

For now, his was the small voice crying in the wilderness, spreading the word of God that some souls would accept, while most ran merrily along the road to Hell. Booth knew that he should mourn for them, but couldn't find it in his heart to grieve.

Was that, itself, a sin?

If so, then Christ himself must be a sinner, Booth decided. God's own son had flown into a rage the day he drove the money changers from his temple, and he'd never asked forgiveness for that righteous tantrum. As to who those vile defilers were, the Bible made it plain.

Whatever Slade, Vandiver, and the rest of them might think, Booth knew who Satan's children were. He'd seen how they corrupted civilized society, boring like termites from within, until it teetered on the knife's edge of collapse.

In Jubilee, he thought, the problem was a relatively minor one. Removing harlots from the small community was hardly any crime at all, though Booth was vaguely frightened and disgusted by the killer's methods. Granted, as a man he was exempt. But he had seen one of the victims, as she'd been discovered, and the sight revolted him. He'd prayed to have the killings stop, then wondered whether they were God's will after all, when they continued unabated.

Impossible to say, since many of his prayers had gone unanswered over time. Prayers for a helpmate who would share his burdens and his bed, give him a son to carry on his name and his crusade. Prayers for a larger, richer congregation to support his vision of a shining tabernacle on the prairie.

Prayers that he might not feel so alone.

Tonight, Booth had a broom to keep him company. His final chore, before he slept, was sweeping out the church. It was a daily ritual, whether or not he'd had parishioners inside, because the grit and dust relentlessly assaulted everything in Jubilee. God's house might not be full on Sundays, but he was resolved to keep it clean.

At first, Booth thought the smell of smoke was an illusion, something that his mind had conjured up to complement his thoughts of Judgment Day and hellfire. Then, he guessed it must be the aroma from MacDonald's restaurant, borne down the length of Main Street on an errant breeze.

And by the time he recognized his grave mistake, it was too late.

The first bright glare of flame came through his office doorway, to the rear, behind the altar. Crackling noises reached Booth's ears a heartbeat later, and he broke in that direction, still armed with his broom, as if he thought a fire was something he could sweep away.

And yes, perhaps he could, if it was small enough.

How had it started? Booth was not a smoker, had not cooked a bite of food since noontime. There should be no open flame at all, in or around the church.

Unless . . .

He reached the office doorway, saw the room on fire from wall to wall, and was recoiling from it when another blast of heat swept toward him from behind. Spinning, Booth saw more flames leaping behind the pulpit, from the baptistery.

A bell might still have saved God's house, but Booth had none. No rope to pull and summon help with pealing notes. Instead, armed only with his faith and long frock coat, whipped off to beat the flames, Booth charged the fire alone.

Fire is the mortal dread of any frontier town. The buildings, mostly made from wood, sunbaked and dried for years or decades, are the next best things to tinderboxes. Once the flames catch on and start to spread, a fair-sized town can disappear within a few short hours. Embers on a night breeze, burning shingles carried on a gust of wind from a collapsing roof, and Hell can spread before its victims scramble from their beds. At best, they lose their livelihoods. At worst, they die screaming.

The central fire alarm in Jubilee—a bell resembling one you might find on a sailing ship—was mounted on a post outside the livery, whether because someone had thought hay might catch fire more easily or for some other reason, Slade couldn't divine. In any case, he wasn't sleeping when the bell began to clang and clamor, summoning the townsfolk to a battle for their very lives.

Slade checked his window first and saw it was the church on fire, flames shooting up the walls, across the roof, making a giant torch out of the belfry. Nothing else was burning yet, but if the belfry toppled left or right they stood to lose the northern side of Main Street.

That would leave the Jubilee Hotel and livery intact, Slade saw, giving him time to save his horse, weapons, and few belongings if it seemed the town was lost. With that in mind, he grabbed his hat and gunbelt on the fly, took time to lock his door against intruders, then ran pounding down the stairs and out into the street.

Most of the town was out and milling in the firelight. Outfits ranged from nightwear to the clothes they'd donned that morning, with a bit of everything between the two extremes. A couple of the working girls from the American Saloon wore sheets twisted around their bodies, toga-style, and nothing else.

There were no rules in a disaster, Slade supposed.

Firefighting on the open prairie was a problem. Some larger towns—like Enid—had fire wagons with water tanks and pumps on board, but Jubilee hadn't advanced to that state of sophistication. The alternative normally called for a bucket brigade, pitching water or sand on the flames in relays.

By the time Slade reached Main Street, the buckets were already coming out. Say half a dozen from the livery, snatched up by people shocked from sleep or pulled away from some other activity, while individuals along the street emerged from shops and homes with buckets of their own.

More would be coming anytime now, Slade surmised, from houses farther back to the north and south.

There was a central well in Jubilee—again, close by the livery—where one man cranked a drum to raise a wooden bucket and another sloshed its contents into waiting pails. Slade recognized one of the hostlers on the crank and wished him luck. At that rate, there'd be little chance to save the church. Indeed, the whole town might go up in flames.

It took another moment to discover that the townsmen had a trick in hand. They started with their buckets full, water in some and sandy soil in others. Each firefighter ran directly to the church and tossed his quenching load before retreating to the well for a refill.

Something, at least, but would it be enough?

Without a bucket of his own, Slade moved off toward the church, where he found Mayor Johansson standing rigid in the firelight, staring blankly as if mesmerized. Slade nudged his arm, then gripped it, shook him, called the mayor by name until he blinked and looked around.

"It's terrible!" he blurted out. "Has anyone seen Pastor Booth?"

Before Slade could reply, a scream cut through the babble of excited, frightened voices, and a human figure limned in fire burst through the front door of the church, streaking across Main Street, the very image of a comet come to Earth.

The huntsman was delighted with himself. He had chosen the perfect diversion, the ideal target. Who in Jubilee, from the supposed cream of the crop to lowly tosspots, would stand by and watch the Mercy Baptist Church consumed by fire?

No one.

He saw the mayor and constable, one watching from the sidelines while the other did his part with pail and water.

Saw the lawman who had come to hunt him. Saw the two saloon proprietors working together for a rare moment in time. Most of the bucketeers were men, but wives shouted encouragement. Whores from the Klondike and American saloons mingled and chattered like a flock of sparrows, showing off their wares as if the whole male population hadn't had a closer look already.

Perfect.

In such confusion, with the stakes so high, it was a relatively simple thing to be invisible. All eyes were focused on the church—already lost, from all appearances—and its immediate neighbors.

It was risky, setting fires in town, but he enjoyed a good blaze on occasion. His establishment was on the other side of Main Street, safe for now, and nothing that he couldn't stand to lose in any case. The huntsman thought of starting over as a grand adventure, every time.

He sidled over to the hookers, took his time, no sudden moves. The trick to blending in was to be mundane and unremarkable. Still, when he reached the group of whores, inhaled their scent, the huntsman found that he could not resist a bit of fun. His fingertips trailed over a bare shoulder, made the harlot jump and turn to face him with a gratifying little gasp.

She recognized him then, relaxed, letting her sheet sag down across the swell of her right breast.

"You spooked me there," she chided him.

"I'm sorry, Molly. Please forgive me."

"Never mind," she said, smiling. "Is this a laugh, or what? Old Boothy won't be sending us to Hell from that depot next Sunday."

"What about the town?" he asked, amazed to find her malice and disinterest in other townsfolk such a mirror of his own.

"Well, what about it? Don't you think they'll put it out?"

The huntsman shrugged. "It could go either way."

"Say, where's *your* bucket, anyhow?" she asked.

"Turns out, my bucket has a hole in it," he said.

"Mine, too," she answered with a sly smile, stepping closer to him.

No clothes to waste time on, thought the huntsman. *It's as if she has prepared herself for sacrifice.*

A scream erupted from the church just then. Molly strained forward, gaping as a human torch burst from the flaming hulk of God's house, stagger-sprinting through the Main Street crowd and trailing sparks.

Hellfire had found the Reverend Booth.

"Jesus! Is that—?"

"The pastor, I'm afraid," the huntsman said.

She turned into his arms, shivering inside her sheer cocoon. "Make him stop screaming," Molly whimpered. "I can't stand it."

"Horrible," he said, smiling inside.

Someone had splashed the preacher with a pail of water as he ran, now others grappled with him, scorching fingers in the process, as they pulled him down and rolled him in the dirt, smothering stubborn flames with jackets they would never wear again.

"I think it's done," he murmured, into curly hair that smelled in equal parts of sweat, tobacco, and some cheap cologne.

"You're sure?"

"I'm positive."

"I never saw the like of that before," she said. "Have you?"

"And worse, I fear. Much worse."

"You up for some distraction?" Molly whispered, while her fingers slid below his belt buckle.

The huntsman met her eyes and said, "I thought you'd never ask."

9

The fire was nearly out by midnight, mostly embers left, and those were being doused and smothered. Mercy Baptist was a write-off, but the town's bucket brigade had saved its neighbors with a minimum of damage. To the west, the hardware store would need new shingles on a portion of its roof, fresh paint along one wall. Eastward, a surveyor's office had been scorched but would survive.

The damage might have been much worse—catastrophic, in fact—but for the draw of gravity. When Mercy Baptist's burning steeple had collapsed, instead of falling to the left or right, it toppled over backward, to the north, and fell on empty ground. Its fall buckled the church's roof and let the walls drop inward, sparing the adjacent structures.

It was mere coincidence, in Slade's view, but some Jubileeans gave full credit to the Lord, as if a giant invisible hand had reached down and given the steeple a shove. He heard the talk but focused on finding the cause of the fire.

Vandiver found him at the northwest corner of the

Mercy Baptist funeral pyre. Slade nodded to him. "You smell that?"

"Kerosene," the constable replied.

"That's my thought."

"Hard to miss," Vandiver said.

"It's not just here." Slade led him past the smoking rubble, to the former northeast corner of the church. Again, the sharp, almost intoxicating scent of kerosene was evident.

"Arson," Vandiver said. "Goddamn it!"

"Set from the outside," Slade added. "Likely not the preacher, then."

"What, Pastor Booth?" Vandiver's frown threatened to tie his eyebrows into knots. "You think he'd burn his own church down?"

"It wouldn't be the strangest thing I ever heard of," Slade replied.

"I can't swallow that," Vandiver said. "What reason would he have?"

"I'm no mind reader," Slade replied.

"And burn himself up, in the bargain?"

"Last year, in Adair, there was a man who burned his own store. Killed himself, his wife, two kids."

"Well, maybe. But a *preacher*?"

"With some strange ideas, you may recall."

"There's strange, and then there's crazy," said Vandiver.

"And it doesn't matter, anyway," Slade said. "He would've poured the kerosene inside."

"So, now we've got a firebug, too, on top of everything?"

"Not necessarily," Slade said. "It's possible—"

A boy ran up to them, all out of breath. He gasped out, "Constable Vandiver! Marshal Slade!"

Vandiver must've recognized the child. He asked, "What is it, Tommy? You should be in bed."

"Doc Wheatley sent me for you," Tommy said, already

picking up his second wind. "He says you oughta hurry, if you wanna talk to Pastor Booth. He's goin' fast."

The curse Vandiver uttered made little Tommy blink, then grin. The constable struck off for Dr. Wheatley's alley office at a jog, Slade on his heels.

Three men had carried Booth to Wheatley's office from the fire scene, once the flames that wreathed him were extinguished. Slade had glimpsed the preacher's blackened face, his hands like claws carved out of ebony, and knew that he would need a miracle to live.

If anyone could call that living.

Entering the doctor's office shortly after midnight, Slade caught the familiar scent of roasted meat he had been dreading. He had smelled it for the first time at a brothel fire, in Tucson. Later, more times than he cared to, standing over ashes of some burned-out homestead where disaster had arrived on horseback and left ruin in its wake.

At least, in those cases, the smell had been dispersed by open air. The doctor's office, by comparison, was closed in, windows shut against the night. There was nowhere for the stench of suffering and death to go.

Wheatley met them in his small reception room, saying, "I thought you might have questions for him. I can't guarantee he'll hear you, much less answer you coherently. Time's short. That's probably a blessing."

Vandiver followed the doctor to his operating room, Slade bringing up the rear. He had nothing particular to ask the dying minister, as he assumed the arsonist—the *killer*, now—had set his fire outside the church, unseen by Booth. There was a chance, of course, that Booth knew something useful. If his brain could spit it out, compel his ashen tongue and vocal chords to speak.

Vandiver stood beside the groaning, blackened mannequin on Dr. Wheatley's operating table. Grimaced as he leaned in close to ask, "Can you hear me, Pastor?"

Booth expelled a ragged, smoky sigh.

Vandiver glanced at Slade, then forged ahead. "Pastor, can you shed any light on who might want to burn the church?"

Slade had some thoughts on that himself but didn't interrupt. He watched Booth turn his head an inch or so, heard crackling noises from the preacher's skin, then saw the gray lips move.

Vandiver stooped to place one ear an inch or so from Booth's face, eyes closed, as if blotting out the sight before him would improve his hearing. So it was that he missed Booth's left claw rising to brush dark fingertips across Vandiver's cheek.

Instinctively, the constable recoiled, gasping. He swatted at his own face, smearing streaks of soot the preacher had deposited, then caught himself and struggled to regain a calm façade.

Too late.

The minister was gone, immune to slights and insults now, presumably no longer racked by animosity toward Jews and Chinamen. Or, maybe he would carry all those traits along with him to someplace else, Slade thought.

No place that Slade would care to go.

"What did he say?" Slade asked Vandiver.

Pale by lamplight in the operating room, the constable replied, "He said it was the Devil."

"Just crazy talk," Vandiver said, moving along Main Street with Slade in the direction of his office and the Jubilee Hotel. "A man dying in pain like that. It broke his mind."

"Maybe."

Vandiver peered at Slade. "Oh, what?" he asked. "You gonna tell me now that Satan burned down Mercy Baptist."

"It's the kind of thing he'd do, if he existed," Slade replied. "But, no. I'm thinking more of someone Booth might *call* the Devil, with his mind half gone."

"You think he saw whoever set the fire?" asked Vandiver.

"Maybe. More likely, he had some idea of who it was. Suspicion, anyway."

"And knowing Booth, if he could talk, he'd blame Amos Shapiro for it. Maybe Hoop Wong's people."

"I think you can rule out the Chinese," Slade said.

"But not Shapiro? Hey, don't tell me you've converted to that Jew-conspiracy rigamarole."

"What I think," Slade replied, "is that your killer set the fire."

Vandiver stopped dead in his tracks and gaped at Slade.

"The same one who's been cutting whores?"

"How many killers have you got in town?" asked Slade.

"You're joshing, right? I mean, he butchers women. Why would he start setting fires?"

"Not *fires*," Slade said. "Just one—at least, so far. As for his motive, I can think of several."

"Go ahead," Vandiver said. "I'm listening."

"We don't know why he kills the women," Slade replied. "One possibility, he wants to terrorize the town. Either he feeds on other people's fear, or he has a reason that we haven't worked out, yet. The fire could be a way of branching out. Instead of waiting overnight to hear what people think about his handiwork, he'd get to watch them scurry."

"So, he'd come to watch the fire," Vandiver said.

Slade shrugged. "I'd say it brought out everyone in town."

"You said there could be several reasons."

"Maybe he was after Booth, specifically. He could've seen me talk to Booth this afternoon and started thinking that the preacher had some information that could hang him."

"Time to deal with that would be *before* you questioned him," Vandiver said.

"Except, the killer couldn't know I would. It was a whim, me stopping at the church."

"Where you heard nothing useful."

"Which the killer wouldn't know," Slade countered.

"Okay. What's another reason?"

"Say he had a grudge against the church, rather than Booth himself. Maybe it stands for something he despises."

"Brings us back to what Booth said. The Devil did it."

"I don't know about the Devil," Slade replied, "but I've met men who nearly qualified. We're looking for one, now."

"What else?" Vandiver asked.

"Maybe thumbing his nose at us. Adding insult to injury. Showing the world—or the town, anyhow—that we're eating his dust."

"Sounds like something the cocky shit would do," Vandiver said.

"And one more possibility," said Slade.

"Which is . . . ?"

"He might've set the fire as a diversion. Send us in a new direction, if he thinks we're getting close to something."

"Close to what?" Vandiver asked. "Myself, I'm still no closer to him than I was when he cut Becky Hatcher."

"Work out what it is that worries him," Slade said, "and we'll be more than halfway home."

"Too bad you're *not* a mind reader," Vandiver said.

"Have to admit," Slade said, "it would be handy now and then."

Nearing the church, with smoke still hanging in the air, Slade saw a gaggle of hookers surrounding a tall man with muttonchop sideburns and shoulder-length hair, all jabbering excitedly.

"Al Loving," said Vandiver, as the tall man spotted them and said something to the collected women.

All at once, the working girls abandoned him, rushing toward Vandiver and Slade. They clamored for attention, talking over one another, sending up a Babel that was gibberish to Slade. Vandiver batted at the air with anxious hands, trying to calm them and bring order out of verbal chaos.

"Hush, now!" he commanded. "One of you go on and spit it out, so I can understand you."

"Mills," a short brunette spoke up, "it's Molly!"

"What about her, Wanda?"

Loving reached them as Vandiver asked the question, speaking up before the woman could reply. "She's gone," he said.

"What do you mean by *gone*?" Vandiver asked.

"Just up and disappeared."

"We come to watch the fire, like ever'body else," the one called Wanda said. "She was right with us when we left the Klondike."

"So?" Vandiver prodded.

"So, she's with us at the start . . . but when it started winding down, she weren't."

"You missed her then?" asked Slade.

"Not right away," Wanda replied. "We thought she'd gone back to her crib, you know. But when we went on back ourselves, she weren't there."

"Checked the privy," said another of them. "Nothin'."

"And there's nowhere else she'd go in town?" asked Slade.

"My girls all live together," Loving said.

"Could've met up with somebody," Vandiver said.

He looked to Slade, catching the drift, as Wanda said, "That's what we're all afraid of."

The secret still eluded him. The huntsman had been rushed with Molly, certainly, and haste made waste, but he had done a thorough job. Delving. Searching. The mystery was still beyond his reach.

So be it. He had not expected miracles.

Still, poor Molly would serve him in a different way, as he'd intended from the moment that his plan was hatched, before he visited the Mercy Baptist Church.

Its immolation had been glorious, a fiery warning in the night to his sworn enemies. They hoped to cage and kill him with the help of their imported marshal, but they had misjudged the huntsman. He was not the lunatic they claimed, a madman baying at the moon.

He had a purpose. No, a *calling*. He'd been chosen by a power greater than himself to carry out a sacred task for all mankind.

The preacher hadn't seen that, wrapped up as he was in reverance for ancient fairy tales and the pursuit of petty influence. Big fish, small pond. Booth had condemned the huntsman from his pulpit, as expected, though his loathing for the so-called victims was apparent. All in all, he was pathetic.

Still, the huntsman hadn't meant to kill him.

That had simply been a bonus.

The huntsman required a distraction. He'd chosen the church for its central location on Main Street—and yes, for its symbolic power, the fevered emotion some townsfolk would feel when it burned. While burning down the livery or hardware store would qualify as an attack, setting the church on fire was an affront to decency itself. It threatened Jubilee's collective soul.

He had expected Booth to be at home, shut up inside his little cottage with the shutters closed and curtains drawn, holding the sinful world at bay. Presumably, some chore had kept Booth at the church beyond his normal time, and he had paid for it.

A little taste of hellfire for the man who'd preached it so convincingly. Why not?

And in his final, agonizing moments Booth had done a favor for the huntsman. Left young Molly shaken, hungry for the comfort of a strong man's arms.

The huntsman had been happy to oblige.

It had been thoughtful of her, turning up in nothing but a sheet. Slicing through clothes and undergarments all took time, and that had been in short supply this evening. Delicious irony, he thought, considering that Molly had provided her own shroud.

The locals would be stunned by his audacity; their borrowed man hunter would be enraged. And angry men were prone to make mistakes, a lesson learned the hard way as the huntsman had pursued his calling over time.

Today, he was as passionate as ever, but he was not angry at the harlots who seduced men to their ruination. Infected as they were with vile corruption, they could no more help themselves than could a mindless parasite. Mosquitos drew their meals of blood from higher animals, while hookers sucked the essence out of men, leaving them hollow shells and easy prey to other forms of vice.

Even though he had failed to find their secret and prepare an antidote, the huntsman knew that he performed at least a small-scale public service. Every leech in human form that he removed from circulation helped society. He might be like the Dutch boy in *Hans Brinker,* stalling the inevitable with his finger in the leaky dike, but at least he'd done *something*.

By the time he'd gone home, washed his hands, and checked his clothes for any wayward stains, the search for Molly had begun. It pleased the huntsman to join in, hearing his worried, frightened neighbors speak of him in abstract terms. They hadn't named him yet. Their fear was not personified, but labeling was generally done by newspapers, and Jubilee had none.

Too bad.

In other towns, he'd thoroughly enjoyed the fruitless speculation of reporters, sometimes doubled up with laughter as they fabricated "evidence." It was a thrill of sorts to walk with strangers on a busy street and know he could stop any one of them at random, tug a sleeve, and introduce himself using a nickname from the headlines. Watch them tremble, gasp, and flee.

Of course, he'd never done that. Never would, no matter how tempting it was. Exposure meant the interruption of his quest, and what else did the huntsman live for, after all? A life in service was his destiny.

He thought of leading the small party to the spot where he'd left Molly on display but squelched that urge immediately. It would only draw attention to him, prompt questions from the marshal. Better if he let another group make the discovery, then joined them in expressing outrage.

As if anyone in Jubilee would truly miss another whore.

Well, he supposed that Molly's pimp would miss the money lost while he sought her replacement. Men like Tewksbury and Loving were another kind of parasite, living on income from the hookers, feeding liquor to the men who were seduced and drained, to make the conquest even easier. The huntsman would have killed them cheefully, with relish, but he had not been called to hunt pimps.

His quest was for the secret that kept victims coming back time after time, submitting to the whores who violated and infected them. When he had solved that mystery, when men of influence around the world were forced to act upon their knowledge, then the pimps would naturally disappear.

Fleas never lingered on a dying mongrel.

"This way!" somebody shouted from the far end of the street. "Down here!"

His handful of companions broke into a run, the huntsman following like cold Death on their heels.

Slade spent his first few minutes at the murder scene, behind the Jubilee Hotel, helping Vandiver shoo the curious away. No matter how they moaned and groaned about it afterward, experience had taught him that most people loved to see dead bodies and the aftermath of violence. They'd hide during a gunfight, then come flocking out to gawk at corpses, crowd around the wounded in pretense of helping, even dig spent bullets out of walls and doorjambs for a souvenir.

There was no doubt that seeing Molly Whittaker—he'd learned her last name from Al Loving when the search began—in her present situation would sicken Jubileeans. Most of them, at least. The killer obviously wouldn't mind, since he'd reduced her to this hideous state. The undertaker, Guidry, might've seen worse in his time, and Slade supposed Doc Wheatley must be getting used to it.

Another day, another woman disemboweled.

Slade felt some queasiness himself, despite his limited experience with madmen and atrocities committed in the long struggle between red men and white. He'd never gotten used to it entirely, which he guessed must mean some vestige of humanity survived inside him.

He hoped so anyway.

Once the vultures were dispersed, he stood with Vandiver, the doctor, Silas Guidry, and the mayor, examining the killer's handiwork by lamplight. Scanning faces in the semicircle ranged around the body, Slade thought all of them looked numb.

Was one of them pretending? Faking it?

"I can't examine her like this," the doctor said at last. "I need more light. If you can help me move her to my office . . ."

Mayor Johansson cleared his throat, fishing for an excuse to get away. Before he had a chance to speak, Vandiver said, "Let's use the sheet. It ought to hold her."

"Right," said Guidry. "Four of us can do it, I believe."

"Well, then . . . um . . . I'll just check the church," Johansson said. "The ashes . . . we can't be too careful."

He was off, then, wobbling on unsteady legs. Part of the act, or was he really sickened to the point of nearly hobbling like a drunkard?

Molly Whittaker had not been fat in life, but deadweight always took Slade by surprise. Each of them took a corner of the sheet, trying their damnedest to avoid the tacky blood, and hoisted her together. They were bound to leave a trail, and didn't want to mark the Main Street sidewalks, so they trudged along behind its row of shops until they reached an alley opposite the doctor's office. Crossing there, they passed within sight of the burned-out church. Two of the townsmen still on duty, dousing embers, paused and doffed their hats out of respect.

"This sumbitch needs to die," Vandiver grunted, walking in the lead with Slade.

"No argument from me," Doc Wheatley said, behind them.

Silas Guidry kept his mouth shut, guaranteed more customers whichever way it went.

There was a tussle getting Molly through a doorway built to pass one person at a time. Vandiver went ahead, then Slade squeezed through, hoping he didn't reach the other side with bloodstains on his shirt or trousers. That thought sparked a pang of guilt, but he suppressed it.

Life went on. For some.

The feet were easier, but only just. Two minutes later, they had Molly on the doctor's operating table, covered in the sheet she'd carried from her crib to watch the fire.

"We know, now, why he burned the church," Slade said.

"For this?" Vandiver asked.

Slade nodded. "This, and showing he can do whatever pleases him, with no one stopping him."

"Goddamn it! And he's right," the constable replied.

"So far," Slade said.

"One thing, at least," said Wheatley. "You can let Heidegger go."

"Hell of a way to clear him," said Vandiver.

Silas Guidry turned to leave, telling the doctor, "I'll come back to get her when you're finished. Sometime in the morning?"

Wheatley nodded. "I'll get started now," he said. "From

what I see, it shouldn't take more than an hour. Two, at most."

Slade didn't envy him and was anxious to be out of there. The smell of smoke and ash on Main Street came as a relief, after the odors trapped inside the doctor's office.

"It's odd," Vandiver said, as they approached the blackened skeleton of Mercy Baptist Church.

"What is?" asked Slade.

"First time I ever hated someone who I've never met," the constable replied. "I really want to kill him, though. You know?"

Slade knew the feeling but chose to say, "That's not our job."

"Unless he happens to resist arrest," Vandiver said, a bleak smile on his face.

"We have to find him first," Slade said. "Back at it, first thing in the morning?"

"Right," Vandiver said. "You're on your own for breakfast, though. The bastard's killed my appetite."

10

The rapping at her door caught Faith Connover staring at her wedding dress. It was a fairly simple gown, a little beadwork on the bodice, with a modest train. Fashion's current trend dictated puffy leg-of-mutton sleeves with tissue paper for support and a high neckline trimmed at the back with a bow. She'd splurged on satin, one extravagance that Faith allowed herself, and picked a shade of coral rather than descend into hypocrisy.

Faith hadn't been exactly chaste these past few years. Her mother might have blushed and scolded her, but Faith herself was born eight months after her parents wed, and no one ever claimed that she was premature. Jim Slade had been her first, and after he was killed, Faith had believed there'd never be another man who satisfied her in that way.

Then, Jack.

She still had trouble, sometimes, understanding what had happened there. At times it seemed bizarre, her love for twins who were completely opposite from one another in most ways, once you got past their faces. Other times, however, it seemed logical—even predestined, if there was in fact a guiding hand in the affairs of humankind.

One of her hands, Ed Murdoch, doffed his dusty hat as Faith opened the door. He had an anxious look about him, not quite worried, but on edge somehow.

"Miz Connover," he said, kneading his hat.

"What is it, Ed?"

"We got a problem, ma'am," he answered.

"Tell me."

"Goes against the grain for me, ma'am. Tattlin'. But you got a right to know what happens on your spread."

"I'm listening."

"The past few weeks," said Murdoch, "little things've come up missin' from the bunkhouse. First a pocketknife from Jeb, next thing old Johnny's watch. Five dollars from my poke, another time."

"You're saying there's a thief."

"Yes, ma'am. But that ain't all of it."

"I'll hear the rest," Faith said, concerned and curious to know what else was making Murdoch so uneasy.

"Well . . . this part ain't easy."

"A quick cut's the best," Faith replied.

"Okay." But still he hesitated, close to half a minute slipping by before he spoke again. "Last night, 'bout nine o'clock, Art went to do some bidness and he seen somebody else behind your house. Up by the bathroom window, there."

Faith frowned, then felt the color rising in her cheeks. From half past eight till nine fifteen or so, she had been bathing. With the blinds drawn, certainly, but still . . . If there was any kind of gap at all between the curtains . . .

"Oh," she said. "I see."

"Yes, ma'am."

"What happened then?"

"Well, Art went over like, to find out who'n he—to find out who it was, but they was gone. He figgered musta heard him comin'. He goes on to look around, and purty soon runs into that Burch Thornton."

"Ah."

The new man, only hired two months before. Twenty-four or -five and lean, at five foot ten. He had a quick smile, but Faith wondered now if it had seemed a little shifty to her when she hired him.

Maybe just.

"So," Murdoch said, "Art asks him what he's doin' round the house and all. Thornton claims that he couldn't sleep and likes to walk it off."

"You don't believe him."

"No, ma'am. I sure don't. Art, neither. He was skairt to tell you, though. Embarrassed, like."

"About the stolen things . . ."

"We snuck a look this mornin', ma'am. While Burch was in the privy, there. Found Johnny's watch. He's likely carryin' the knife. Reckon my fiver's gone."

"You'll get it back, out of his severance."

"Yes, ma'am. I thank you."

"Does he know you're onto him, about the stealing?"

"Doubt it. He was laughin' up a storm like always over breakfast."

"Right. No point in dillydallying. Wait here a minute, and we'll have a word with Mr. Thornton."

"Yes, ma'am."

Faith went quickly to her bedroom, opened up the night-stand drawer, and found her Smith & Wesson Safety Hammerless revolver. She checked the pistol's load, found six .38-caliber rounds in the cylinder, and tucked it underneath her belt, around in back, before returning to the porch.

Jim's death and everything that happened afterward had driven home a lesson.

There was no such thing as too many precautions.

•   •   •

Slade spoke to Dr. Wheatley on his way to breakfast at MacDonald's. Wheatley looked wrung out and faded, like a man who'd spent a long night dodging sleep, afraid of what he'd see in dreams. Slade knew the feeling, though he'd managed several hours after all and woke, if not refreshed, at least prepared to face another day in Jubilee.

The doctor's findings came as no surprise. Slade had already seen the worst of it and simply needed conformation of the rest. Wheatley supplied it, telling him the killer had removed the victim's womb and ovaries.

"No child this time, thank God," he said. Almost a sigh.

"What would he likely . . . what he takes?" Slade asked.

Wheatley, already pale, had lost another shade of color as he said, "I'm not sure that I care to know."

Vandiver kept his word and didn't show for breakfast. Slade, despite the recent assault on his appetite, ate steak and eggs with a small loaf of rye bread some six inches long. Black coffee helped chase any lingering cobwebs out of his head and prepared him to visit the Klondike Saloon.

Barrooms are generally drab by daylight, and the Klondike offered no exception to the rule. Fresh sawdust would be sprinkled on the floor by sundown, girls and a piano player sprucing up the place, but at the moment it was dead, smellling of sweat, stale beer, and last night's smoke—tobacco and the church—all mixed together.

"Marshal Slade, I've been expecting you."

Al Loving came out of a back room, pushing through a curtain made from strings of many-colored beads. Slade guessed that it would catch and play with the lamplight, hinting at exotic pleasures to be found beyond, though he supposed most of the sweaty work was done upstairs.

"Is it convenient?" Slade inquired, not really caring one way or the other.

"Absolutely," Loving said. "To catch this lousy prick, my time is yours."

"I understand you've lost three girls out of the five, so far."

"That's sadly true," said Loving, while he poured himself a double shot of whiskey. He tipped the bottle Slade's way. "Something on the house?"

"No, thanks. A little early for me."

"Fine, fine. You have questions?"

"Just a few," Slade said. "You keep track of the customers who hire your girls somehow?"

"Indeed I do. Up here," said Loving, as he tapped his temple with an index finger.

"Nothing that would be written down?"

"You mean like who poked who at one o'clock on Friday the thirteenth, last year?" A smile, as Loving shook his head. "Nothing like that, Marshal."

"Too bad."

"You're working up to asking me about my customers," said Loving. "Whether any of them likes to hurt the girls or asks for anything unusual."

"You got me there," Slade said.

"I don't know if you've ever hired a woman, Marshal. Not my business, though I'd offer you a goodwill discount. Most men go with whores for two main reasons. One, they need relief and either don't know anyone in town or have no social skills where so-called ladies are concerned, out in polite society. Or two, because they have some fantasy they can't get satisfied at home. Something the wife won't go along with."

"Or that might land them in trouble," Slade suggested.

"That could be," Loving agreed. "Of course, I wouldn't go along with anybody damaging my girls. Beyond that, what the two of them work out is up to them."

"I'm guessing you'd remember anyone you had to escort off the premises for getting rowdy," Slade remarked.

"And you'd be right. Downstairs, they pay for anything they bust up, one way or another."

"Money, or a session with your bouncers?"

"That's the ticket."

"And upstairs?"

"Man hurts one of my girls, he isn't welcome back," Loving replied. "No matter what he pays before I boot his ass outside."

"You have many of those?" asked Slade.

"Not locals," Loving said. "There was one, maybe two, three years ago, but someone caught him dealing off the bottom of the deck at the American. He isn't with us anymore."

"The others?"

"Drovers, passing through," said Loving. "Some of them forget what being human's all about, out on the trail. Since we've been open, I've banned maybe five or six. None of them stuck in Jubilee."

"You're in for the long haul?" Slade asked.

"I'm working on it," Loving said. "But who knows, really? I could change my mind tomorrow."

"What I need now," Slade informed him, "is to ask your girls some questions."

Loving smiled and said, "Suits me. Let's go and wake 'em up."

Faith didn't believe she'd need the Smith & Wesson, couldn't picture Thornton getting rowdy with her in the presence of her other hands, but why take chances? Anyway, she wasn't showing off the gun or making it provocative, just bringing it along the way she'd carry any other tool around the ranch.

She found the hands just saddling their horses for the day's work, riding fences, checking on the stock before they separated to perform specific chores. Art Hanes and Johnny Gray were first to spot her approaching with Murdoch beside her, exchanging glances and shifting easily toward where Burch Thornton stood, just tightening his saddle's billet strap.

Faith saw the young man's shoulders stiffen, head cocked slightly as if listening for footsteps at his back, but he continued with his task until he got it right, then casually turned to face her. Faith supposed it was her own imagination, thinking that he blushed at the sight of her. She wondered what he'd seen last night, if it had been the first time he'd been spying on her, and she felt the color rising in her own face. Anger and embarrassment together.

Anger won.

"G'morning, Boss," said Thornton, not quite smirking.

"It's good-bye," Faith said. "You're leaving us today."

"That right?"

"It is."

He looked around, saw how the other hands had circled him. He still had the nerve to ask, "How come?"

Beside him, Johnny Gray opened a hand. His pocket watch swung brightly on its chain, glinting with sunlight.

"Thieves don't work for me," Faith said. "You're done."

"Ain't that a shame."

"There's still the matter of a jackknife and five dollars," Faith pressed on. "The money will be coming from your severance. I'll need to check your pockets for the knife."

He grinned at that, lewdly, and thrust his pelvis forward. "Come ahead, then. I been lookin' forward to it, after what I seen—"

If there was more, he didn't get a chance to finish it. Ed Murdoch took a long step forward, snarling as he slammed his right fist into Thornton's face. The Peeping Tom went down, cursing, fumbling to reach his pistol as he wallowed in the dust.

The sound of half a dozen pistols cocking stopped him with his Colt still holstered. Faith's Smith & Wesson made no sound, since it was hammerless and double-action, but Burch Thornton saw it leveled at his face.

"I won't forget this, bitch!" he hissed.

Art Hanes was drawing back a boot to kick him in the ribs when Faith said, "No! Just search him, then escort him off the property."

Rough hands hauled Thornton upright and disarmed him, prior to turning out his pockets, scattering small change around his feet. Jeb Danson found his pocket-knife and aimed a dark stream of tobacco juice at Thornton's boots.

"Mount up," Ed Murdoch ordered. "And we'll relieve you of that Winchester, unless you wanna try and use it."

"Those damn guns are mine!" Thornton protested.

"Bill me for them when you've settled somewhere far away," Faith said.

Slouched in his saddle, sleeving bright blood from his lips, he glared at Faith and said, "You haven't seen the last of me. None of you."

"Thanks for that," Faith answered him. "Next time, we'll just start shooting and assume it's self-defense."

"My finger's gettin' itchy, standin' here," said Johnny Gray, his watch in one hand while the other rested on the curved butt of his six-gun.

"He gets this one chance," Faith told her men. "And after this, no more."

"You just remember what I tole ya," Thornton said and spurred his gelding northward, toward the open plains and Kansas in the distance. Three of Faith's hands trotted after him, not pushing it, but keeping him in sight.

"You done the right thing, ma'am," said Murdoch, at her elbow.

Faith watched Thornton dwindling in the distance, followed by her trackers, and replied, "I guess we'll see."

• • •

The huntsman trailed Marshal Slade as far as the Klondike Saloon but did not follow him inside. He had work to do, keeping up appearances, and bellying up the the bar at that hour would strike the wrong chord. He would be greeted, recognized, remembered for behavior that was out of character.

And when he wasn't seen at work on time, the same as always, it would be another cause for comment. After last night's events, suspicion would be automatic. Anyone found missing from his normal post in Jubilee—except for Pastor Booth, of course—or who behaved in a peculiar manner would be under scrutiny.

Not only from his neighbors, but from Mills Vandiver and from Marshal Slade.

The huntsman had rehearsed that morning, with a mirror, to perfect his attitude. Although his church attendance had been spotty—limited to major holidays and special celebrations—weddings, funerals—he must be seen to mourn the preacher's passing and lament the loss of Mercy Baptist Church. To smile at the wrong moment, much less chuckle at a private joke, would mark him as a suspect.

At the same time, he must demonstrate sufficient outrage toward himself, his so-called crimes. That part was easy, since his miserable childhood had been dedicated to self-loathing, conquered only when he learned that others were to blame for all his quirks and insufficiencies. Turning the fury outward was a lifesaver, but he could only vent it under special circumstances, with a proper audience of one.

Barely eight hours since he'd set the church afire and culled young Molly from the harlot herd, he was primed to go again. That urge was dangerous, the huntsman realized. If he surrendered to it, he might very well go raving down the street, slashing at every female he enocountered, until someone gunned him down.

Which simply wouldn't do.

The huntsman thought that he was making progress

toward unveiling the harlots' secret, but he still had far to go. It might take years—decades—to document his findings in sufficient detail for society, the lords of science, to acknowledge what he'd found.

It was a burden he could bear.

In that respect, at least, he had the patience of the saints.

As for Marshal Slade . . . that was another matter, altogether. He could not afford to have the lawman idling in Jubilee indefinitely. While the huntsman loved a challenge, Slade concerned him. He was not the standard urban copper, whom the huntsman had befuddled and humilitated in his other outings. Some—like Abberline in London—had been better educated, likely more experienced, and he'd defeated all of them. Left them grasping at straws and theories when he moved on to new hunting grounds.

Something about Slade was different. He seemed to be a plodder, but the huntsman would have bet his last week's earnings that Slade rarely lost his man—or woman, if it came to that. And unlike others who had failed to truncate his experiments, he sensed that Slade would be as happy killing him as taking him to jail.

That was a thing he loved and feared about the West. Its guns and attitudes. If he was caught performing one of his exploratory operations, he'd be shot or mobbed and killed, no question. Even if he was arrested, held for trial, the huntsman knew that frontier denizens were fond of private intervention. Sometimes made a public spectacle of executing miscreants, after a period of torture that included townsfolk young and old.

It was a risk the huntsman took, and he had made a promise to himself. If capture in the West was unavoidable, he'd press the issue. Force a quick end for himself.

Trust someone else to understand and carry on his work.

But for the moment, he could help himself by getting rid of Marshal Slade. And being an extremist by his very nature, he immediately thought of an extreme solution.

Nothing that would point the finger his way. Quite the opposite in fact. It would invite more marshals into Jubilee, but they would need time to assemble, make the trip, pick up where Slade left off.

And in the meantime, he might shed his latest false identity.

Move on and find himself another operating theater.

Loving had five hookers remaining at the Klondike. Wanda was the one who'd raised the first alarm the night before when Molly went missing. The rest were introduced to Slade as Cassie, Jo-Beth, Norma Jean, and Blaze. All five were bleary-eyed from loss of sleep and none too pleased at jawing with a lawman when they'd normally be bundled up in bed—alone, for once.

Al Loving had excused himself at Slade's request, Slade watching him to make sure that he didn't flash some signal to the girls or glare at anybody in particular. The pimp seemed honestly intent on winding up the murders, nailing down the killer, but Slade wasn't taking anything on faith at this point in the game.

Instead of singling Wanda out, he asked, "Which one of you was first to notice Molly gone, last night?"

They hesitated, cutting glances back and forth, before Blaze said, "I must've been. One minute, she was standing right behind me. Next time, when I turned around, she wasn't there no more."

"And did you mention it to anyone, right then?" asked Slade.

Blaze shook her head, bronze waves of tangled hair in motion, as a tear escaped from her left eye and spilled across her cheek. She swiped it clear and stiffened, staring back at Slade.

"You gonna say it's my fault, now?"

"Not even close," he said. "I'd like to know what came

to mind, though, when you found her missing. It might help me."

Blaze softened, shrugged. Told Slade, "I didn't really think about it at the time. You know, she coulda walked around to get a better look, whatever. Maybe gone back to her crib."

"Okay. Was anybody else around there with you? Maybe someone that you didn't recognize?" asked Slade.

"Mister," said Wanda, "we know everyone in town."

"'Cluding the mayor," said Cassie, with a wicked smile.

"All right," Slade said. "Someone you *did* know, then? Aside from each other and Mr. Loving, was anyone hanging around with you?"

Around the circle, muttered negatives and shaking heads. Slade let it go and changed directions.

"What I need to ask you now is personal," he said. "This person that I'm looking for is obviously down on working girls. Which doesn't mean he's not a customer, between these other times. I need to know if any of you's run into a . . . client who was *different*."

"Than what?" asked Norma Jean.

"Than normal," Slade replied.

"What's *normal*?" Jo-Beth challenged him.

Slade thought about it for a second, then refined his question. "Someone who's inclined to hurt you for the fun of it, not accidentally or when he's sloppy drunk and clumsy."

More looks passed around the group, then Wanda said, "I guess we all have, one time or another."

"Make it recently," Slade said. "In Jubilee, for starters. Take it back six months or so before the killings started. Anybody new and mean, or somebody who changed on you in a surprising way?"

"No one like that, for me," said Wanda, and the others joined her in denials, one by one.

Running short of notions, Slade threw out a long shot.

"Well," he said, "has anybody threatened one of you? Or

maybe all of you together? Maybe threatened Mr. Loving or the Klondike, that you know about?"

"Only the preacher," Blaze replied. "But he was getting roasted when the bastard carried Molly off."

"I'm thinking that she may have gone with him for money," Slade replied.

"That leaves the field wide open," Wanda said.

"Okay. And I suppose there's no great competition with the girls across the street, at the American?" Slade asked, scraping the bottom of his barrel.

"Not so you'd notice," Blaze replied.

And smiling Cassie added, "Hell, Marshal, there's always pricks enough to go around."

Slade wasn't sure if he was blushing, but it felt that way.

And felt that he was failing, too.

II

Ben Tewksbury would never be mistaken for Al Loving. Shorter by six inches, with a barrel-shaped torso above slender legs, he might have looked comical but instead exuded a sense of physical power. His short, sandy hair was thinning on top, while a bristling ginger mustache matched his eyebrows. His face was round and quick to smile, but it reminded Slade of something he had seen once in a zoo.

Maybe a crocodile.

The American Saloon was similar in layout to the Klondike—and to every other halfway decent joint he'd ever drunk or gambled in. Barroom downstairs with cribs above for any extra business customers could manage or afford. The placement of the stairs was different, as were the decorations on the walls—running to posters for performances of fancy plays back East—but overall, the gambler in Slade felt like he'd found another home.

Which wasn't right, he knew.

Home was with Faith, a two-day ride from Jubilee and all its craziness.

"Marshal, we meet at last," Tewksbury said, pumping Slade's hand, releasing it on the downstroke as if to fling it from him.

"After last night's shivaree," Slade said, "I figured it was overdue."

"Indeed. We've grown accustomed to some terrible events, but that . . ." Tewksbury shook his head and found his smile again. "In any case, welcome to the American!"

"I understand you've lost two girls to Loving's three, so far," Slade said.

"The first and fourth," Tewksbury said. "Poor Becky Hatcher, almost six weeks gone, then Thelma Lou."

"Last name for her?" asked Slade.

"She never shared it with me."

"And you didn't ask?"

Tewksbury shrugged. "These girls don't come from high-falutin backgrounds, Marshal. They've been knocked around and seen life on the ugly side. Most aren't inclined to talk about their pasts, and I don't pry."

"Were you aware of anyone who had it in for either victim here? Maybe someone who'd roughed them up or threatened them?"

Tewksbury frowned, seeming to think about it. Finally, he said, "Most of the boys who go upstairs are drunk, you realize. They want to have some fun, and some of them are rowdy. Others find they can't manage, you know?"

He raised a fist, showed Slade a drooping index finger.

"So?"

"So, we've had incidents, of course," Tewksbury said. "But nothing close to this, or that would lead me to expect it. Nothing for the murdered girls specifically, that comes to mind."

"And you'd remember? You're around most of the time?"

"I *live* here," Tewksbury replied. "With my girls and Dan, the bouncer. Like a family."

Slade let that pass. "I suspect it made you angry when you heard that Thelma Lou was giving it away."

"To Heidegger, you mean?" Tewksbury shook his head. "*They* thought it was a secret, Marshal, but I run this place and I don't miss a thing."

"So, how'd you feel about it?"

"Not my business," Tewksbury replied. "She worked her shift, the same as everybody else. Put money in my pocket every night. If she'd been humping Otto on the house while we had customers, I would've kicked her out, not dressed her like a sow for market."

"How do you get along with Mr. Loving at the Klondike?" Slade inquired.

"Friendly enough. I'd rather have the whole town to myself, and so would he, but neither one of us is hurting. Or, we *weren't*, until this bloody business started."

"And it's never crossed your mind that Loving may have killed your girls or had it done, to hurt your business?"

"Did it cross my mind? Hell, yes! And then it kept on going. Look," Tewksbury said, "we're businessmen. Both rough around the edges, and we don't take any shit. But killing girls like that to hurt somebody else's trade? You'd have to be insane."

"Or want to make it look that way," said Slade.

Tewksbury shook his head again. "I can't speak for Al Loving, Marshal, but I don't believe he'd pull something like that. And if I thought he *had*, I wouldn't try to pay him back in kind. I'd be down at the Klondike with my Schofield .45 to call the rotten bastard out."

Slade read his face, considered it, then asked, "You mind me talking to your girls?"

"Just talking? There's no charge for that, Marshal," the pimp replied. Laughing again. "My house is yours. Come on upstairs."

• • •

Tewksbury's surviving stable included six women of various ages. Rose was the youngest, still in her late teens, while Clara was edging toward forty. Between them, Jane, Annette, Louise, and Sherry covered the spread, showing wear on their faces and grim resignation in posture. None of them struck a seductive pose for Slade, but they relaxed a little when Tewksbury left them on their own.

To break the ice, Slade said, "I know you all must be upset about what happened to your friends, Becky and Thelma Lou. I'm here to stop it, if I can."

"Not doin' any good so far, are you?" asked Jane. "Couldn't keep Molly off the chopping block."

"You're right," he granted. "Two suspects so far, and now it looks like neither one did any of the killing."

"Hell, I never thought that Otto murdered Thelma Lou," said Rose. "The dumb kraut loved her, head over heels."

"And how did she feel?" Slade asked Rose.

She shrugged, one shoulder only, saving energy. "Liked him enough to hump him without charging for it. What's that tell you?"

"She was never giving up the life," Jane said.

"You don't know that," Rose challenged her.

"Nobody leaves the life," Annette declared.

That silenced them, all glum-faced, until Slade asked, "Do you know of anyone who threatened Thelma Lou or Becky? Anyone at all who worried them?"

Head shakes around the circle, then Jane said, "We talk about the funny ones, you know. There's always something, but I don't recall them being scairt of anybody."

"Becky didn't scare," said Rose. "She had that baby face, but wouldn't let a guy do anything she didn't like. She had that razor." Looking for agreement from the others. "You remember?"

"Ivory, the handle was," said Shelly.

"Never saw her use it," Clara added, "but she showed it to a couple drunks and backed 'em down."

"I understand that she was found beside the livery," said Slade.

A couple of them nodded. No one spoke.

"So," he pressed on, "any idea what she was doing there, at night?"

After a moment's silence, Rose replied, "She liked to go for walks sometimes, after the bar shut down and everyone went home. Told me it helped her sleep."

"I guess it would," said Clara.

"Meaning what?" asked Slade.

"Nothin'."

"If you have any information that can help me end this, now's the time to share," Slade said.

Clara looked nervous, glancing at the others, then replied, "All right. I followed her one time. She didn't just go walkin', if you want to know. She went to see a Chinaman."

"What for?" asked Jane.

It would've been Slade's question, so he waited.

"Not for business," Clara said. "At least, not ours. He sold her something in a little bundle and she brought it home. Later, I smelt it through the wall, while she was smoking it."

"You're talking opium?" Slade asked.

"What else? She coulda got tobacco at the gen'ral store."

Slade frowned, thinking he'd need to have another talk with Huping Wong. There was no law against selling or smoking opium in Oklahoma Territory, or anywhere else in the United States so far, but Slade worried about Wong's failure to mention dealing with Becky Hatcher. Then again, Slade hadn't asked the proper questions.

Something he could remedy.

"You think one of the celestials killed her?" asked Shelly.

"No reason to think so," Slade said, "but I'm talking to everyone."

"Reverend Booth thought they might've," Annette interjected. "He told me."

"You knew him?" asked Slade.

"You're surprised," she replied. "That he'd let me in church."

"Well . . ."

"I didn't go down there on Sundays," she said. "But I saw him alone, now and then. Went around to the back, like, when no one was lookin'."

"I'll bet," Shelly said.

"It was nothin' like that," Annette said. "We just talked about things."

"With a hand in his pants," Rose suggested, grinning.

"Not a bit!" Annette flared, then slumped back in her seat. "He was hopin' to save me, I think."

"Did it work?" Clara asked.

"Reckon not," Annette said, with a sad smile at Slade. "I'm still here."

Slade reached the mayor's home at noon, straight up, and saw Vandiver trudging toward him from the other end of Main Street. Visiting Hoop Wong, perhaps? Some kind of business at the livery or at the blacksmith's shop?

The constable looked better than he had the previous night, but the incessant string of incidents in Jubilee had clearly worn him down. In just the short time Slade had known him, Vandiver seemed to have shrunk inside his own skin, losing some part of his essence.

Was it simple weariness? A sense of guilt for failing to corral the killer . . . or some other cause?

Before they could do more than nod at one another on the doorstep, Mayor Johansson stood before them, beckoning them both into his house. His pretty wife was hovering, wearing a smile that managed to be sad and sunny, all at the same time. The mayor, for his part, looked like he had seen the future of his own career and didn't like it one damned bit.

When they were seated in the parlor, the obligatory coffee placed in front of them with thanks for stopping by, Johansson fixed his eyes on Slade.

"Well, Marshal? Have you any news?" he asked.

"Nothing that puts us any closer to the killer," Slade admitted. "What I've learned today is that the victims weren't harassed or threatened prior to being killed, as far as anybody knows."

"Except Long Liz," Vandiver said.

"You fined Christofides for belting her around," Slade told the constable. "Unless we break his alibi, there's nothing else to charge him with."

"Damn it!" Vandiver's shoulders slumped another quarter inch or so.

Slade forged ahead. "Aside from that, I questioned Tewksbury and Loving. Neither one of them appears to have a motive for the killings. No peculiar rivalry between them, and their trade's about the same. Again, no threats from either one toward girls who work across the street. They're tough men, and I wouldn't be surprised if both got bloody hands, somewhere along the way, but this is different. They're pimps, not—"

"Please!" Johansson interrupted him. "They're *business* men!"

"Have it your way," Slade said. "Long story short, I don't think either one of them's behind the killings. As for Pastor Booth—"

"It can't be him," Johansson said. "For heaven's sake, man, he was burning up on Main Street when the last who— when this Molly person died!"

Slade held the mayor's eyes for a moment, then continued. "As I was about to say, I've learned that he was meeting privately with one of Ben Tewksbury's girls, after hours."

"Oh, Lord!"

Johansson slumped back in his chair, while Vandiver made an intensive study of his dusty boots.

"The girl in question—no point naming her—denies any kind of, er, scandalous contact. She claims that the preacher was trying to 'save' her from something or other. My point is, he may have been meeting with others and no one the wiser. He could've learned something or formed some idea who the killer might be."

"Hard to buy that," Vandiver replied. "I talked to him plenty, since this business started, and he never mentioned anything. You questioned him, yourself. He sent you after old Shapiro and Hoop Wong."

Slade didn't mention Clara's observation about opium in Jubilee. Instead, he told the constable and mayor, "It's just a thought. The business about Jews and Chinamen was mostly prejudice. If he suspected someone else was killing girls in town, he'd have to give a reason why he thought so. That could turn around and bite him, if he got the information from a hooker while he's preaching night and day to run them out of town."

"All right," Johansson said. "Let's grant that, for the sake of argument. It doesn't help us any, though, since he's *dead*!"

Slade nodded. "True enough. We'd have to know who he was talking to, first thing, then find out what they told him—that would take some trust, right there—and *then* work through whatever Booth decided it might mean."

"A waste of time, in other words," Johansson said.

"For me, at least," Slade granted. "It would take some-body local, who's acquainted with the girls."

His eyes cut back and forth between the mayor and the constable until Johansson blurted out, "Don't look at me! Sir, I'm a family man. I've never paid a penny for—"

"I'll ask around," Vandiver said. "Can't promise it'll help, but what the hell. No stone unturned."

"Good man," Slade said.

"I don't feel good," Vandiver said.

"And Marshal, what will you be doing in the meantime?" asked Johansson.

Slade reflected, stroked his bristling chin, and told the mayor, "I think I'll get a shave."

The barber's shop, beside Shapiro's Dry Goods, wasn't large, but it was sparkling clean. The implements were polished, and the floor looked clean enough to eat from, if you were too drunk to stand. Slade couldn't spot a smudge of any size on the front window or the mirror mounted on a wall behind the barber's chair.

"Good afternoon, sir! Here you are, at last!"

Slade recognized the Irish brogue and thought its owner looked the type, from ginger hair slicked down and neatly parted in the middle, to the matching eyebrows, lightly freckled nose, and narrow gap between his two front teeth. He wore the standard barber's uniform: white shirt beneath a vest, a garter on one sleeve, dark pants and shoes.

"It takes some time for me to get around," Slade said.

"But now you're here. That's all that matters, eh?" A hand shot out toward Slade. "Connor MacGowan, at your service. Any questions you might have, I'll do my best to answer up."

"Appreciate it," Slade replied. "But first, I need a shave."

MacGowan's laugh exploded in the smallish shop.

"In that case, sir," he said, "you're well and truly in the perfect place. Be seated, if you please."

Slade doffed his hat and hung it on a stand beside the door, then sat down in the barber's chair. MacGowan pumped a pedal with his foot, to raise the chair by six or seven inches, then retreated to collect a hot, wet towel from a steamer on a nearby shelf. Slade winced as it was draped across his face, then let himself relax, enjoying it.

"You've come a long way on a hard road," said the barber, somewhere behind Slade and to his left. "No end in sight, I fear."

Slade heard a rhythmic clinking sound, ceramic noises, as MacGowan whipped up shaving lather in a mug. Muffled beneath the towel, "I'd like to talk to you about that, if I may."

"O' course you can," MacGowan said. "Feel free."

"In my experience, a barber hears all kinds of things," Slade said. "Town gossip. Whispers. Sometimes things he wasn't even meant to hear."

"It happens," said MacGowan. "That's a fact, sir. Anywhere I've worked, I've come away with secrets dropped by gentlemen."

"You've been around, I take it?"

"Oh, indeed I have. And then some, sir."

"I've traveled some myself," said Slade. "Around the States."

"I've gone a good deal farther, sir. I signed on in my youth as a ship's barber. Shaved my way around the world, I did, and never sorry for it. Not a minute's worth."

"I can't top that," Slade said, his own voice sounding louder to him as MacGowan peeled away the towel. "But getting back to Jubilee . . ."

MacGowan started lathering Slade's face with deft strokes from a soft brush, covering his cheeks first, then Slade's lips, chin, jawline, and at last his throat.

"I wish that I could help you, sir. It's terrible what's goin' on in town. Just terrible! I've been keepin' my ear to the ground, sir, believe me. Everyone talks on and on about the murders, but they don't say anything of substance, if you follow me."

Slade followed him, all right. Under the barber's voice, he heard MacGowan start to strop a razor's blade.

"The poor girls from the barrelhouses were a sad lot, in themselves," MacGowan said. "Now, with the minister gone up in smoke, we'll have a whole new round of worried talk, but where's the answer to our misery? Perhaps with you, sir. Just hold still now."

Being shaved was an experience Slade always found difficult to quantify. His life was literally in another person's hands—often a total stranger's—and the luxury of being pampered for a while couldn't erase the thought that someone held a razor to his throat, could press a little harder, slice instead of scraping, and be done with him for good.

Hadn't there been a barber once, who killed his customers? In Europe somewhere, wasn't it? And something darker still . . . about meat pies?

Slade pushed the thought away, and when the razor cleared his lips he said, "So you've heard nothing useful, basically?"

"A lot of stuff and nonsense I'm afraid, sir," said Mac-Gowan. "People throwing stones at neighbors who they've never liked. I doubt they can remember why, but such is life. I'll keep on listenin' for certain, sir. And just another minute now, if you could be especially careful not to move . . ."

The huntsman watched Slade leave the barber's shop. There was no point in trailing him along Main Street. No matter where he went in Jubilee, he'd hear the same thing from the yokels.

Speculation. Supposition and exaggeration. Outright fabrication. Nothing worth a damn to help him close the case.

Still, it was troublesome to have him lurking in the background, poking into every nook and cranny, sniffing after secrets. God knew there were plenty of them to be found if he looked closely enough and asked the right questions.

Could they lead him to the huntsman? It was doubtful.

Still, he would feel better with the lawman gone.

Granted, eliminating Slade would be a risky proposition. He was dangerous, clearly a man who'd killed and would not hesitate to pull a trigger if the need arose once more. He was alert, on guard, but there were ways around that. Ways to do him in, the huntsman felt assured, with just the right amount of planning and audacity.

The danger: getting rid of one marshal would only bring another down upon him, likely more than one to settle up the score. But it would buy him time. Two days for news to reach the court in Enid, and another two, at least, for reinforcements to arrive in Jubilee. If they were standing by and ready, that is. Otherwise . . . well, who could say?

The huntsman's choice, once he'd eliminated Slade, would be to run or stay and see what happened next. He'd never been a master horseman, but in four days minimum he could be well up into Kansas and away, a hundred miles or more from Jubilee. How would they track him, once he'd shed his latest temporary name? There was his trade, of course, but even that was flexible. And he had cash enough on hand to live a while without employment, in a pinch.

It was decided, then. He would eliminate the lawman at his soonest opportunity. Perhaps that very night, if Slade was careless in his wandering through Jubilee. The smallest lapse in vigilance would serve the huntsman's purpose, if he was prepared.

And afterward . . . well, who could say? He might not be required to run. Might stay in Jubilee, continue his experiments and find the secret he'd been seeking for so long. How wonderfully ironic if the answer waited for him there, when he'd failed to unearth it in some of the world's greatest cities.

So it ever was. A treasure hidden where the prospector would least expect to find it. His advantage was that no one else had cared to look before him. They were too intoxicated by corruption to imagine life without it. Purity of essence was beyond the grasp of common men. A genius was requird to lead the way, and even he had found the going rough so far.

What of it?

No historic triumph had been made without great sacrifice. To be remembered, heroes must risk everything—their lives, their very souls—on behalf of others, flying in the face of danger. How else were they measured, after all?

His course of action chosen, now the huntsman turned his thoughts to the mechanics of its execution. While he favored knives—indeed, required them for his examining his harlots—it would be a grave mistake to challenge Slade with steel alone. The lawman would probably shoot him before he could even draw blood.

Something else, then.

A little surprise that the marshal would never suspect.

12

Night crept into Jubilee like something hungry from the prairie, sneaking along alleyways and side streets first, then edging onto Main Street when it passed unchallenged. People hurried on their way, pursued by shadows. Shopkeepers who might have kept their doors open past closing time the week before now locked up on the dot. A couple that Slade passed—the blacksmith and the barber's shop—had closed up early, seemingly for lack of trade.

His third night in the town, and Slade was sick of it already, but he couldn't leave. He hadn't done his job yet. Worse, he had begun to question if it *could* be done.

At least by him.

He'd spent much longer periods of time pursuing killers. Three nights was a drop in the bucket for something like this, whatever *that* meant. The closest he'd come to something like this in the past was a kill-crazy family roaming the badlands and picking off families on remote homesteads. They'd left a clear trail, etched in blood, and he'd followed it—after a couple of costly false starts—to the end of the line.

In Jubilee, the killer wasn't going anywhere. He circled like a hungry fish concealed by muddy water, rising up to snatch his prey, then sinking back into the murk, unseen. He might as well have been a ghost, for all the tracks he left behind.

Unlike the Bender family, whose talent for deception had been concentrated in a single member of the tribe, the juggernaut of Jubilee was capable of passing neighbors on the street, conducting business with them, maybe even socializing at a level that seemed ordinary. Everyone in town knew everybody else, at least by sight and for a greeting on the street. If there had been a snarling maniac among them, he'd have been eliminated after one or two killings, and Slade would not be there.

He'd be at home with Faith, a married man.

That made him hate the killer even more, another steady drip of acid etching and corroding the façade of objectivity Slade wore when he put on his badge. Judge Dennison warned constantly against emotional involvement with a victim or a case, but warnings only went so far. As long as marshals were recruited from the human race, they would have feelings—good and bad, noble and base. The trick was not to act upon those feelings, if they put you on the wrong side of the law.

Like pistol-whipping some mean drunk who beat his wife and children, for example. Or shooting a rapist instead of arresting him so he could hang. Slipping the other way sometimes, from sympathy, and counseling a person who could just as easily have gone to jail.

Slade walked a fine line in some cases, figured that all lawmen did at one time or another. By the very definition of the job, he dealt with people at their worst, both predators and victims. Some were helpless, hopeless, shattered. Absolutely vulnerable. Others didn't give a damn about the trauma they had caused—or gloried in it, drawing twisted sustenance from someone else's suffering.

Slade treated each case as a separate, distinct event and gave each job his best. He had a decent record, though a few men whom he'd hunted had eluded him. It didn't take a genius to escape from Oklahoma Territory, just a strong horse and a rider with a fair head start.

But Jubilee was different.

The killer wasn't running. He was taunting Slade and every other person in the town, assaulting and insulting all of them each time he plunged his blade into another victim. The slayer's fixation on working girls did nothing to relieve the town's "decent" inhabitants. Each new attack, compounded by the burning of their church and murder of their pastor, was another nail sunk into Jubilee's casket.

And could that be the point? Had Slade been looking at the murders from a skewed "normal" perspective? Was it the killer's intent to destroy Jubilee from within?

Passing MacDonald's, where he'd eaten supper two long hours earlier, Slade frowned and shook his head. It made no sense, inflicting slow death on a minor frontier town by way of murdered hookers when another fire or two would do the trick in nothing flat. Whether the killer simply hated prostitutes or Jubilee itself, burning the town would solve his problem.

No.

If someone hated a specific town, why not just leave? The only reason to remain while wreaking havoc was *revenge*.

For what?

More questions for Vandiver in the morning, finding out if anyone had been run out of town for some vice-related infraction, or maybe had a loved one punished more severely. Blood feuds didn't spring from arid ground. They festered and emerged from open wounds.

Slade reached the Klondike, found it doing moderate to average business, and decided that he might as well go in.

With any luck, he might rub shoulders with his quarry. Smell his guilt or spot the bloodstains on his hands.

More likely, he'd just have a beer.

The huntsman's chosen weapon was a .52-caliber Spencer carbine. The gun measured forty-two inches from muzzle to butt and weighed eight pounds empty, eight and a half with a round in its chamber and seven more waiting to go in the stock's magazine. Its lever-action mechanism let a practiced shooter fire eight shots within some fifteen seconds.

That was for emergencies, however.

On a hunt, it paid to aim.

Choosing a stand was equally important and uniquely difficult when hunting in a town. He couldn't simply hide and blaze away from any alley's mouth or doorway along Main Street. Slade was armed and dangerous, unlike the whores he studied—although Becky Hatcher had surprised him with a razor, on his first time out in Jubilee.

No, thank you. Getting killed was not part of the huntsman's agenda that night or anytime soon.

He'd thought about the Jubilee Hotel, wondered if he should find a spot across the street and wait until the lawman finally retired, frustrated by another wasted night. The huntsman noted two fair vantage points from which he could observe Slade's second-story window, but he also found the curtains drawn. Without a clear view of his target, it would be a futile exercise.

Another thought: the restaurant. How shocking it would be to plug Slade as he sat, stuffing his face with other diners. Second thoughts, however, told the huntsman that a sniping at MacDonald's would increase the odds of someone noticing his muzzle flash and maybe even coming after him. The very last thing that he wanted was a running gunfight through the town, where he might be cut off, surrounded, killed, or captured.

So, the street, then.

With no decent leads to follow, Slade had been reduced to standing watch at one saloon while Vandiver covered the other. Whether he hoped to catch the huntsman operating or was simply burning off his nervous energy, it had the same result. He was exposed sporadically for several hours, between supper and the time he went upstairs to bed.

The huntsman watched Slade turn into the Klondike, wondering how long the marshal would remain inside. Slade was not seeking recreation, certainly would not avail himself of Loving's harlots. Maybe he would have a drink or two, try to relax a bit without losing his edge. He struck the huntsman as an individual who rarely dropped his guard, and then only by small degrees. Slade seemed to lead a life of vigilance, with one eye always watching for a threat, his hand invariably near a gun.

In some ways, he supposed they were alike.

Slade rode in search of evil, as it was perceived by his employers and his conscience, meting out the wrath of modern law. The huntsman's cause was more exalted, but he still devoted every fiber of his being to salvation of his race and the society it had created. Under altered circumstances, he imagined that they might be allies, but that notion would remain a fantasy.

Tonight, instead of following his calling, seeking out the harlot's secret scourge, he had a man to kill.

While Slade idled in the saloon, his nemesis would find the perfect sniper's nest and lie in wait, prepared to strike no matter which direction Slade took from the Klondike's bat-wing doors.

Al Loving's girls were working at the Klondike, picking up the slack for those he'd lost in recent days. Slade hadn't seen enough of Jubilee to judge a normal crowd for the saloon, but there were five men playing poker when he entered, all well-lubricated, and another dozen ranged along the bar with drinks in front of them. It wasn't what he'd call a joyful group, but none of them appeared to be in mourning, either.

Was the man Slade hunted there among them?

Was he sizing up another victim even now, dark thoughts of butchery concealed behind a normal face?

A few years back, in Dallas, Slade had seen a so-called "medium" enthrall a paying crowd by talking to their loved ones who had passed away. Or so she claimed, at least. Most of the spirit messages were vague and could've fit a hundred people picked at random, but she nailed a couple of peculiar names and warned one woman that her children were in danger. Two days later, on the verge of leaving town, Slade saw a story in the newspaper describing how that woman went home from the theater and found a small fire burning on the back porch of her home, three kids asleep inside with grandma.

It was spooky, but it didn't do Slade any good tonight. He didn't have a medium to ask the murdered women who had killed them—and, the truth be told, he didn't have enough faith in the Great Beyond to trust a message if he received one.

But he would have checked it out. Just playing safe.

Slade drank a beer, saw Loving on his way out, and confirmed that the bartender was alert to any move against the working girls.

The killer didn't work that way, of course. He didn't want an audience, just privacy and time enough to satisfy his sick desires.

Whatever *they* were.

Slade still had no clear idea of what could motivate such crimes. Hatred of women topped the list, but why the emphasis on whores? There was a greater risk attached to going after married women in their homes, but Slade didn't believe the killer's choice of targets was a simple matter of convenience.

Something was still eluding him. If he could grasp it, Slade thought he would be a long step closer to his man.

Out through the swinging doors, he turned right, moving westward toward a point where he would cross Main Street and enter the American Saloon. One more beer ought to settle him, Slade thought, and he'd have done his duty for the evening without accomplishing a blessed thing.

He hadn't seen the constable so far tonight. Slade guessed that Vandiver was feeling beaten down, hating the looks that people gave him on the street, unwelcome sympathy mixed in with scorn because he hadn't caught the killer yet. Slade felt some of the same looks turned his way and shrugged them off. He had a job to do and wouldn't let himself be caught up in the social side, with all its drama and recriminations.

Slade was stepping off the sidewalk, with a talior's shop behind him, when a rifle cracked across the street. He missed the muzzle flash but moved on instinct with the first crack of the shot, before its echo rattled off the storefronts on his side of Main Street.

Ducking, diving, rolling, Slade dropped flat behind a nearby water trough with Colt in hand. The bullet meant to kill him cracked a window of the tailor's shop and drilled a headless dummy decked out in a fancy suit. The dummy toppled over backward with a secondary crash.

Slade's problem now: the shot told him his unseen adversary had a high-caliber rifle, and the trough concealing him made poor cover. A slug might pass completely through it, even filled with water. Barring that, another shot or two could tap the trough and drain it in a hurry, leaving Slade with nothing but two narrow planks of wood to hide behind.

And hiding didn't suit him, in his present mood.

Slade didn't know if his assailant with the rifle was the same man who'd been killing girls in Jubilee, but he was anxious to find out.

And either way, he owed the bastard one.

*   *   *

The huntsman saw his target spin and dive for cover, mouthed a curse that would have startled his acquaintances in Jubilee, and cranked the Spencer carbine's lever-action mechanism to reload its chamber. By the time he lined up for a second shot, though, Slade was gone.

The water trough.

There'd been no time for him to reach the nearest alley, and the front doors to the shops along Main Street were all securely locked this time of night. He still had time before the sound of gunfire brought men spilling out of the saloons and rousted sleepy merchants from their beds.

The trough was easy. Roughly man-sized, when he thought about it. He sighted down the Spencer's twenty-inch barrel, remembering to squeeze the trigger, not jerk it.

The carbine kicked against his shoulder and he saw the bullet strike downrange. A square hit on the flat side of the water trough, but no reaction from the man concealed behind it. Had the bullet penetrated far enough to reach Slade, or—

The huntsman was cocking his rifle again, prepared to fire one more shot before fleeing, when Jack Slade erupted from cover. Flame blossomed from his right hand with a pop of sound that forced the huntsman to recoil involuntarily, wasting his third shot on the stars.

Then the huntsman was running. He knew beyond a whisper of a doubt that if he tried to stand and duel with the lawman, he would die.

Unthinkable.

His work was not complete. It would be tragic for humanity if he was interrupted now, before the breakthrough that he sensed was close at hand.

The roof he'd chosen was a flat one, with an empty shop beneath, the owners sleeping in their tidy house a block south of Main Street. There was no one underfoot to hear the huntsman race across the rooftop, to the ladder he'd left standing against the shop's back wall.

Descending in a rush, he nearly dropped the carbine. He cursed again, but saved it from a fall that might have damaged it. The spent round in its chamber made the weapon useless, but he pumped the lever action once more as he reached the bottom of the ladder, turning back toward home.

The ladder—stolen from the livery—would tell Slade nothing, so he left it. If the lawman blamed one of the stable's hostlers for the shooting, so much the better. As long as he escaped from Slade tonight, survived this reckless episode, the huntsman could revise his strategy.

He was a genius, after all.

But Slade was coming, might have crossed Main Street already. He'd have marked the huntsman's place on that third shot, if not before. Would he go up to check the roof or guess that he'd already missed his man?

The ladder might be useful there, as a diversion, but it wouldn't distract Slade for long. He could sweep the empty rooftop with a single glance, assuming he went up at all. And from the high ground, he might see the huntsman scurrying away.

Damn it!

He had a choice to make: keep running to his sanctuary now, or go to ground and hide. Perhaps cut back to Main Street and pretend the rifle fire had brought him out to look around, see what was happening.

Scratch that. The Spencer was a surefire giveaway. Slade merely had to sniff the carbine's muzzle and he'd know it had been fired. It wouldn't matter if the huntsman killed him on the spot, then, since he'd be surrounded by a crowd of neighbors that could turn into a lynch mob instantly.

Concealment was the ticket. He must reach his home and stash the weapon, then return and mingle with the Main Street crowd, all innocence and outrage at the latest crime.

If he could only reach his hideaway before the lawman glimpsed him, took a lucky shot, and brought him down.

Panicked and hating it, the huntsman ran as if the very hounds of Hell were snapping at his heels.

Slade charged along an alleyway between two shops, a grocer's and a shoemaker's. It was pitch-dark inside the alley, with a hint of starlight at the other end but no moon out to help him make his way along. Slade stumbled once, on something that he couldn't see, but kept himself from falling with a hand thrown out against the nearest wall. He felt splinters gouge his palm and swallowed back an angry curse.

He'd made enough noise as it was, to mark his passage for the sniper. When he cleared the alley, *if* he cleared it, he would be an easy target for a rifleman, either above him or on level ground. To hedge his bet, Slade sprang ahead and hit the ground beyond the alley belly-down, rolling to leave his Colt free for a quick response to any hostile fire.

And felt a damn fool in the silent night, no threat confronting him.

Back on his feet, he spied the ladder and was forced to make a choice. Assume the sniper had already fled, or risk leaving him on the roof where he could shoot Slade in the back, going away.

No choice at all, in fact.

It was the first time Slade had climbed a ladder with a pistol in his hand, but it worked out. A little slower than he would've liked, between the ladder's trembling and the need he felt to check behind himself each time he topped another rung, afraid of someone coming up behind him and below. Then, at the final moment, lunging upward to the roof's edge with the Colt extended, to discover—nothing, once again.

Fuming, Slade put the Colt away and scrambled down

the ladder, cut his climbing time in half, then had to guess which way the sniper would have run from there. It was too dark to look for footprints in the dust, and who could say how many people tramped along that path behind the shops on any given afternoon, regardless.

Slade felt a mounting anger at himself for having botched it when the killer—or, at least, a would-be killer—was so close at hand. He strained his ears for any sound of fleeing footsteps, but whatever sound there may have been was lost amid the voices raised on Main Street.

Still, he tried. Chose east as his direction on a whim and jogged along past three shops, peering into shadows all the way and finding no trace of his man. Another alley yawned ahead of him, and Slade was ready with his pistol when a man stepped out of it, holding a long gun ready at his hip.

"Slade?" Mills Vandiver challenged him.

"It's me," Slade answered, disappointed as his last hope turned to smoke.

"What'n hell's all this?" the constable demanded.

"Someone took a couple shots at me," Slade said. "I lost him in the dark."

"Where was he firing from?" Vandiver asked.

"Back this way. I can show you."

First, though, Slade took time to check Vandiver's weapon. Saw it was a double-barreled shotgun, not the piece that had been blazing at him moments earlier. Thus satisfied, he led Vandiver back to where the ladder stood and pointed toward the roof.

"Up there."

"And he was using a repeater?"

"Had to be," Slade said.

"So, maybe if we have a look upstairs, we'll know what he was using," said Vandiver.

Slade followed the constable this time. The darkness wasn't much relieved on top, but with a little work they found two cartridge cases. Each of them retrieved one, waiting while Vandiver struck a match and held it close to gleaming brass.

"A Spencer rimfire," he announced. "Plenty of gun to do the job, if he could aim."

"He rushed it," Slade surmised. "Or maybe I was lucky."

"Maybe he's more comfortable with a knife," Vandiver said.

"We don't know it's the same man," Slade replied.

"Who else? He wants to kill you off or scare you off, one or the other."

"I don't scare that easy, Constable."

"I hope not. This would rattle me, I have to tell you."

"Anyone you know in town who has a Spencer?" Slade asked.

"Not offhand," Vandiver said. "We can't go house-to-house, the way I'd like to, but I'll ask around."

Slade nodded. It was all that he could ask for, at the moment. Thinking that it might be best for all concerned if he sat back and let the killer try again. Be ready for him next time. Finish it with blood.

But whose blood would it be?

13

Next morning it was Mayor Johansson who surprised Slade over breakfast at MacDonald's, coming through the doorway with a pinched look on his face and waving off the waitress when she tried to greet him. Slade kept working on his ham and eggs, tracking Johansson from the corner of his eye until the mayor stood over him, his shadow falling on Slade's plate.

"You want to have a seat?" he asked. "Or will this be a speech?"

Johansson sat across from Slade, his chair legs scraping on the wooden floor, and leaned in to impress Slade with his level of intensity. Oddly, it had the opposite effect, making the mayor seem nervous, frayed around the edges.

"Marshal Slade," he said at last, "this thing has gotten out of hand."

"Which thing?"

Johansson squinted back at him. Replied, "All of it. Everything. These killings and the incident last night."

Slade nodded. "I'd say you're right."

"I am?"

"You bet. 'This thing' got out of hand the minute that you had a second murder and forgot to ask for help. You had five weeks to find the killer. I'm just starting my third day."

"And are you making any progress?" asked the mayor.

"I'd say so."

"Based on what?"

"First off, the fact he tried to put me down last night."

"You think that was the same man, then?"

"I hope so," Slade replied. "If not, you've got *two* lunatics in town."

"What if he tries again?"

"Best thing that I could hope for, I suppose," Slade said.

"Marshal, this town is not a shooting gallery!"

"You're right," Slade said. "Until last night, it seemed more like a slaughterhouse."

Johansson blanched at that, whether from shock or anger Slade couldn't have said. Nor did he care, if truth be told. It was Johansson's fault—and Mills Vandiver's—that the first two acts of butchery passed unreported. Slade couldn't say what might have happened if he'd been called in after the first or second murder, but there was a chance three other women still might be alive.

"You're blaming me for this!" Johansson said, aghast.

"There's blame enough to go around," Slade said. "The killer started it, and he's the one who needs to hang for what he's done. You and your constable decided it was best to wait and see what happened next. You made that choice after the first kill, and the second. It took three to make you ask for help, and that's on you."

"My job," Johansson said, "is watching out for the development and the prosperity of Jubilee."

"How's that been working out for you?" asked Slade.

Johansson took a moment to compose himself. When he could speak without his voice cracking, he said, "I came to ask you if it's possible to say when all of this may be resolved."

"No, sir, I couldn't say. Our man is getting shaky, but he's still calling the shots. With any luck, maybe he'll snap. Make a mistake. Might tip his hand somehow or make a run for it."

"Christ, don't I wish!"

"Do you keep track of people here, in Jubilee?"

"Keep track?" Johansson frowned, confused. "I'm not sure—"

"Do you know who comes and goes?" Slade clarified.

"Oh, well . . . of course, we greet new citizens and welcome them to town. As for departures, there's no special ceremony, but the better known among our residents would tell their friends good-bye, you know. Some kind of send-off might be organized. That sort of thing."

"You're talking families," said Slade.

"Well, yes. I would presume so."

"What about a loner? If he wasn't someone prominent, how long before you'd miss him?"

"I suppose the first time he missed work," Johansson said.

"Assuming that he works for someone else."

"Or, if he had a shop, when it was closed."

Slade picked a shop at random, pressing on with it. "Let's say the cobbler is a single man."

"He's not," Johansson interrupted.

"Make believe he is. One day you need a shoe fixed, and his shop is closed. How long before somebody checks and finds that he's skipped out?"

Johansson frowned. Replied, "If you mean calling at his home, I really couldn't say."

"Meaning that someone could be gone already, since last night."

"You think the killer's run away?" Johansson sounded almost hopeful, now.

"I think you need to sit down with your constable and think of some way to find out," Slade said.

"Yes, well . . . I'll do that. Certainly. Good-bye!"

Johansson rose and hurried from the restaurant without a backward glance. Alone once more and satisfied with the result, Slade turned back to his cooling ham and eggs.

Twenty minutes later, he was at the livery. Slade checked in on his roan, considered taking her to get some exercise outside of town that afternoon, then walked around behind the stable for another chat with Huping Wong.

Slade found the Chinese elder sitting on a squat three-legged stool outside his humble residence, smoking a pipe that must have measured eighteen inches from its bit out to the ornate bowl. Slade couldn't tell if it was made from bone or ivory.

He sniffed the air, Wong watching him, and said, "Tobacco."

Wong expelled a puff of fragrant smoke and nodded, just as one of his young watchdogs stepped out of the house.

"You're missing one today," Slade said.

"One is enough, I think," Wong said.

"Suits me. We need to talk about your business, Mr. Wong."

"Which business? Laundry? Cleaning round-eye shops?"

"The opium was what I had in mind," Slade said.

Wong smiled and said, "You want to know about the dream poppy? My country banned its use when yours was still a colony of England. Punishment for growing opium or selling it was death. Then come the British traders of your Queen Victoria."

"Not my queen," Slade corrected him.

Wong shrugged. "All round-eyes look alike. The queen says we must buy her opium. When the Daoguang Emperor refuses, it is war. We fight three years against the dream poppy and lose Hong Kong to Queen Victoria. Then comes Taiping Rebellion and we are defeated once again, by Queen Victoria, the French, Russians, and soldiers of your own United States. More opium is coming, and we lose more ports—Danshui, Hankou, Nanjing, Niuzhuang, and more. All round-eye navies own the Yangtze River now. Is victory for you. You wish to know of dream poppies, maybe ask Queen Victoria."

"Thanks for the history," Slade said. "Right now, we need to talk about the opium you sold to Becky Hatcher."

"Names I do not care to know."

"Well, have you sold to more than one of the saloon girls here in town?" asked Slade.

"Is not a crime to sell in your America," Wong said.

"That's right. It's not," said Slade. "I just need information, and my reason's still the same."

"Killer of five now, and the God man maybe, yes?"

"It looks that way," Slade said.

"Almost kill you, last night," said Wong.

"You're keeping track."

"We watch the round-eyes from necessity," Wong said. "Their fear may turn against us. We stay ready."

"And the working girls?" asked Slade.

"Imagine their life," Wong replied. "If it was yours, would you not seek escape in poppy dreams?"

"I might," Slade said.

"You will not be surprised if they do likewise, so?"

"And are the ladies there your only customers?" Slade asked.

Wong puffed a while, then said, "Dream poppies help with many ailments, not just rotten life. Make pains subside, bring sleep."

"And once you've used enough, it's hard to stop," said Slade.

"Is why my country said no more. But thanks to Queen Victoria, we share the blessing now."

"I'll have to take that up with her, next time I see her," Slade remarked. "About your other customers . . ."

"Round-eyes like privacy, you understand? I tell you names, next thing, no more *celestials* in Jubilee."

Without a high card in his hand, Slade played a deuce. "The whole town saw me coming here," he said. "Suppose I let it out that you already gave me names."

Wong smiled and raised an eyebrow.

"Careful who you tell," he said. "Same hammer fall on you as on Chinee."

"Word to the wise, eh?" Slade observed.

"The wise don't need a word," Wong said, and then returned his full attention to the pipe.

The double funeral that afternoon could fairly be described as curious. Under other circumstances, Slade supposed some Jubileeans might have balked at burying a preacher and a hooker in a single ceremony but the recent crimes had shocked the town into a kind of numbness where such vain considerations didn't matter.

Plus, the man who likely would've railed the loudest was, himself, one of those being planted—which left Jubilee short one funeral orator. Guidry, the undertaker, had volunteered with some reluctance to perform the eulogies, but he'd been edged out at the last minute by Mayor Johansson, anxious now for any chance to speak his piece before a crowd.

Slade had considered skipping the funeral—he wasn't local, barely knew the preacher, hadn't even met the murdered woman—but he knew that the majority of townsfolk would attend, the killer probably among them, and he hoped that studying their faces might enlighten him somehow.

What was he looking for? A gloating smirk?

Unlikely. Neither should he see regret, since he imagined that his quarry was immune to it. He was a decent actor, though, to pass among his neighbors unnoticed with so much blood on his hands. There was a chance he'd overdo it, mourn a smidgen too extravagantly for his personal position in the town, and thereby give himself away.

Slade had a rule of thumb for funerals. When preachers

and politicians died, even their bitter enemies from life lined up to say nice things about them. Maybe they were lying, maybe everybody knew it, but the people left behind were generally disinclined to speak ill of the high-and-mighty dead.

In public, anyway.

It was another story altogether for a working girl. In larger towns, and under other circumstances, Slade would have expected no one at the graveside seeing Molly off, except her fellow hookers and, perhaps, her pimp. If he was sober, had the energy to dress himself, and felt like turning out.

But Molly Whittaker, without intending it or taking any action on her own, had changed all that. Slade knew it might be mere coincidence—he hadn't seen the other victims buried, after all—but having died the same night Pastor Booth went up in smoke, and being buried at the same time (though in plots removed from one another by some fifty feet), she had transcended any hint of public scorn.

Slade wondered how the men who'd paid for Molly's favors would react, some of them likely standing next to wives and children in their Sunday best. His best surmise was that the stiffest poker faces probably concealed the greatest sense of guilt.

Or was it sweet relief that now, no one would ever share their dirty little secret?

That sparked another thought. Somewhere, sometime, Slade knew he'd heard a theory that the first Ripper, in London, wasn't just a crazy man. That he'd been killing certain hookers chosen in advance, because they shared a common secret. Something about Catholics and kings?

The details presently eluded him and were in any case irrelevant. But, he was moved to wonder, what if something of the same sort was occurring here and now, in Jubilee? It seemed unlikely, with the victims culled from two competing brothels, but the women could have talked among themselves. Most likely had, in fact, since they'd be shunned by "decent" females.

And the preacher? Was his murder simply a diversion, or should Slade rethink the possibility that he'd been privy to a fatal secret, too?

He was distracted by a rasping sound, glanced up, and saw Johansson in his place midway between the graves, Bible in hand, clearing his throat. When everyone had hushed, the mayor began.

"My friends and fellow citizens of Jubilee, we gather here today in sorrow for a double loss. We know not why this blight of violence has fallen over us, but I have faith that Providence will see us through this trial and soon restore the peace, prosperity and happiness we all deserve."

Not bad, Slade thought. He let Johansson's voice fade as the mayor launched into scripture, scanning faces in the crowd. Was *he* a killer? Or the fellow standing next to him? Was there a secret Mark of Cain he should be able to detect, simply by looking at a guilty man?

I wish, he thought and bit his lip to quell a bitter smile.

With the eulogy completed, no one lingered long at either grave. A couple of the girls who'd worked with Molly scattered wildflowers over her casket. Pastor Booth, for his part, seemed to have no special friends among the mourners.

That did not surprise the huntsman. He had known Booth's immolation would astound and shock the town, but he'd expected no great outpouring of grief over the preacher's passing. Booth had been a stiff-necked, doggedly opinionated and outspoken man. Within the limits of his personal experience, the huntsman thought that Booth had never formed a thought that didn't spew directly from his mouth, without a thought for anything resembling tact. That quality had put some people off, doubtless made some of them despise the preacher in their hearts, but none had ever raised a voice against him publicly.

Now he had been removed.

Another of the huntsman's public services.

He had examined Slade during the funeral oration, saw him peering into faces as if they were windows to the soul, and wished him luck with that. His own face was a mirror that reflected the emotions of whomever he was speaking to, at any given moment. Years of diligent rehearsal had prepared the huntsman to pass any inspection with flying colors.

Right up to the moment when he slipped his blade between a subject's ribs.

It had been touching, he supposed, when Molly's cohorts dropped their weedy blooms into her grave. A couple of the other women at the gathering—a pair of so-called honest ones—were moved to tears by the display. The huntsman had considered dabbing at the corner of one eye, scratching an itch in fact, but stopped himself.

Too much.

No one in Jubilee would think it normal for him to go weepy at a funeral, much less one held in honor of a prostitute. He daren't make a wry remark about this one, as he had done when Becky Hatcher turned up inside out, because the time for bawdy revelry had clearly passed in Jubilee.

These were the days of blood and fear.

The huntsman's time.

It was a fact, and undeniable, that he enjoyed community reactions to his so-called crimes. On one or two occasions he'd surrendered to a whim and penned some hurried notes to scribblers of the press, then watched a swarm of rank impostors take his name in vain, claiming the credit for his deeds—and other things he'd never have imagined.

It was fun, all right? Who ever said that science had to be a dour and joyless occupation, after all?

Leaving the town's small cemetery—small but growing, thanks to him—the huntsman trailed Slade at a distance, ambling at a pace he judged to be sedate, mournful without the added touch of lethargy. He did not mind that other townsfolk passed between him and the object of his scrutiny.

Where could the lawman go to hide in Jubilee?

Small towns were interesting. While the huntsman found a wider range of subjects in great cities, and felt more secure himself, a small community reacted both more quickly and more viscerally to reports of his experiments. Those who had seen his work firsthand, he thought, might never be the same again.

All to the good. They ought to thank him, if they had their wits about them. But instead, they clamored for his blood. Spoke openly of hanging him, or worse, once he had been identified.

No worries there, the huntsman thought.

His mask was still securely fixed in place. No one who patronized his place of business, or who passed by him on the streets of Jubilee, would feel the slightest tremor of suspicion in his company.

Why should they?

He had been rehearsing for this role since he was born.

Indeed, sometimes the huntsman thought he might have played it in another life, or many other lives, before his present incarnation. That idea was pleasant, but it also troubled him.

If he'd been searching out the harlot's secret for a hundred or a thousand years, why had he failed so far?

Gripped by determination to succeed this time, at last, the huntsman followed Slade down Main Street, already devising his next plan to throw the marshal off his scent.

Vandiver met Slade on the sidewalk, stepping from his office as the mourners filtered back along Main Street. He had a sheepish look about him and avoided making eye contact with any of his neighbors when they passed.

"How'd Roland do?" he asked, as Slade approached.

"Half politics, half Holy Ghost," Slade said.

"That's typical," Vandiver said. "Sometimes, I think he honestly believes God wants him to be mayor of Jubilee."

"If that's the height of his ambition," Slade replied, "I'd say it was a modest goal."

"Oh, he's a climber," said the constable. "He had to start somewhere, I guess."

"And finish here, if he's associated with these killings in the public mind."

Vandiver nodded. "It's not exactly what you look for in a governor or senator."

But if he wrapped it up somehow—or got the credit for it, anyway . . .

Slade frowned at that. It wouldn't fly, no matter how he tried to look at it. Johansson couldn't pull the crimes himself, then solve them, without going to the gallows. End of story for a would-be statesman. On the other hand, if he had someone else killing the women for his benefit, bizarre as it might sound, why would the killer put his own head in a noose without naming the mastermind behind him?

It was ridiculous. Which didn't mean some idjit might not try it, all the same.

"You pick out any likelies at the funeral?" Vandiver asked.

"Not one. It was a long shot, anyway," Slade said.

"I guess. Still more than I could think of." Staring down the length of Main Street toward the empty plains beyond, Vandiver said, "You know, I'm sick of this."

"So's everyone in town," Slade said.

"I don't just mean the killings. Jubilee and all of it. Pretending I'm a lawman."

"Aren't you?"

"Why? Because I wear a piece of tin?" Vandiver shook his head, half smiling. "Hell, you saw through that five minutes after you hit town. If I was any kind of real lawman, I woulda gone out after Chris the day Long Liz was killed."

"You had a point, about the jurisdiction," Slade replied.

"I had a damned excuse," Vandiver said. "Don't try to sugarcoat it for me."

Slade had no reply to that. He let Vandiver talk.

"I'd leave today," the constable pressed on, "but how'n hell would that look? Two more killings, and I run away? Next thing I know, you'd be out looking for me, thinking I'm behind all this."

"It crossed my mind," Slade told him, honestly.

"O' course it would," Vandiver said. "Who better to be pulling shit like this? Put on a badge and cover for yourself. It wouldn't be the first time, eh? You know they used to call the Earp brothers the fighting pimps. Them and Doc Holliday ran half the whores and faro games in Tombstone."

"Yeah, I've heard that," Slade replied.

Vandiver had a point. Half of the West's most famous lawmen had been outlaws, too, at one time or another. Ben Thompson, in Texas, had served time for murder before he was Austin's city marshal. Jim Courtright was another, doubling as a marshal and a hired assassin until liquor and a faster gun put him away.

"You're sticking, then," Slade said. Not asking.

"Looks that way. We catch this prick, and then I'm gone."

"Free country," Slade replied.

"I used to think so," said Vandiver. "Now, I just don't know."

"Meanwhile."

"Meanwhile," Vandiver echoed, facing Slade, "be smart and watch your back. Somebody wants you gone."

"Won't be the first time," Slade replied.

14

Sunset over Jubilee held no attraction for Jack Slade. Facing his fourth night in a town where it appeared no one was safe, he missed Faith more than ever. Wished that he could put this place behind him, ride all night and through tomorrow, till he fell into her arms exhausted and found peace.

Not in the cards, he thought, watching from his hotel room's window as the shadows of another haunted evening crept along Main Street. The shops were closing early, but it hardly mattered, since their customers were all intent on getting home as soon as possible, racing the dusk to put locked doors between themselves and darkness.

Slade had napped a bit that afternoon, not usual for him, but with another night of prowling set before him, he'd decided he could use the rest. Amazingly, no one had interrupted him with news of any fresh atrocities.

Like ghosts and vampires, he supposed the killer only worked at night.

No, that was wrong. To pass for human in a town like

Jubilee, a man would have to be employed, or else display some evidence of wealth that would explain an idle life. Since no one in the town stood out as filthy rich, that meant the slayer had a job. He offered goods or services for sale by day, and earned enough to keep from being put out on the street and starving.

Which was not to say he worked *in town*, but Slade had talked about the local cowboys with Vandiver, learning that the Bar-B was the only spread of any size in the vicinity. The other farms were family operations, one or two employing younger men from Jubilee who rode out for the day but slept in town. Vandiver had been watching out for late arrivals since the second killing and had seen no deviation from the Saturday furloughs Tom Gallagher had described.

So, working days and killing nights, the madman ought to look rundown and haggard, needing sleep. *He ought to look like me,* Slade thought and nearly smiled, before remembering that crazy people generated extra energy. He'd heard it said that a lunatic possessed the strength of ten normal men, and while that likely wasn't gospel truth, Slade had dealt with people before who were off their nut, and he didn't crave another round.

The first excuse he gives you, use the Colt, Slade thought.

But he would have to find the bastard, first.

Hungry despite the grim turn of his thoughts, Slade grabbed his gunbelt from the bed and buckled it in place. Made sure to double-check the Peacemaker before he donned his hat and locked the door behind him, headed for the stairs.

The hotel clerk was never sure exactly how to act with Slade. He had the basic courtesy down pat, and any hotel man was glad to have another paying customer who caused no fuss, but every time they met, Slade saw the apprehension in the clerk's gray eyes. He would be thinking someone might come after Slade at the hotel, next time. Shoot out the windows, maybe set the place on fire.

If he'd been just another drifter passing through, the

clerk would probably have given him the boot—or asked Vandiver to explain why it was inadvisable for him to hang around. The badge spared Slade from that, but not from worried glances, smiles that faltered, or an attitude that seemed to ask him, *Why in hell are you still here?*

Good question.

He was there because he hadn't done his job yet, and there was no end to it in sight.

Tonight, therefore, he would be on the street again, showing himself and giving anyone who cared to try his luck another chance to frame Slade in his sights. He thought about the Spencer rifle, made for killing buffalo long distance, and it made his skin crawl. Still, what other options did he have?

Whatever else was on the killer's mind right now, he was obsessing over Slade. The fire at Mercy Baptist had been staged to let the slayer snatch another victim out from under Slade's nose, as it were. Showing superiority. The next night, he'd tried killing Slade and bungled it. That had to sting, and if his quarry had an ego even half the size that Slade imagined, he would have put it right. Either take Slade out of the picture or make some substantial gesture of contempt for all the town to see.

Sooner the better, Slade thought, as he left the hotel's lobby, stepping onto Main Street. Dusk had reached his doorstep, and he counted only half a dozen people on the street, all busy locking doors or looking over their shoulders.

He wondered whether Jubilee would ever make a full recovery and finally decided that he didn't care. It was a harsh admission, but an honest one. His oath of office bound him to protect these citizens of Oklahoma Territory from the monster who was stalking them, but that aside, Slade had no personal investment in their future. If they all dried up and blew away to fertilize the prairie's grass, he wouldn't miss them one iota.

They were keeping him from Faith.

And at the moment, thoughts of them were keeping him from supper.

The huntsman watched Slade through a window facing Main Street, saw him crossing to MacDonald's restaurant again, and watched him disappear inside. He seemed to be the only customer so far, which meant he wouldn't have to wait as long as usual for service, but the food Jory MacDonald served was copious and tasty, plenty there to keep Slade at his table for a while.

What did he have to rush for, anyway?

The huntsman knew what Slade was thinking, feeling, as he ordered from the menu chalked on Jory's wall. He'd had enough of Jubilee and wanted to go home but couldn't with the huntsman still at large. After last night, the lawman would suppose his last, best hope lay in exposing himself to another attack. He'd be out and about through the night, being seen, with his heart in his mouth and a hand on his pistol.

Good news for the huntsman, since he had decided to try yet another approach.

No diversion this time, just a full-on display of his genius and stealth. Let Slade parade himself on Main Street, rattling doorknobs, ducking in and out of alleys like a stray cat. It would all avail him nothing.

Getting ready for the night, the huntsman checked his gear. Blackjack and derringer. Two knives. Bottle of chloroform. A folded dust rag. Leather gloves. Distributing the several items in his pockets, where they could be easily retrieved but didn't make his pants or jacket bulge and sag in a peculiar way, took several moments longer. Posed before a full-length mirror, he rotated slowly, trying different angles, until he was satisfied.

All set.

Tonight would be a test of both his ingenuity and skill. His plan called for him to invade a hornets' nest, select his prize and spirit her away, perform his usual inspection—always hoping for the best, of course—and then . . . deliver a surprise.

He would test the lawman, see what he was made of where it counted, beyond a fast draw. Galling, of course, that he had missed what should have been an easy shot last night. But there was no embarrassment beyond his own, since no one else in Jubilee knew who had sniped at Slade.

The Spencer was concealed once more, secure from prying eyes along with sundry souvenirs and objects of investigation. For a while, last night, he'd thought the marshal and Vandiver might go door to door through Jubilee, questioning residents and merchants on their whereabouts, but nothing of the kind had happened. By the time they thought of it, he guessed, too many had been in the streets, responding to the gunfire.

Chaos saved the day—or night—again.

Once, in another city far away, one of the coppers tracking him told reporters that the huntsman had the Devil's own luck. He hadn't been sure what that meant, at the time, since Satan was famous for losing his battle with God and being evicted from Heaven. Later, he'd decided that it must mean he was guided and protected by a higher power, misinterpreted as evil by police since it prevented them from catching him.

The huntsman had been called to serve mankind, and something greater than himself meant to ensure that he succeeded. It was obvious.

Leaving his shop through the back door, he walked parallel to Main Street, westbound, until he reached the rear of the American Saloon. Inside, he heard the muffled tinkling of piano music accompanied by strains of forced laughter. The yokels would have a good time if it killed them.

Or somebody else.

He tried the back door on a whim and was surprised to feel the knob turn in his hand. Unlocked. It was an almost shocking lapse under the circumstances—or, perhaps, more proof that he was being guided on his way to ultimate success.

With one hand in his pocket, ready with the derringer, he cracked the door and peered inside. No one was there to intercept him as he crossed the threshold, closed the door behind him, and moved casually toward the service stairs. The barroom sounds were louder now, but still felt distant as he climbed the steps, ascending toward his destiny.

The second floor included ten small bedrooms for the harlots and their customers, together with a larger suite of rooms where Ben Tewksbury slept. The huntsman had been here before, a business errand, and he knew the layout well enough. Concealment was provided by a broom-and-linen closet halfway down, just room enough inside for him to stand and listen as the whores went back and forth with idiots in tow.

The only challenge now, to pass the time without being discovered. Standing with the longer of his knives in hand, prepared to strike without a heartbeat's hesitation if the door was opened from outside, the huntsman waited, humming softly to himself. Imagining the sense of triumph that he would experience if this time he succeeded and revealed the harlots' secret.

Would he even recognize it at a glance? Might he would require a magnifying glass or microscope to verify his first impression?

No. It must be obvious, or he could not reveal it to a world of ignorant, shortsighted men whose collective knowledge of science was nil. So obvious, in fact, that when he saw it for the first time, the huntsman himself would be humbled at having failed to find it earlier.

Perhaps tonight, within the next few hours.

And for Jack Slade, the surprise of a lifetime.

• • •

At half past midnight, Slade decided that he ought to be in bed. A final pass along Main Street, from end to end, and he'd call it a night. Brush off the disappointment of a wasted night and try to dream of Faith.

He'd been on edge since finishing his beefsteak supper at MacDonald's, half convinced that Jubilee's madman would feel compelled to take another shot at him. The bad news, from a man hunter's perspective: no one had.

Somewhere around eleven, he'd watched Vandiver remove a rowdy drunk from the American Saloon. The guy was three sheets to the wind and then some, raving at Vandiver in a slurred voice, calling out his failures as a lawman. When the lush asked why Vandiver picked on honest men and let a killer roam the streets unhindered, Slade knew that the constable was close to lashing out. He'd been prepared to intervene, but Vandiver had managed to control himself, sending the drunk home with a shaking that could easily have been much worse.

Now, ninety minutes later, Slade couldn't help wondering how long the town of Jubilee would last. No one could fully trust his neighbor, with the killer still at large. But even if they caught the crazy scum tomorrow, would it help? Suspicion had become a habit now, would have to be unlearned, if that was even possible. Some Jubileeans would regard the town itself as tainted, maybe cursed. Slade couldn't guess how many would sell out and leave, eventually, but he wouldn't bet a month's pay on the town's odds of surviving for another year.

Slade had finished one whole side of Main Street and was turning back toward his hotel when the commotion started. Just a scream, at first, rising from everywhere and nowhere, all at once. A second later, and the high-pitched wail was followed up by other rising voices emanating from Ben Tewksbury's saloon.

Slade jogged in that direction, keeping watch on alleyways and shadows as he went. He couldn't guess the trouble from a distance, but he knew that if their killer was involved, the bastard liked diversions. Tricks and ambushes. It might be his style to pull something, cause a ruckus, then lie waiting in the dark for Slade to walk into his gunsights.

Not tonight, Slade thought, slowing his pace and keeping to the shadows where he could. Balancing urgency and caution, he still reached Tewksbury's place within a minute of the first long scream.

Business at the American Saloon had been declining when he'd left the place, around midnight, but now Slade walked into a scene of turmoil. Tewksbury was coming down the stairs, yelling at somebody behind the bar—two of his girls, Slade saw, huddled behind the burly bartender. Three other girls were clustered on the second-story landing, shifting worried eyes between their boss and something farther down the hallway to their left. Three paying customers remained, one of them making for the door as Slade came in.

Slade buttonholed the man and asked him what the trouble was. The patron swallowed hard, then said, "One of the women's missin'. Jesus, what a thing!"

"You'd best go home," Slade said and let him slip into the night. Slade reached the bar as Ben Tewksbury did, voice rising to compete with the proprietor's interrogation of his girls.

"What's happened?" Slade demanded.

"There you are!" Tewksbury said, red-faced. "It's Rose. The stinking sumbitch took her out of here. She's gone!"

Slade saw the sassy blond once more, in memory, and felt his stomach tighten. Moving past Tewksbury, toward the stairs, he asked, "Has anybody searched the place?"

"Hell, yes!" Tewksbury snapped. "I'm telling you, she isn't here!"

"All right," said Slade, now halfway up the stairs. "Who noticed she was gone, and how?"

"Annette went in to bum a smoke and found . . . well, look. See for yourself."

The girl was gone, not butchered here, but Slade still braced himself. He guessed that her small room had been tidy when the struggle started. Now, her bedding had been lashed onto the floor and there were crimson speckles on it. Blood, about the quantity Slade would expect if someone had been punched to settle them.

And something else.

"You smell that?" he asked Tewksbury.

"I do. It's fading now. You should've smelled it first thing, when Annette called me."

"Is she the one who screamed?"

Tewksbury nodded. "Panicked at the sight of the blood, I guess. These days, can't say I blame her."

Slade was working on the smell, a sickly sweet aroma coming from . . . the bed? No, more specifically, the space beneath it. Kneeling on the plain wood floor, he drew back Rose's tangled, bloodied sheet and found a piece of rough cloth lying there. Damp to the touch, and when he lifted it . . .

"It's this," Slade said, holding the rag aloft for Tewksbury to smell.

"What *is* that?" asked the pimp.

"I thought you might have some idea," Slade said.

"Not kerosene. It's . . . hell, who knows?"

Slade checked the window, found no fire escape or ladder standing by.

"They didn't jump from here," he said. "Could he have carried her downstairs?"

"Not down the *front* stairs," said Tewksbury. "But the service stairs, I guess so."

"Then we need to hurry."

Slade pushed past him, running by the time he hit the balcony, the damp cloth still clutched in his hand.

They were too late, of course. It felt like fate to Slade, but he was sick of it, regardless. Down the dusty path from the American Saloon's back door, past silent shops, he ran with Tewksbury and the remaining barroom patrons, seeking any trace of Rose.

They found her lying huddled, almost on the back step of the general store.

Tewksbury had a lamp from the saloon, snatched up in passing. Its pale light revealed blood first, a lot of it, before Slade's eyes could make sense of the damage wreaked by steel. There hadn't been sufficient time for Rose's killer to inflict all of the savage wounds they'd found on Molly Whittaker, but he had done enough to sicken Slade and spur Tewksbury to a rage of cursing.

Slade was looking for a way to cover her, the flimsy nightgown cut to shreds, when one of Tewksbury's customers started to retch. That set off the other one, staggering off a few paces to bring up his supper and beer, while Slade wrinkled his nose at the new wave of smells.

"Go on home!" he snapped at them. "Right now!"

They were staggering off into darkness on unsteady legs as Slade rose, turned his back on the ruins of Rose.

"Hold up the light," Slade said.

"What?" As he raised the lamp, Tewksbury squinted, following Slade's eyes. "What's that?"

Beneath the smooth line of the dead girl's jaw, a flat steel shaft protruded, glinting in the lamplight. Slade bent closer, recognized it as the handle of a small knife, buried in her throat.

Another round of swearing from her ex-boss as Slade straightened and turned to face him.

"She was how old? Seventeen?" he asked.

"About that," Tewksbury replied. Reading the look on

Slade's face in the lamplight, he added, "Hey, I don't pick them, you know. *They* pick *me*."

"You're a prince," Slade said. "Now, when you're done with the excuses, go next door and fetch the doctor, will you?"

"You mean undertaker, don't you?"

"No, I said—"

"I'm here," a voice behind Slade said. "What's going— Oh, dear Lord!"

Doctor Wheatley stood in shirtsleeves at the edge of light cast by Tewksbury's lantern, staring down at Rose's supine form.

"I heard your voices," Wheatley said. "I thought . . . I didn't know . . ."

Slade frowned, bent down, and pulled the slender knife from Rose's throat. Her flesh was unresisting. Wheatley focused on the blade as Slade held it aloft, between them.

"Do you recognize this, Doctor?"

"It's a scalpel," Wheatley answered, almost whispering. "For use in surgery."

"That's right." The words were barely out before his eyes narrowed. "Now, wait! You don't think—"

Stepping closer, Slade held up the cloth he'd found in Rose's room. Still slightly damp, though it was drying quickly.

"Smell that for me, would you, Doctor?"

Cautiously, as if expecting Slade to strike him, Wheatley leaned forward and sniffed at the cloth. His nose wrinkled before he recoiled.

"Chloroform," he declared.

"Are you sure?"

"Of course. There's nothing else quite like it."

"It's used to knock out patients for an operation, isn't it?" asked Slade.

"That's not the only use," Wheatley replied. "But yes, for anaesthesia during surgery and childbirth."

"Right."

Beside Slade, Tewksbury was fuming. "Scalpel? Chloroform? A body nearly on the doctor's goddamned doorstep? You son of a—"

"Hold it!" snapped Slade. "You calm down, now, and wait."

"Wait for what? It's plain as the nose on your face that he—"

"What?" Slade challenged. "That he *what*?"

"That he killed Rose, goddamn it!" Tewksbury lashed back.

"Killed . . . killed," Wheatley stammered. "I never . . . I swear, I . . ."

"It's not plain to me," Slade announced, "but it bears looking into."

Tewksbury gaped. Said, "You've got to be—"

"Quiet! You wanted to fetch Silas Guidry? Well, this is the time. Do it now."

"And what about *him*?"

"He'll be coming with me. You go on, like I said."

Tewksbury left, reluctantly, taking his lantern with him. Stranded in the dark with death and Dr. Wheatley, Slade said, "Doctor, get your coat. Lock up and come with me."

"Where are we going?" Wheatley asked.

"To jail," Slade said. "The only place in Jubilee where you'll be safe tonight."

15

Burch Thornton left his horse a half mile out, tied to a spindly tree in an arroyo where it could graze while he handled his business. Walking in was risky—snakes, the chance that he would fall and snap an ankle, plus a threat of being shot on sight—but Thornton knew his odds were better this way than on horseback.

He had let a full day pass since he was booted off the spread and out of work, then he could wait no longer for a taste of sweet revenge. Faith Connover owed him for the humiliation he had suffered and the steady income he had lost. Her fault, all of it.

In Thornton's mind, there had been nothing wrong with stealing from his bunkmates. If they left their valuables lying in plain sight, or carelessly concealed, what else should they expect? From talking to them, Thornton knew that none had shared his background, coming up from nothing and convinced that he was worth precisely that: nothing. None of them had been beaten down and broken till they fled their so-called homes at nine years old and started living hand-to-mouth by any means available.

Some of the things he'd done to stay alive and give himself some ease would make a buzzard sick, but Thornton took it all in stride. The only crime in stealing, as he saw it, lay in getting caught.

As for the other, sneaking out to catch a glimpse of Faith while she was bathing, that was only natural. What real man wouldn't seize the opportunity if it was offered? Thornton guessed the other hired hands had been looking in on her for years, some of them maybe doing more than that. Murdoch had only squealed on him because he was the new guy and they didn't like to share.

Bastards.

He couldn't deal with all of them tonight, the way he would've liked to, but at least Thornton could show them that there was a price attached to making him feel small. When he was done, the bitch who'd fired him wouldn't recognize her precious spread. Some of her flunkies might not have a place to work.

And it would serve all of them right.

The trick was getting in and doing what he'd come to do without somebody spotting him. Thornton had no doubt that the hands would work him over good and proper if they caught him. Some of them—likely the ones he'd stolen little trifles from—might shoot him for the hell of it, before good-hearted Faith could intervene.

Good-hearted, shit!

If she was all that sympathetic, why, she could've overlooked a little window-peeping, maybe even called Thornton inside and given him a ride for old time's sake. But, no. Whatever he might say about the other hands around the place, Thornton knew Faith was fiercely loyal to her lawman. It was a lucky break for him that Mr. High-and-Mighty Slade was out of town the morning he got fired.

The marshal likely would've whupped his ass into the middle of next week.

Or tried to, anyhow.

Thornton had heard the stories about Slade and what a hand he was with guns, but he imagined most of that was puffery, conflated out of all resemblance to reality. So, Slade had killed some men. Who hadn't?

Nobody was bulletproof.

The quickest way to soften up a hard case was to shoot him in the back. No fuss, no muss, and very little risk of getting shot yourself.

When he had closed the distance to a quarter mile or less, a pair of riders passed to Thornton's left and went on without seeing him. Good thing for him they didn't bring a dog along on night patrols.

Speaking of watchmen, Thornton knew he'd come too late to get another look at Faith Connover in the buff, but maybe he could roust her in a nightgown, at the very least. The main thing was to pay her back for firing him, and all the others for the way they'd treated him like dirt.

That was a bad mistake on their parts.

The plan had come to him in Enid, while he spent his last few bucks on rotgut at the Lazy Eye Saloon. Not sharing his scheme with anyone, in case the word got back to someone at the courthouse and they gave his name to Slade. An easy in-and-out, if he did everything just right, Thornton would be miles away before they got around to blaming anyone.

Of course, they'd all suspect him. To avoid that, he would have to wait for months, but who had that much time to spare? Forget that crap about revenge being a cold dessert, or whatever it was old-timers liked to say. Thornton was steaming with embarrassment and meant to make it right before his fury had a chance to fade.

At last, he saw the house, the barn, and other outbuildings.

Some of them fairly new, rebuilt after some trouble on the place with Mormons, as he understood it, not too long before he'd hired on at the spread. Thornton wished he had seen that, but the way his luck ran, he'd have been one of the guys the crazy bastards killed.

My turn tonight, he thought and started creeping toward the barn, barely a hundred yards in front of him.

Faith dreamed a wedding from a storybook, the kind where princes find their true loves sleeping off a curse or evil potion and revive them with a kiss. The costumes weren't exactly right, of course. Her prince had managed to forget his polished armor and had trail dust on his boots, while Faith was barely wearing anything at all. Some kind of flimsy little thing that she could see through, in the dappled sunlight. Lying on a rough stone pallet, it was cold, and she'd been waiting for a long, long time.

Anxious, she glanced around and couldn't find the minister who was supposed to lead the ceremony. Was he late, or had she missed the wedding altogether? Jack was at her side now, touching her, and it appeared they were proceeding to the honeymoon without further delay.

And that was fine.

As Jack leaned down to kiss her, Faith smelled something, started to recoil, and winced at the collision of her skull and stony bed. She frowned at Jack and asked him, "When did you start smoking?"

When he answered, with his lips almost against her own, he gave a jarring shout of—

"Fire! Wake up! The barn's on fire!"

Faith bolted from her bed—not stone at all—and snatched a robe to wear over her nightgown, rushing to her southward-facing window first, whipped back the curtains, dazzled by the sudden glare of firelight in her eyes.

The barn was burning, true enough. Not totally engulfed

by fire, but flames were gnawing at the east wall, spreading from the southeast corner, leaping toward the eaves. Even without the window being open, she could hear the panicked squeals of horses from inside.

With a curse, she left the window, found her boots and jammed bare feet down into them. To hell with blisters. She was thinking of the animals, their helpless terror, while a portion of her mind tried to imagine how the fire had started.

Never, under any circumstances, was an unattended lamp left burning in the barn at night. There'd been no storm, which ruled out lightning strikes. It wasn't hot enough for stacked-up bales of hay to smolder on their own. Which only left . . .

Faith hit the porch running, to find her hands scrambling for buckets and water in various states of undress. Ed Murdoch, in his union suit, had only buttoned one side of the flap in back, but there was no time for a laugh at his expense. Robe billowing around her as she ran, Faith sprinted for the barn and through the broad front doors that someone else had opened.

Jeb Danson met her just inside, caught her left arm, and tried to drag her out again, but Faith broke free and snapped at him, "The horses!"

"Ma'am, we're trying," he replied, but Faith was past him, homing on the corner where the flames were eating though the walls, smoke pouring through the cracks.

Faith started opening the stalls, standing aside as horses galloped past her, toward the night's clean air. She freed the nearest to the conflagration first, then worked her way backward along the right-hand stalls, with Danson helping her, soon joined by Johnny Gray. The rest were outside, hauling water, and she prayed they'd bring it soon.

Before it was too late.

A bay mare brushed against Faith in her panic, sent her reeling to the ground, but she leaped up again and shook it off. Bruises could stand along with blisters in the waiting line. If she could only save the horses, frightened living things, the barn could always be replaced.

Not cheaply, mind you. But she'd had experience, and recently, with renovating damage caused by fire and axes, by malicious men.

She almost thought of something, then, but lost it in her haste to save a jet-black gelding, rearing in his stall as waves of heat washed over him. Danson got there ahead of her, was fumbling with the latch, smoke in his eyes, until Faith's nimble fingers managed to release it.

Two more horses on the barn's side nearest to the fire, an Appaloosa and a gray. Once they were freed, she could release the others, maybe save them all before a portion of the roof collapses or flames spread to the hay bales stacked along the barn's south wall.

Maybe.

Outside, she heard Art Hanes and Murdoch shouting back and forth as they sloshed water on the fire. Impulsively, she grabbed Jeb Danson by the belt, used all her strength propelling him in the direction of the open doors.

"Go help them!" she commanded. "Douse the fire!"

He hesitated, staring at her, then gave her a jerky nod and ran to do as he'd been told. Faith turned back to the stalls, coughing as smoke swirled in around her and the fire sucked oxygen out of the barn.

It was a race, now, with the flames and time itself, to save the dozen horses still remaining in the barn and save herself.

A race with Death.

Burch Thornton huddled in darkness beyond the firelight, trembling with a jumble of emotions, torn between fear and excitement. He'd been on his way to set the house afire, then hesitated when the barn went up so fast and everyone responded quicker than he'd planned. The more he thought about it, hiding in the shadows, he was thinking that he'd have to go *inside* Faith's house to get it burning, and the thought of being trapped in there had nearly made him wet himself.

The barn would be enough, he reckoned. Knew how it would pain Faith when she heard the horses wailing with their almost-human voices, battering against their stalls. If he could only break her heart for what she'd done to him . . .

He hadn't counted on his ex-boss running from the house in boots and nightdress, with a robe flapping around her, charging straight into the fire. That made him think she must be downright crazy, over and above her hardnosed attitude toward letting Thornton glimpse a little skin. Risking her life for animals was something that a lunatic or sloppy drunk might do, not someone in her right mind with a spread to run and hands depending on her for their daily bread.

Crazy.

He had another chance to light the house, then, but the fear was strong in Thornton and he couldn't follow through. Hating himself for that, the yellow streak he'd never shaken from the time he'd fled his miserable childhood home down to the present, left him feeling small, more furious than ever at himself, at Faith, the whole damned world around him.

Who could he blame for what he was?

His old man, sure. A heavy-handed drunk who hated everyone and made damn sure that it was mutual. His mother, drab as dishwater and just about as helpful when it came to sheltering her firstborn from abuse. The strangers who had used and schooled him once Thornton was out and on his own. He hadn't known what Hell was, after all, until he had to earn his own keep and hang on to what he got by any means available.

All that had made him mean and sly, but somehow none of it had made him strong. He shied away from fights, unless he had a chance to catch an adversary by surprise and strike the first decisive blow. He'd never faced an armed man in a stand-up duel of any kind—and never would, if he could get away with hiding in the shadows, backshooting his enemies.

Why risk a crippling injury or death when he could be the one delivering the punishment to helpless victims? Any idiot could get his brains blown out. A smart man watched his back, and everybody else's, looking for his opening.

Horses were breaking from the barn now, one by one, and galloping away into the night. No one was taking time to stop them, more intent on saving those still trapped by walls and flame. Burch Thornton felt a pang of disappointment in addition to his other mixed emotions. He had nothing personal against the horses; they were simply Faith Connover's property, which he'd decided should be stripped from her as punishment for treating him like garbage.

Well, at least she'd lose the barn. And if she stayed inside too long, fighting the fire, she might be—

Thornton's fear came back, full force. He hadn't planned on killing anyone tonight, though it was always a potential option in most any situation. Still, if Faith took crazy chances, then it wasn't really his fault, anyway.

Try selling that in court, he thought, and knew it wouldn't go to trial if Faith burned up and someone figured out that he had set the fire. In that case, Jack Slade would be looking for him. Might forget to bring his badge along but damn sure wouldn't leave his guns at home.

Of if Judge Dennison kept Slade away from him, what then? Some other marshals tracking Thornton everywhere he went, until they ran him down and either shot him in his tracks or brought him back to hang.

And that was worse.

Like anybody else, he had enjoyed his share of public executions. He had laughed at poor dumb bastards wriggling on the rope like fresh-caught trout. But even as he joined the other ghouls in celebrating frontier justice, Thornton's cowardice came back to haunt him, with a small voice in his head telling him he could die the same damned way.

Something to think about, when he was being careful not to leave a trail.

He'd just about decided it was time to leave, give up watching the show and clear the property before somebody stumbled over him by accident, when he saw Danson clear the barn, carrying Faith. She wasn't burned, as far as he could tell—although her robe and nightgown had been smudged with soot—but she was lolling in Jeb's arms, a limp feeling about her, maybe from the smoke she would've breathed.

He waited, watching, hate-filled as her savior set Faith down, not sitting in the dirt but stanting upright with Jeb's arm around her waist. Same crybaby who missed his stupid pocketknife and paved the way for Thornton getting fired.

An impulse sent his right hand sliding toward the pistol on his hip, but Thornton didn't figure he could make a shot from that range, much less two, and then escape the other hands. Whether they shot or lynched him, either way, he'd wind up dead for nothing.

Cursing silently, he faded back into the dark.

The dizziness was fading now. Faith wasn't sure where it had come from, possibly a combination of the heat, the smoke, and being jostled by the bay mare, but she'd lost her bearings, felt the ground beneath her feet slide out from under her, gray haze that wasn't smoke obscuring the firelight in the barn.

Next thing Faith knew, she was outside, leaning on Jeb, his arm around her, keeping her upright. Her legs felt weak, but they would still support her. Muttering her thanks to Jeb, Faith pulled away from him, stood on her own, and focused on the barn.

A piebald mare ran past her, then no more. Ed Murdoch,

coughing heavily, was last out of the barn. When had he gone inside? For that matter, when had Jeb Danson doubled back to rescue her?

"That's all of 'em," Ed wheezed, approaching Faith and Jeb. Art Hanes and Johnny Gray still ran a two-man fire brigade, shuttling between the yard pump and the barn with buckets, but they obviously couldn't save it.

"Stop!" Faith called to them, feeling the near-sob in her voice. "It's too late, now!"

Reluctantly, they quit the endless shuttling back and forth from pump to flaming barn and came back to join Faith and the others where they stood, watching the fire.

When it collapsed, Faith knew, the barn would not endanger any other buildings on the property. Rebuilding it would not be cheap, but she had money in the bank and would apply herself to working with the men. Her mind was working on another problem now.

"We need to find out how it started," she declared.

Silence among her hands.

"An accident, you think?" she asked of no one in particular.

"It happens," Murdoch said. His face and tone were glum.

"A lantern burning in the barn?"

"No, ma'am," Danson replied without a beat of hesitation. "I checked that, like always. There was nothing lit in there."

"Unlikely it would just go up, then," Johnny said.

"God*damned* unlikely," Hanes said. Quickly adding, "Sorry, ma'am."

"I would agree that it's goddamned unlikely," Faith said. "But if it was set—"

"Whoever done it's probably still close!" Murdoch concluded.

"We should look, while there's still light," Hanes said.

"Get to it," Faith instructed. "I'll get dressed and join you."

"Ma'am," Jeb Danson said, "with all respect, I think we'd all feel better if you went back in the house and locked the door behind you."

"Hide out, you mean?"

"No, ma'am. It's just that—"

"What about the house?" asked Murdoch. "I can see the door open from here. We all been busy with the barn. Somebody coulda—"

"Snuck inside," Gray finished for him. "Better have a look, in case."

"And now you'll say I ought to wait out here, alone?" Faith challenged them.

When no one spoke, she led the way back to her home, Danson and Murdoch flanking her, while Hanes and Gray ran back to get their pistols from the bunkhouse.

The search was swift but thorough, moving room to room, opening closets, cupboards, peering under beds, Jeb Danson scrambling up into the attic. All the windows were secure, the back door locked from the inside, no sign of an intruder anywhere. Faith's natural relief was tempered by depression that the search was even necessary. She felt violated, in a way that called up memories of Danite gunmen battling to invade the house and slaughter everyone inside.

This time, no enemy.

Or, rather, none that she could see.

But if the fire was set deliberately . . .

"Burch Thornton," she blurted out when they were reassembled in the living room, her men preparing to disperse and search the property.

"Makes sense," said Murdoch. "He's the kind to hold a grudge."

"And sneak around behind your back at night," Jeb added.

"If he's here, I want him," Faith instructed.

"Does it matter if he's breathin'?" Hanes inquired.

Faith felt as if ice crystals had begun to form around her heart, the numbness spreading.

"If you find him," she replied, "give him a chance. Don't put yourselves at risk, though."

If she was passing sentence on a man, it didn't bother Faith. She couldn't prove Thornton had set the fire unless her men caught him in the vicinity. In fact, she didn't know if *anyone* had set the blaze deliberately, but searching for an arsonist made sense, before the might-be prowler had a chance to slip away.

Too late, she thought, chiding herself. A full half hour and counting had elapsed since she was wakened by the fire alarm from her peculiar dreams. Thornton or someone else could easily have sparked the fire and fled within that time, might be crossing the limits of her property by now if he was mounted.

And what kind of fire starter would walk from Enid, much less somewhere else even farther away, just to burn down her barn?

No one.

Setting the fire required a certain malice that she'd recognized too late in Thornton. He was capable of this, she thought—which didn't prove that he was guilty.

Catch him first, then prosecute.

And let him rot in prison with the other scum.

Faith thought of Jack, wished he was there to help her, feeling anger as she swiped unwelcome tears off of her cheeks.

The ranch was hers. She would defend it, with her men, a part of proving she was worthy to possess the land and profit from it.

But again, she wished with all her heart that Jack was safely home.

16

"How many out there now?" asked Slade.

Vandiver checked the window, frowned, and said, "About a dozen, give or take."

"You need to break them up and send them home," Slade said.

"I can't tell people where to stand or send 'em to their rooms like they were kids," the constable replied.

"You can if that's a lynch mob forming up," Slade said. "In fact, your badge requires it."

"Don't you try and tell me—"

Mayor Johansson gripped Vandiver's arm to silence him, turning to Slade. "Marshal," he said, "there's nothing to be gained by arguing among ourselves right now."

Slade felt his anger simmering and tried to tamp it down.

"You're right," he said. "We've got a situation that needs handling before it slips out of control."

"We have good people here," Johansson said. "Our town is small, I grant you, but it's not some Dixie backwater. We don't have lynchings here."

"You never had a string of crimes like this before," Slade said. "Your town's on edge, ready to crack. It's why you sent your message to Judge Dennison."

"Agreed. And we've established that I should have sent it sooner," said Johansson. "If the voters turn me out come next election, that's the price I pay. But in the meantime, can we *please* find out what's going on with Dr. Wheatley?"

Slade glanced toward the door that separated Mills Vandiver's office from the town's two holding cells. One of the cells was occupied, the other vacant.

"What we have," Slade told Johansson and Vandiver, "both of you already know. A scalpel and rag that someone doused with chloroform, both tools for surgery. Of course, there's no law that restricts their sale, and anyone could steal them, if it comes to that. They don't prove that your doctor murdered Rose, or anybody else."

"But they're *suggestive*," said Johansson.

"Tell me, Mayor. Would you say the killer's smart or stupid?"

"Well . . . I'd say he was insane."

"Amen!" said Vandiver.

"In what he does," Slade said. "But I mean *how* he does it. Has he left you any clues before that led you anywhere? Has he been clumsy?"

"Well, if you put it that way—"

Interrupting him, Slade said, "But now, he leaves us proof that chloroform was used, he leaves a scalpel, *and* he leaves the body right next door to where he works and lives. That is, if he's the doctor. Does that sound like evidence of guilt to you? Or does it sound more like a frame?"

"A frame?" Johansson frowned. "I don't—"

"Stuff planted by the killer," Vandiver interpreted, "to make the doc look guilty when he's not."

The mayor's frown deepened. "Marshal, if you think that's true, you'll need to prove it. Have you questioned Dr. Wheatley yet?"

Slade fought an urge to sigh and roll his eyes.

"I was about to, Mayor, when you showed up. And them, out there." He nodded toward the window and the street beyond, where townsfolk had begun to gather moments after he arrived with Wheatley.

Clutching his dignity, the mayor replied, "I'd say you should get on with it. You needn't fear intrusion by a mob, as you're implying. Not in Jubilee."

"If I were you," Slade told Johansson, "I'd be out there warning everyone that lynching is the same as murder, and Judge Dennison will hang them for it. No exceptions. Anyone who agitates a mob and then stands back to watch it work is facing time at Leavenworth."

"I won't go out and threaten people who elected me!" Johansson said.

"Word it any way you like," Slade said. "Or wait until they cross the line. Then you can bury them. I would've thought you'd had your fill of funerals by now."

"I'll speak to them, as friends and my constituents," Johansson finally conceded. "While you question Dr. Wheatley."

Realizing that he'd get no more out of the mayor, Slade turned to Vandiver. "You've got a rifle and a shotgun on the wall, there," he observed. "You keep them loaded?"

"Just the twelve-gauge," said Vandiver.

"My advice, take it or leave it," Slade said, "is to load the rifle. When you need it in a hurry, there's no time for fumbling around and dropping cartridges."

"I can do that," Vandiver said. "Don't guess you need my help with Doc?"

"I'll call you if I do," Slade said and turned back toward the cells.

A lantern lit the cell block, standing out of reach for any normal arm beyond the bars on Wheatley's cell. The doctor sat upon a simple cot, pushed back as far from Slade and freedom as the walls would let him go.

"You think I killed that girl," he challenged Slade. "Who was she?"

"Rose, form the American Saloon," Slade said. "I never heard her last name, but I'll get it for the trial."

"What trial?"

"For murder," Slade replied. "Six counts. No, seven, with the preacher. And an arson charge."

"My God! You're saying that I burned the church?"

"I'm saying that the killer did. If you're not him . . ."

"Of course I'm not!"

"It looks bad, Doctor. I was talking to the mayor, outside. A scalpel used to kill the victim, after she was chloroformed. I grant you, now, it's funny that you'd drop her almost on your own doorstep."

"Funny? I'd have to be a madman."

"Which the killer is," said Slade.

"Perhaps, but is he stupid?" Wheatley asked, echoing Slade's own words from moments earlier. Could he have heard somehow, through the connecting door, though it was closed? "Tell me, Marshal, would I point the finger at myself?"

"You might," Slade said, "to raise that very argument."

"Create suspicion to divert suspicion?" Wheatley snorted a derisive laugh. "And make myself a damned pariah in the town?"

"Let's get it straight. You're saying that you didn't murder Rose."

"I haven't murdered *anyone*," Wheatley replied. "Not here in Jubilee. Not anywhere."

Why add that final bit? Slade asked himself. *Unless . . .*

"You're British," Slade remarked.

"Yes, we've established that."

"You knew about the Ripper when I mentioned him. His other nickname. Red Jack, was it?"

"Yes."

"And all the theories about him. Who he was, what made him kill."

"One can't have lived in London at the time and missed all that," Wheatley advised.

"So, you weren't just in England, but in London when the crimes were going on."

"That's right. So what? At least four million people live in London."

"One of them the Ripper. Or, he used to be," Slade said. "They never worked out why the murders stopped, I take it?"

"There was talk of suicide or someone in his family committing him to an asylum. If he was arrested on another charge, he may have gone to prison. Then again, he might have died."

"Or moved away," Slade said.

"So, that's it? Since I come from London, I'm the Ripper?"

"No proof, in itself," Slade said. "But when you come from London, where the killings stopped, and they start up again in Jubilee, I'd call it one hell of a strange coincidence."

"Five years between the crimes," Wheatley reminded him.

Slade nodded. Asked, "And how long have you been in Jubilee?"

The doctor's shoulders slumped. "Eight months, next week," he said.

"Where were you, prior to that?"

"I came into the States from Canada," Wheatley replied. "I've spent time in Chicago, Kansas City, and St. Louis."

"None of them appealed to you?" asked Slade.

"Too crowded, if you must know," Wheatley answered. "I was tired of London's overcrowding when I left. The air and rancid smell that comes in off the Thames. Did you know they call London 'The Smoke'?"

"I didn't," Slade admitted. "So, you left there for your health?"

"And peace of mind. Each of the cities that I've visited in your country—*my* country, now, unless you plan on hanging or deporting me—has been a smaller version of the place I left. Chicago's stockyards. Much the same in Kansas City. River traffic and the mobs of Irish in St. Louis. Where's the peace and quiet in all that?"

"You're bound to make less money here," Slade said.

"Don't count on that," Wheatley replied. "Each of the cities that I mentioned has got doctors by the hundreds. I'm the only one in Jubilee."

It sounded plausible enough to Slade, but what else would the killer say to cover his perambulations?

"I don't know if Jubilee will have you, after this," he told Wheatley. "I need to check some things before I make my mind up, one way or another. If it seems to me you've been set up, I'll make my feeling known. I can't swear it'll help you with your neighbors."

"And if you conclude I'm guilty, Marshal?"

"Then, you take a ride with me to Enid and we let Judge Dennison decide what happens next."

"You won't find anything to hang me with," said Wheatley. "Not unless somebody planted it."

Natural confidence, or was he hedging? Setting up a possible defense?

"I won't find anything, for sure, unless I go and look," Slade said. "You should be safe here. I'll be back to see you soon."

Johansson was nowhere in sight as Slade closed the connecting door behind him, but Vandiver had removed his rifle from its wall rack and was loading it.

"What happened to the mayor?" Slade asked.

"Went home, I guess," the constable replied.

"He talk to them, outside?"

"Said something, but I didn't catch it."

"No one comes through that door for any reason but the mayor and me," Slade said. "We clear on that?"

"I hear you," said Vandiver.

Knowing he would get no more from arguing, Slade left the jail, ignored the questions called out from the crowd—two dozen people now, at least—and struck off up Main Street toward Silas Guidry's funeral parlor.

Slade had never seen the undertaker smile, no great surprise within their limited acquaintance, but Guidry's face was even more solemn than usual tonight. They stood together on the threshold of the room where Guidry worked on silent customers, Slade trying not to look at young Rose on the operating table. Trying not to smell her.

"It's unusual, I know," he said. "Beyond the call of duty, you might say. But if I don't find out, it's possible the wrong man may be punished for this crime."

The undertaker glanced off toward his latest guest and shook his head. "I just . . . you know that Dr. Wheatley normally looks into that."

"I understand," Slade said. "And *you* know I can't ask him this time."

"Lord have mercy," Guidry muttered. Then, "All right, sir. Tell me again, what am I looking for?"

"The killer normally takes something from his victims," Slade replied. "According to the doctor, it involves the . . . female parts."

"Lord, Lord!"

"I need to know if anything is missing. Can you tell me that?"

"It should be possible," said Guidry. "Poor thing's opened up, already."

"How long will it take you?" Slade inquired.

He thought that Guidry shuddered before he said, "I would imagine half an hour, at the most."

"Okay." Slade checked his pocket watch and said, "I'll see you here in thirty minutes. Thanks for helping out."

"Too late for any help," said Guidry. "All that I can do is help her rest in peace."

Slade's next stop was the doctor's office. He used Wheatley's key to enter, lit a lamp, and took it with him as he roamed from room to room.

Searching.

To make a case in court, he should've had a warrant, but Judge Dennison was flexible in that regard, particularly in emergencies where he determined there were "exigent circumstances." Slade had been forced to look it up the first time Dennison had used the phrase, and found that *exigent* meant "urgent."

Which, Slade thought, was presently the case.

If Wheatley was the killer and he'd brought Rose nearly home to gut her, there'd have been no time for him to slip away and hide his nasty little souvenirs in some other location. Anything he'd taken from the body would be somewhere in his office or the living quarters just above it.

And, if he was Slade's man, there might also be some relics of his former kills.

That was the kind of evidence required to hang a man who slaughtered women as if they were livestock. Other things that might put Wheatley on the gallows: any bloodstained items that a normal doctor's office shouldn't have lying around, uncleaned, and operating tools that fit the victims' wounds. The last bit might be useless, since no one had bothered measuring the wounds on victims one through five, as far as Slade knew. He could ask Doc Wheatley, but it almost made him laugh to think of asking his prime suspect to assist with the investigation.

Slade began his survey in the operating room, checked all the things in plain sight first, then started going through the drawers, the doctor's bag, and so on. While he rummaged, Slade was picturing the foggy nighttime streets of London, where a faceless figure hunted working girls.

Was it coincidence that Wheatley lived and worked in

London while the Ripper's crimes were happening? Four million people called the city home, and countless others passed through every day, on ships and trains, in carriages, transacting business, or simply moving on to someplace else. How many men were in the States right now who'd spent some part of 1888 in London town?

Slade couldn't answer that, but it inspired another question. Wheatley claimed that he'd spent four years working in Chicago, Kansas City, and St. Louis prior to winding up in Jubilee. It *should* be possible to check and see if there'd been any homicides in Red Jack's style in those three cities, during that time frame. Judge Dennison could wire the local courts or the police chiefs, make the inquiry official.

And if Wheatley had been leaving other bodies in his wake, it couldn't be coincidence. If that turned out to be the case, he was as good as dead.

Slade finished with his search, still empty-handed. Checked his watch and found he was ten minutes over time. In his mind, Silas Guidry's answer might determine whether Slade held Wheatley or released him.

If the killer had removed something from Rose and Wheatley hadn't stashed it anywhere, it stood to reason he was innocent.

Conversely, if the maniac had mutilated Rose *without* claiming a souvenir, it left the question of the doctor's guilt unanswered, hanging there and open to interpretation, either way.

That wouldn't help Doc Wheatley with his neighbors, but at this point, Slade wasn't convinced that anything could save the doctor's reputation there, in Jubilee. He might become another victim of the madman, driven into exile, hounded by suspicion anywhere he went, for the remainder of his days.

Disgusted with himself for failing to discover anything and thereby solve the riddle, Slade blew out the lantern, locked the doctor's door from the outside, and started back toward Silas Guidry's shop.

•   •   •

The huntsman listened to his neighbors muttering on Main Street. They were losing precious sleep to mount a vigil at the jail—for what? To learn if they'd misplaced their trust in a physician who was privy to their most intimate secrets? Who had touched them in places normally reserved for husband or wife? To learn if he was innocent or guilty?

And could anything that Jack Slade found, in fact, prove innocence?

It seemed unlikely to the huntsman. If the lawman came to them with nothing, what did that mean? It was tantamount to scanning the horizon and announcing that you saw no Indians, therefore no Indians existed.

Utter rubbish.

No one would accept that or be mollified. They wouldn't let the doctor back into their lives, their homes, the heart of their community. In fact, they still might drag him out of jail and hang him, overrunning Slade and Mills Vandiver if they tried to stem the tide. A veritable Roman circus come to town.

And afterward? What then?

The huntsman reckoned they would have to live with it, the knowledge that he'd turned them into animals no better than himself. That wouldn't help him find the harlots' secret, but it was amusing nonetheless. When they looked back on it, in years to come, he'd wager none of them would laugh.

A fitting end, perhaps, to his experiments in Jubilee, still incomplete.

Coming back from Guidry's funeral parlor to the jail, Slade noted that the crowd outside had tripled, at the very least, since he'd brushed past them on his exit. None of them were armed, as far as he could tell. There were no ropes in evidence, no torches. Still, experience had taught him that it didn't take a crowd long to become a mob.

One rousing speech could do it, sometimes just a single word. Depending on their mood, the watchers might disperse without a whimper, or they might become enraged and storm the jail bare-handed, howling for their pound of flesh.

Slade thought about retreating to his hotel room and picking up his shotgun but decided time was more important than the extra firepower. With that decided, he picked up his pace, clomping along the wooden sidewalk toward the jail.

Someone spotted him when he was still a block out from the crowd. Slade heard a man's voice say, "He's coming back!" Another chimed in, "Here he is!"

The faces swung around to track him, but the crowd hung tight together in the street, its front rank still a long pace from the sidewalk and the constable's threshold. Slade reached the office, glanced in through the lighted window. Vandiver peered back at him, the sawed-off twelve-gauge clutched in sweaty hands.

He wouldn't want to kill his friends and neighbors. Hell, who would?

Only the monster who had brought them to their present state.

"It's late," Slade told the crowd, "so I won't keep you waiting. Most of you know more about the killings here in town than I do. You've been living with them longer, anyhow. You've likely heard the killer likes to take a little something from his victims while he's operating on them."

Angry murmurs from the townsfolk, sickened looks on all the faces Slade could see. When no one interrupted him, he forged ahead.

"Well, Silas Guidry tells me nothing's changed. The same thing, more or less, was taken from the girl he killed tonight."

More volume to the muttering, more rage behind it.

"Now," Slade said, raising his voice, "I've just come back from searching Dr. Wheatley's office and his home. You can believe me when I say that I looked everywhere a person could hide anything. You name the spot, I checked it, large or small. And what I found was . . . nothing."

Silence from the crowd, at that. Slade let his own voice fill it.

"When I tell you *nothing*, that's exactly what I mean. Nothing from Rose, who died tonight, or any of the other women who've been killed. The murderer's been taking souvenirs or trophies, call it what you will. There's absolutely nothing to suggest that Dr. Wheatley is involved in any of these killings."

"What about the scalpel?" someone called out, halfway back among the upturned faces.

"And the chloroform!" another voice chimed in.

"Both things that anyone can buy, borrow, or steal," Slade answered. "I can't tell you if the scalpel's new or old, but Mr. Guidry says it likely didn't make all of the wounds he found on Rose this evening. Long story short, and sparing details for the ladies gathered here, he says the blade's not long enough."

"Why leave the body on his doorstep, then?" a third voice challenged.

"That's a question all of you should keep in mind," Slade said, "before you rush to judging anyone. Why *would* the doctor leave her where she was and point the finger at himself? If that makes sense to anybody here, I hope you'll explain it to me."

More angry, frightened muttering, before a voice spoke up, away to Slade's left side. "Well, Jesus!" said the man. "If Wheatley didn't kill 'em, who in hell's been doin' it? Can't anybody tell us that?"

"If I could point a finger and be sure of it," Slade told them all, "I'd have the killer sitting in a cell tonight. Truth is, we still don't know."

"Fat lot of good that does us," said a slender, worried-looking woman, down in front.

"I realize it doesn't help, ma'am," Slade replied. "All I can do is make a promise to you—and the killer, if he's listening. I'll be here until this is all worked out. The man responsible for all this pain and suffering will either ride my dust to Enid and the gallows, or I'll bury him right here, in Jubilee."

17

"You mean . . . I'm free to go?" asked Denton Wheatley.

"Nothing to hold you on, just like you said," Jack Slade replied.

The doctor looked suspicious now. "It's not some kind of trick?"

"No trick," Slade said. "It may not be a favor, either."

"I don't understand."

"Your neighbors are upset, to say the very least," Slade told him. "I've explained to them how there's no evidence you were involved in any of the crimes, and then I sent them home. That obviously doesn't mean you're in the clear."

"But you just said . . ."

"With them, I mean. I can't predict how any one of them—or all of them together—may react to your release. They're angry, frightened, frustrated. A potent combination. And you have to figure most of them have guns."

"You're saying I'm not safe in Jubilee?" the doctor asked.

"I don't predict the future, Doc. What I *can* say is that in your place, I'd watch my back and sleep with one eye open for a while."

Wheatley's tone was bitter as he said, "All this, because I was arrested falsely."

"Nothing false about it," Slade replied. "We both know that. You were detained pending investigation, and you've barely been locked up three hours. If you want to sue for loss of sleep, you'll have to file the papers with Judge Dennison, in Enid."

"This isn't just another joke to me, Marshal!"

"You find somebody laughing, let me know," Slade said. "He'll likely be the man I'm looking for."

Wheatley brushed past him, headed for the outer office, where he stopped at the sight of Mills Vandiver and the mayor. Addressing both of them at once, he said, "Apparently, I'm innocent."

Johansson wore a pained expression and began to say, "Doctor—"

But Wheatley cut him off and turned to the constable. "I trust that I can count on your protection if the townspeople ignore what they were told by Marshal Slade?"

"My job is keepin' peace," Vandiver answered. "I've been doing what I can, one man alone. Somebody bothers you, you come and let me know, all right? I'll see what I can do to help."

"That's very reassuring, Constable. Perhaps I should acquire a set of pistols, to protect myself."

"You'd be within your rights," Vandiver said.

"You want me to," Slade said, "I'll walk you to your office. Get you past the dark parts for tonight, at least."

"No, thank you," Wheatley answered stiffly. "If I'm bound to be attacked on Main Street, why not get it over with? Perhaps you and the constable can manage to arrest my murderer, in lieu of others."

That said, Wheatley left the officer without bothering to close the door behind him. Mayor Johansson muttered something under his breath and began to wring his hands before he caught himself and stopped it.

"What's that, Mayor?" Vandiver asked.

"I said that's goddamned marvelous! We'll lose our only doctor, now. He can't stay, after this. What kind of town survives without a doctor? Can you tell me that?"

"He may not leave," Vandiver said.

"And if somebody kills or injures him? What then?" Johansson challenged.

"Well, um . . ."

"Then you lock them up," Slade said. "The same as you would any other criminal."

"Of course," Johansson said. "Just what we need. Give up our doctor, while we build a bigger jail."

"One thing," Vandiver said. "If he *does* leave, we've still got Connor."

"Who?" Johansson asked, sounding exasperated now.

"Connor MacGowan," Vandiver replied.

Slade frowned at that and asked, "The barber?"

"Sure," Vandiver said. "You know, across the water where he comes from, barbers do a lot of surgery themselves. Been going on for years and years, from what I understand."

Johansson shook his head again. His shoulders slumped. "I'm going home," he told them. "Not that I'll find any peace and quiet there, God knows. Have to repeat the whole damned thing for Emmeline, then listen to her fuss and fume. I doubt I'll get a wink of sleep."

"Good luck with that," Slade said. "I'll make another pass around downtown before I hit the hay."

"Do us a favor while you're at it," said Johansson, from the open doorway. "Catch the killer, and you'll be a hero to this godforsaken town."

• • •

The huntsman was a night owl, always had been. In the cities he'd inhabited, he found it comforting to walk the streets for hours after dark. You met a special kind of human in the shadows, primal folk, often surviving by their wits and hand to mouth. Many were predators, but they had never frightened him.

The ones who tried to take advantage of him soon learned their mistake.

There wasn't all that much to see in Jubilee, of course, by day or night. The town was growing at a reasonable pace—or had been, until recently—but it was small, remote, and fairly primitive. There was no maze of paved or cobbled streets where footsteps echoed through the midnight stillness, no damp mist to fold around him like a sentient cloak. No gentlemen out late, dallying with their mistresses or lounging overlong in houses of debauchery.

The Klondike and American saloons were shoddy imitations of the places he had seen in London, Paris, other cities. In a great metropolis, the opportunities for degradation were unlimited. Whores by the thousand, representing every age, race, sex. Vile gateways to perdition that delighted him no end.

The huntsman realized that he was running out of time in Jubilee. Even without the interfering U.S. marshal, he would soon run out of harlots at his present pace. A few more weeks, at most, and then his larder would be empty.

Now, it seemed, he must abandon Jubilee and find another place to practice his experiments. Keep searching for the secret that eluded him.

Time was the key, and freedom. He would never manage to accomplish anything from prison, much less from a hanged man's shallow grave. The law of averages was working for his enemies in Jubilee. The best thing he could do was slip away.

But first . . .

It would be useful if he found a way to throw the lawmen off his track. Present them with an answer they could live with, to the riddle that bedeviled them.

Why not?

The obvious solution lay before him. He had used it once before, in London, where he understood that some detectives were relieved to close his case, albeit unofficially. Their colleagues who resisted were, of course, no closer to an actual solution than they had been back in '88.

Nor would they ever be.

Such fantasies they spun around his work, blaming a Jew, a Freemason, an heir to England's throne. The huntsman laughed each time another theory surfaced—but he kept it to himself, unleashed his glee in private, keeping up his "normal" face before the world at large.

Having decided on a course of action, nothing now remained but execution of the plan. Why not be done with it tonight and take advantage of the passions simmering in Jubilee? The night's events would make his farce more plausible. If he could dupe Jack Slade, the mayor and constable would quickly fall in line, trumpet their victory to anyone who'd listen.

Afterward, the huntsman could restrain himself—with difficulty, it was true, but all the same—and let a decent interval elapse before announcing that he meant to leave. Excuses would be made: a distant relative in need of help, perhaps, or simple weariness at all the bloodshed he had seen in Jubilee. A need to start afresh.

That much, at least, would be the truth.

A fresh start for his quest, in a new hunting ground. Perhaps the secret waited for him there, wherever *there* happened to be.

Unfold a map and jab a finger at it, with his eyes closed. If the choice failed to excite him, try again, as often as was necessary.

It was good to have a touch of mystery in life. A bit of

something unresolved, unanswered. He was doing Jubilee a favor, if his neighbors only knew it. They could trade on his atrocious reputation for the next decade, at least. It was his parting gift, to let them take his name in vain.

A final gift of blood.

Dr. Denton Wheatley made it from Vandiver's office to his own without encountering another soul. Along the way, he had imagined window curtains twitching as he passed, believed he could feel hostile eyes upon him, but saw nothing when he turned to check.

All fantasy, perhaps.

But when the sun rose in a few short hours, and the town began to stir again . . .

For once, he was not looking forward to the daylight. Wheatley almost wished it would stay dark forever—or, at least, that his detractors would sleep long enough to wake refreshed, convinced that his detention and the rest of it had been an idle dream.

No hope of that, he thought. And then, *I'm finished here.*

So be it. He had pulled up stakes before, and more than once. He was no stranger to the road and new beginnings. If he traveled far enough, the next town would know nothing of his troubles here in Jubilee. He'd be accepted as a friend and asset to his new community.

The muffled rapping on his door surprised Wheatley. He hesitated, then crept toward the stairs, descended slowly from his modest living quarters, until he could see the entrance to his waiting room. The top half of the door was glass. And peering through it, a familiar face.

One man alone. No mob behind him, and he wasn't scowling, didn't seem to have a weapon. He caught sight of Wheatley on the stairs and raised a hand in greeting. Was about to knock again, more tentatively, until Wheatley closed the gap, unlatched the door and opened it.

"Good evening, Doctor. Or, perhaps I ought to say good morning."

"It *is* late," Wheatley agreed.

"I didn't wake you, did I?"

"No, no. I just . . . well, I've only been home for a little while."

His caller nodded. "I heard all about it," he replied. "It's scandalous, them treating you that way!"

"Well . . ."

"So, I told myself you might do with a visit, never mind the hour. Something that would lift your spirits, eh?"

"That's very kind of you, but . . . well . . . yes, all right. Won't you come in?"

"A pleasure," said his visitor. The door was barely shut and latched behind him when the caller drew a silver flask from somewhere underneath his jacket. "Just a little something for the chill," he said, smiling.

Wheatley considered it, then said, "I don't mind if I do."

"You'll have a glass, no doubt," the caller said.

"Oh, yes. Um . . . here's one."

"All we need, Doctor. I'll take mine straight."

Wheatley's unexpected guest poured him a generous measure of some pungent liquor, then stepped back to wait while the doctor tried it. It burned going down, but the fire quickly mellowed and spread a warm glow through his vitals.

"All better?"

"It's a special mixture of my own," the caller said.

"You *made* this?" Wheatley was surprised. "I must say you're a man of hidden talents."

"So they tell me." As he spoke the visitor capped his flask and slipped it back into his coat, out of sight.

Now Wheatley frowned. "None for yourself?"

"The truth be told, it's too strong for me. I don't mind the brandy, right? But when it comes to strychnine . . . well, a fellow has to draw the line somewhere. Don't you agree?"

Strychnine?

"I'm bound to tell you, I've heard better jokes," said Wheatley.

"I'd agree with you, if I was joking. It should hit you any second now."

As perspiration broke out on his face, Wheatley tried to recall the properties and symptoms of the poison known as strychnine. It was a colorless crystalline alkaloid, sometimes prescribed in small doses as a stimulant, a laxative, or to relieve stomach problems. In larger quantities of half a grain or more it caused muscular convulsions leading to death from asphyxiation or sheer exhaustion.

"If this is supposed to be funny—"

"No, Doctor," his guest interrupted Wheatley. "It's supposed to be fatal. Not my normal style, as you'll have heard from Whitechapel and hereabouts, but one tries to adapt, eh?"

Whitechapel!

The first cramp lanced through Wheatley's abdomen— *so soon?*—and he gasped at the pain, doubling over. The empty glass tipped from his hand, cracking in half as it fell to the floor. Wheatley staggered, mind reeling, groping for an antidote and coming up with none. He had no drugs on hand to block the onset of convulsions, and could not have self-administered them in his present state, regardless.

Hopeless, Wheatley lunged away from his deadly guest, toward the stacked set of shelves where he kept medicines. A wild swing of his left arm brought the bottles crashing down, some splashing liquid on the walls, while others left the floor dusted with multicolored powders.

Wheatley's knees buckled, and he collapsed beside the mess that he had made.

"I'll leave you to your packing, then," his caller said, chuckling as he retreated toward the exit.

As the door snicked shut behind him, Wheatley clenched his teeth and reached out with a quaking hand.

•   •   •

Slade judged his last circuit of Jubilee to be a waste of time, but he was wide awake and hoped the extra bit of tramping up and down Main Street would help him to unwind. Another murder—and another suspect snatched out of his grasp—was working on his nerves.

Slade wondered if he'd been guilty of underestimating his quarry. The killer was certainly crazy, but still far from stupid. Unless Dr. Wheatley was both a talented actor and criminal mastermind, Jubilee's madman had a taste for offering innocent men up as suspects, while he went on with his work. He didn't seem to plan on seeing them convicted—at least, not in Otto Heidegger's case, where the killing continued while he was in jail—but the ruses were distracting. They muddied the water and heightened the tension in town, turning one neighbor against the other overnight.

How long could it go on?

If Slade had been a hooker, he'd be looking for another town in which to ply his trade. And if they all left town—or, God forbid, if they were all killed off—what, then? Would the night prowler turn on respectable women? On children?

Without a grasp of his enemy's motive, Slade couldn't make an educated guess about the man's next move. And he still thought it *was* a man, despite contrary arguments where London's Ripper was concerned. He'd asked around concerning midwives and found none in Jubilee, though certain women were prepared to aid their married friends in childbirth, if the doctor asked for help.

The doctor.

Slade thought Wheatley might as well pack up and leave, after tonight, but he would leave that to the man himself. Perhaps he still could eke a living out of Jubilee, at least prolong departure for a while, until he formulated other plans. The best thing for him, Slade supposed, would be to get as far away as possible from Oklahoma Territory and erase his months in Jubilee from any subsequent discussion of his background.

Still uneasy with his own role in the doctor's downfall, wondering if he had been too hasty marching Wheatley off to jail, Slade decided to pass by the physician's office once more, on the return trip to his hotel room. He wouldn't knock, wouldn't disturb Wheatley in any way, but he could check the nearby streets and alleys for potential stalkers. Round them up, if they were there, and give them hell.

Crossing Main Street, he saw faint lamplight at the end of Wheatley's alleyway. Slade would have been surprised to find the doctor sleeping, doubted that he'd get a wink at all tonight, after the ordeal he'd endured.

Could have been worse, Slade told himself. *That could've been a real mob at the jail. Or someone could've sniped him on the walk back to his own place.*

It could still happen, Slade knew. From now on, every minute he spent in Jubilee carried potential danger for the British medic. If he chose to stay, for God knew whatever peculiar reason, Wheatley could expect gray hair, ulcers, and headaches without end.

If he was lucky.

Taking his time and moving quietly, Slade passed along the alleyway to Dr. Wheatley's door, peered through its upper pane of glass—and saw one of the doctor's feet, just visible around the corner of the doorway leading into his examination room. Was that a tremor in the leg, or Slade's imagination?

Frantically, he tried the door and found it locked. Stepped back and drew his Colt, swung it against the glass, and reached in through the opening he'd made to free the latch. A moment later, he was standing over Denton Wheatley, bending down to feel the doctor's neck.

No pulse.

Slade sprinted back to Main Street, raised his Colt, and fired a shot that echoed through the haunted town.

• • •

Slade let the mayor of Jubilee cope with his people, standing in the alley outside Wheatley's office, holding them at bay, while Mills Vandiver and the undertaker joined him to examine Wheatley's corpse.

"No marks on him, that I can see," said Silas Guidry. After pinching Wheatley's arms, his neck and legs, Guidry went on. "You see how stiff he is, from head to toe? If he'd been dead twelve hours, I'd say it was rigor mortis, but you say he was alive—how long ago? An hour and a half?"

"If that," Slade said.

"So, poison, then," the undertaker said. "In my opinion, anyhow. I'm not a qualified physician, but I've never seen or heard of any ailment that can make a body stiff like that within the time allowed."

"Lockjaw," the constable suggested.

"No, sir. That will make you stiff, all right, but it has other symptoms leading up to it over a period of days. The doctor would have felt them coming on and would have taken steps, I'm sure. Also, there needs to be a wound that wasn't cleaned. I'll look him over for you, but I don't expect to find one."

"So, what kind of poison, then?" asked Slade.

He'd seen the broken drinking glass as he stood over Wheatley's body, moments earlier. Had moved it to a nearby sink, and now experienced a pressing urge to wash his hands.

"From the condition of the body, I'd say strychnine," Guidry answered. "Makes the body look like this. I've seen it used in suicides, oh, half a dozen times. I always wonder whether they regretted it, when it was already too late."

"So, you think this was suicide?" Vandiver asked.

"I didn't say that. But the doctor could have strychnine in his pharmacy."

"What for?" asked Slade, surprised.

"It's also used for medicine," Guidry replied. "I wouldn't want to try it, personally."

"Well," Vandiver said, pointing toward the array of spilled and broken bottles on the floor, "if he had any, I suppose its mixed up in that mess."

Slade scanned the drift of many-colored remedies, all wasted now, with Wheatley's outflung hand—the right—stained brightly from thrashing around in his death throes.

Thrashing? Or was he—

"What's that?" Slade asked himself, circling the body, crouching near the point where Wheatley's right hand had rested before Guidry turned him over.

"Scrape marks," said Vandiver, dismissively.

"No," Slade replied. "It looks like he tried to write something." He squinted, then almost recoiled. "Does that say *Jack*?"

Guidry and Vandiver leaned closer, peering at the chicken scratches in the powder. "Well, it could be, I suppose," Guidry replied.

"Could be most anything," Vandiver said, "if you use your imagination hard enough."

"You think he was writing to you?" Guidry asked.

The thought hadn't occurred to Slade, and now it shocked him. "No," he said. "I doubt it. But if it *is Jack*, could it be *Red* Jack? Jack the Ripper?"

"What, from England? Jesus, that's a stretch," Vandiver fairly snorted. Hesitating then, he said, "Oh, wait! You think he was *confessing*? Woulda made more sense to write a note before he took the poison, don't you think?"

"It would," Slade said, "if he was trying to confess. What else is there? Something beside the Jack."

"If it *is* Jack," Vandiver said.

"Could be three letters," Guidry said, getting into the spirit of the thing. "Maybe a *B-A-R*?"

"Well, there you go," Vandiver said. "He's gone to meet Jack at a bar. You better hurry, or you'll miss him, Slade."

Ignoring him, Slade said, "Trying to spell out something else, before the final spasms took him. *B-A-R*. What could it be?"

"His cell had bars on it," Vandiver said. "We've got two bars in town. Then there's the Bar-B spread a few miles out. Most of the homesteads hereabouts have barns."

Slade shook his head. "The only thing you've said that fits would be the Bar-B, if he's blaming Chris Christofides."

"Who has an alibi, you said." The constable reminding him.

"That's right. And why would Wheatley pick him out? He couldn't know who did the crimes unless he'd witnessed them."

"Or met the killer here, tonight," Guidry remarked.

"What do you mean?"

"Well . . . never mind. It's probably far-fetched."

"No, tell me," Slade insisted.

"Well, the doctor had to know the way he'd die from strychnine. Some folks know and choose it anyway, I grant you, but if it was me, and I had access to all kinds of drugs and medicine, I'd pick something less painful. Something that would send me off to sleep without the rest of it."

Slade saw where he was going. "But if someone else came by—"

"And what?" Vandiver asked. "Held Wheatley down and poured the strychnine down his gullet?"

"Maybe slipped it to him somehow," Slade suggested. "In a drink, let's say."

Unconsciously, he wiped his fingers on his trouser leg.

"To kill him . . . why, again?" Vandiver challenged.

"Why? Same reason that he left the butcher next to Thelma Lou. Same reason that he dragged Rose nearly to the doctor's doorstep, leaving clues that pointed us toward Wheatley."

"I don't see—"

"The bastard's playing games. That's what he does," said Slade.

"Or, Doc was guilty all along."

"Then we should find his souvenirs," Slade said.

"The *pieces*?" asked Vandiver. "Lord almighty! I don't even want to *think* about what he might've been doing all this time, with those."

Neither did Slade, but there was something wrong. He couldn't bring himself to view the doctor's sudden death as suicide.

Not yet, at least.

Maybe tomorrow, in the light of day, he'd have a change of heart, but Slade thought the odds were against it.

There was something missing, maybe right in front of him, but something that he'd overlooked. What was it? Maybe it would come to him in dreams, if he could get to sleep after the latest shock.

Not likely, Slade decided, but he had to try.

"Okay, he's yours," Slade told the undertaker. "If you find anything else, we'll talk about it in the morning."

"Suits me," Guidry said. "I'll call my boy to get him out of here."

"We'll need to keep this place closed off," Slade told the constable. "You don't want anybody coming in and grabbing potions off the floor. No telling what could happen."

"Right," Vandiver said. "Brett Gavin is our carpenter. I'd better go and wake him up."

Slade passed the mayor outside, brushed through the clutch of townspeople who'd pressed into the alley without answering the questions some of them called out to him. He didn't think he'd find relief in sleep tonight, much less an answer to the riddle that bedeviled him, but he was finished with the town for now. He had to get a stout door closed and locked between himself and Jubilee before he faced another jolt.

Before another person died.

18

Peering over untouched ham and eggs, Roland Johansson said, "It seems to me the mystery is solved."

"How's that?" Slade asked around a bite of sausage.

"Well . . . it's obvious." Johansson looked around, lowered his voice before explaining. "Dr. Wheatley—if he *was* a doctor, if we even know his real name—lived in London when this Ripper person was murdering women, the same way ours were killed in Jubilee. When you arrested him, he panicked. Must've thought he'd hang, and chose his own way out."

"Mayor, you're forgetting that I turned him loose because we didn't have a shred of evidence to hold him on," Slade said.

"But he was worried you might *find* some," said Johansson.

"He could just as easily have moved away," said Slade. "We even talked about it, whether anyone in town would trust him after Rose."

"But he knew that leaving was the next best thing to a confession," said the mayor. "And if he stayed in Jubilee, he'd have no patients. People here would watch him night and day. He couldn't make a move—and damn sure couldn't feed his ugly fantasies."

"So, he just killed himself," Slade said.

"Why not? It wouldn't be the first time that a cornered criminal took the easy way out."

"Strychnine's not easy," Slade replied. "Trust me on that."

"It was the only means at hand," Johansson said.

"Assuming that he had some."

"Can you say he didn't?"

Slade considered it, then shook his head. "Can't say he didn't, with the state he left his office in. And that's another thing."

"What is?" Johansson asked.

"Just think about it. You decide to kill yourself with poison, right? But then, instead of sitting down to wait it out, you run around and smash things like a crazy man."

"Convulsions," said the mayor, with perfect confidence. "I spoke to Silas Guidry. He described strychnine's effects. Makes sense to me."

"Then, there's the writing in the powders that he spilled," Slade said. "He has all night to write a note, but waits until he's nearly dead to scribble on the floor. Does *that* make sense to you?"

"Why not, Marshal? He was a crazy man, just like you said. Some brilliant notion strikes him at the final minute, and he tries to spell it out."

"By writing *Jack*?" asked Slade.

Johansson shrugged and took a small bit of his eggs.

"Mills thinks it was the start of a confession. *I am Jack the Ripper*, or whatever. Then again, it could have been addressed to you."

"We talked about that. I don't buy it," Slade replied.

"It hardly matters now, does it?" Johansson asked.

"Nope. Not unless we want to know the truth."

"The man is dead. We can't go on rehashing every thought that may have crossed his addled mind."

Ignoring that, Slade said, "Then, there's the last thing that he wrote. The letters *B-A-R*."

"What of it?"

"I believe he died before he had a chance to finish, Mayor. I believe he meant to tell us who Jack is."

"All right, let's go with that," Johansson said. "But say that *he* was Jack. The *B-A-R* could be the start of his real name. For all I know, our Denton Wheatley was really Barnabus Barker. Who knows what his name was? *Who cares?*"

"I do," Slade answered. "If the Ripper's still alive and here in Jubilee."

Johansson blanched and hissed across his plate, "You have no evidence of that!"

"Not yet. But I'm not satisfied that Dr. Wheatley killed himself or that his death closes the case."

"Marshal, don't you have somewhere else to be? Something to do?"

Slade thought of Faith and almost smiled.

"Damn right I do," he answered, through clenched teeth. "But I can't get around to it until your problem's settled here."

"I hate to see you waste your time," Johansson said.

"Appreciate it," Slade replied and focused on his breakfast.

Thinking to himself, *It's mine to waste, as long as we're not wasting any other lives.*

The huntsman peered through double window glass—his own, and the front window of MacDonald's restaurant— watching as Jack Slade finished breakfast. Wondering exactly why in hell the lawman hadn't left for home, first thing.

His mind coughed up successive possibilities. Maybe there were reports to write and certify, before he went back to report the case was solved. Maybe he planned to stay for Rose's funeral and see her killer buried. That could fit his personality.

Or maybe Slade had doubts about the doctor's suicide.

That notion made the huntsman grimace. He had gone all out with his latest red herring, first pointing evidence in Wheatley's direction, then helping his sacrificial goat shuffle off the mortal coil in convincing style.

Well, at lead *he* had found it convincing.

But if Slade disagreed . . .

The huntsman felt a sudden urge to flee, put Jubilee behind him, strike out for the Great Unknown without direction or a plan in mind. He'd wind up somewhere, couldn't wander off the far edge of the Earth as ancients had believed, and when he was established with a new identity, he could resume his quest for answers to the harlot's secret.

No.

With Wheatley dead, apparently by his own hand, things would return to normal over time in Jubilee. If Slade questioned the suicide, the worst thing he could do was run away and thereby cast suspicion on himself. The huntsman thought that he should simply wait it out, let time elapse and tempers cool.

Jack Slade would tire of waiting. Other felons would require his presence elsewhere. Even if the murders haunted him forever—and the huntsman hoped they would—Slade couldn't simply camp in Jubilee until doomsday.

Or, if he did, what of it? Given time enough, the huntsman could make some excuse for moving on. Declining business or a family emergency. Perhaps he'd say the dreadful murders had depressed him and he needed somewhere fresh to try his luck. To breathe clean air. Slade couldn't force him to remain in Jubilee without sufficient evidence to charge him with a crime.

Yes, it was best to watch and wait. Lie back and bide his time. But something in that plan chafed at him, ran against the grain.

He craved dramatic action, something that would shake Slade off his back for good and earn his personal crusade some recognition, in the process. Not his name, of course. That would remain a secret to the moment of his death. The Jubileeans who survived would think of him as the madman who made their town a living Hell, but *catching* him was something else.

Watching Slade leave the restaurant at last, well fed and ready for another day, the huntsman turned his thoughts to planning out his farewell gift to Slade and Jubilee.

It must be something no one would forget, surpassing anything the huntsman had achieved before. Something to send shock waves across the territory and beyond, focusing fear and anger there while he escaped, to carry on his sacred mission.

When it came to him at last, the huntsman smiled, then laughed aloud. He was alone, and just as well, since any patrons might have reckoned him insane.

The plan was radical, a total deviation from his normal mode of operating, but he thought—he *knew*—that it could work. There was a lure that Slade could not resist, and once the huntsman had a chance to face his nemesis across the supine body of his final victim, he would be in absolute control.

As it was meant to be.

Slade understood Johansson's urge—his need—to put the murder case behind him and get on with normal life in Jubilee. It would remain for time to tell if that was even possible, with all the fear, anger, and stark suspicion that had built up in the town over the past month and a half. Since Slade had arrived, the mayhem had accelerated to a frantic pace.

The stain of violence pervaded everything.

Perhaps it always would.

The toll so far: six ladies of the evening killed, along with Jubilee's sole minister and doctor. One church destroyed. Two men—the butcher, Otto Heidegger, and cowboy Chris Christofides—still likely viewed as murder suspects in the eyes of some townsfolk. Whether those two could stay in Jubilee or its environs and earn a living was a nagging question.

So, it was convenient, comforting, to say the case was settled now, with Denton Wheatley's death. But it was only settled if it was beyond a reasonable doubt that the doctor had killed himself.

And Slade had doubts.

He'd laid them out for Mayor Johansson, and he could think of nothing else as he walked down to check his roan mare at the livery. If he was right, and Wheatley was a murder victim rather than a suicide, then nothing had been gained. No one in town was safe.

He'd gone back to the doctor's office one more time, donned gloves and sorted through the mess of shattered bottles on the floor where they'd found Wheatley's rigid corpse. Slade checked the labels, read the ones that were in English, hoped he wasn't missing something vital with the Latin tags. Some ninety bottles, overall.

And no strychnine.

From there, Slade had conducted a more thorough search. Not certain if the doc could gulp a fatal dose and hide the evidence before the spasms hit him, Slade checked every cabinet and cubbyhole, upstairs and down. He'd peered under the bed and riffled drawers of clothing, all in vain.

Then he told the mayor and got the answer he expected. Just because Slade hadn't found a strychnine bottle on the premises didn't mean the medic had been murdered. Wheatley could have masked the poison with a false label or used no tag at all. Even if Slade had swept up all the powders

strewn on Wheatley's floor and somehow managed to identify each one—a task that would require a master chemist,
he supposed—absence of strychnine from the mix would
still prove nothing. Mayor Johansson would contend that
Wheatley swallowed the last dose that he possessed to end
his life.

And maybe that was true.

Was there a chance that he was working overtime to keep
a mystery alive where none remained? Why would he? Possibly because he'd failed to catch the killer on his own and
thus felt cheated and reluctant to accept the easy answer. To
move on.

Or was it something else?

Faith sprang to mind. Slade missed her terribly . . . but
was he somehow frightened, at the same time, by the prospect of their wedding? Would anxiety over the altar walk
prompt him to stay in Jubilee, hunting a killer who was
dead and marked for burial tomorrow?

No. The very notion almost made him laugh aloud.

Faith was the best thing in his life. He couldn't say the
only thing, as some young grooms proclaimed, all starry-
eyed, for both of them would still be individuals with active
lives. But Slade wasn't afraid of marrying, in any sense.

He simply couldn't bring himself to ride away from Jubilee while he believed a savage killer was alive and well
somewhere within the town.

He'd ruled out any farmers, ranchers, or their cowboys
from surrounding spreads. The pace of violence had been
so steady in the past three days that nightly trips to town
and back would be required of any slayer in the hinterlands.
He would be missed by family, coworkers, an employer,
and unless there was some great, unthinkable conspiracy to
cover for him, he would be exposed.

No, it was someone living in the heart of Jubilee. Killing
the town slowly, from the inside.

And Slade knew that he couldn't rest until he ran the bastard down.

Emmeline Johansson didn't like to think about the things that had been happening in Jubilee. Her husband had to deal with them, of course. It was expected of him, as the mayor, even though Mills Vandiver was legally in charge of keeping peace and catching criminals.

And now, Jack Slade.

Emmeline Johansson liked to think about Jack Slade. His rugged face and trim, athletic form. The way his gun-belt rode lean hips and seemed to put the slightest hint of swagger in his walk. He had a deep voice that could catch a woman by surprise and tickle her in places where—

Embarrassed by her fleeting fantasies, she blushed and was relieved to be alone at home, where Roland couldn't see her.

Not that he'd have noticed, anyway. For long weeks he had been consumed by worry, for the town and for himself. The second gruesome murder proved the first was not committed by some drifter, passing by. The killer was in Jubilee, or near enough to prey at will on women from the town's saloons.

Emmeline was not among the Mercy Baptist women who dismissed the dead as sluts who got what they deserved. Some of that talk was spawned by bitterness, from women who suspected that their husbands may have patronized the Klondike and American saloon facilities. Others were so immersed in the condemnatory side of scripture that they had lost touch with love, forgiveness, all the things that made faith wonderful.

Most of the hard-nosed talk had ended with the third killing, and all of it was silenced by the awful, agonizing death of Pastor Booth. Losing the town's one minister *and* church had been a shock, to say the least. Whether a person had agreed with Booth or not on any given topic, he had been the moral heart of Jubilee.

Without him, could the town survive?

And now, the doctor! Roland thought he was the murderer and had killed himself to cheat the hangman, but Emmeline wasn't convinced. She'd overheard her husband whispering to Mills about the doubts Jack Slade had raised. They seemed convincing, and a part of her was nearly desperate to think Wheatley was innocent.

Emmeline had visited the doctor's office twice, once for a chest cold, once for female difficulties. Wheatley had examined her, had touched her intimately, and in each case had prescribed a remedy that put her right. It sickened her to think that she had lain under a monster's hands, the same hands that had slashed and—

Dizzy from the mental images flooding her brain, Emmeline paused in the midst of preparing her flower arrangement for supper. Each day, when the blooms were in season, she prepared a centerpiece for the dining table she shared with Roland, eating meals that lately were consumed in brooding silence.

Still recovering, she was surprised to hear a rapping at her kitchen door. Most callers came to the front door, from Main Street, though occasional deliveries were made out back. Emmeline approached the door with caution that would not have been her habit two months earlier. Before she touched the latch or knob, she asked, "Who is it?"

From the other side, a male voice spoke a name she recognized. Relieved, Emmeline opened the door. Offered a smile she'd learned to practice, as a politician's wife.

"Good morning."

"Same to you, ma'am. Is your husband presently at home?"

"I'm sorry, no," she said. "Is he expecting you?"

"Not exactly," said her caller, as he drew a wicked-looking knife from underneath his coat. "It's you I've come to see."

Slade was sitting in a corner at the Klondike, sipping beer, when Mills Vandiver pushed in through the bat-wing doors. Daylight behind him made his face a blank until he spotted Slade and headed for his table. Only then could Slade make out his grim expression, lips drawn back from clenched teeth, spots of agitated color on his cheeks.

"Been looking for you everywhere," the constable announced. He sounded almost out of breath.

"You found me," Slade acknowledged.

"Emmeline Johansson."

"What about her?"

"Gone," Vandiver said. "She's disappeared."

"In Jubilee?" Even as Slade replied, a niggling dread made him regret his flippant tone.

"I mean to say that she's been taken," said Vandiver.

"When?"

"Can't tell you that. Roland got home about ten thirty and found her gone, then called me. I've been the best part of a half hour looking for you."

Slade left his beer and beat Vandiver to the exit, let the constable jog to catch up with him outside. Roland Johansson met them on the front porch of his home, wringing his hands and pacing like a bobcat in a cage.

"We have to find her!" he told Slade, his tone brooking no argument.

"We will," Slade answered. "Are you sure she's not out visiting or shopping?"

"No, for Christ's sake! Come inside and see!"

Slade trailed the mayor into his house and past the parlor, to the kitchen, where he found a two-word message carved into the wall above the stove, presumably by knifepoint.

Come alone, it read.

"He's taken her, for God's sake!" It was strange to hear Johansson almost sobbing, now.

"Who's taken her?" Slade asked, unnecessarily.

"The killer, damn it! Who else?"

"If the killer's dead—"

"So, I was wrong! You need to hear it? There! I should have listened to you!"

"Not my point," Slade said. "It shouldn't matter. Just the opposite, in fact. If he killed Wheatley, and he knew you bought it, why do this? It works against him. Ruins everything he planned."

"Because he's nuts," Vandiver suggested. "What else?"

"We're wasting time," Johansson said. "I need to meet him. Maybe he wants money, for a getaway. I have to go alone, but *where*?"

"He's not asking for you," Slade said.

"What? I don't understand. He took my wife!"

"She's bait," said Slade. "It doesn't mean that you're the fish."

"Make sense! If not me, who?"

"It's Slade," Vandiver said, with dawning recognition.

"Slade?" Johansson looked befuddled now. "For God's sake, why?"

"He's finishing the game," Slade said.

"What game? This isn't sport to me."

"You're not a psychopathic killer," Slade replied. Thinking, *At least, I hope you're not.*

If he was wrong, Johansson could have staged this scene, along with Wheatley's so-called suicide. Using his wife as bait would break the hooker-killing pattern, but it might well serve some secret need.

"All right, then. Say you're right," Johansson granted. "Where in hell are you supposed to find him, then?"

Thinking aloud, Slade said, "He must have left us something. Otherwise, we have to search the town from door to door."

He looked around the tidy kitchen, seeking anything that might pass for a clue. Another note would be too obvious. The mayor would certainly have found it. Possibly some object out of place, or . . .

"Is this yours?" he asked Johansson, stepping toward the counter where a cutting board and butcher's knife lay side by side.

"The knife?" Johansson asked. "We've had it for—"

"No, *this*." Slade pointed now.

Johansson stared, then shook his head. "No. No, it isn't."

"Well, then," Slade replied.

And palmed what might have been a coffee cup but wasn't.

"Hey," Vandiver said. "Is that—?"

"A shaving mug," Slade said, already moving toward the door.

19

It galled Slade when the pieces started clicking into place at last, through no achievement of his own. He told himself it wasn't his fault, anybody could've missed it. Anybody *had*, in fact—and, he suspected, not only in Jubilee.

A barber who had shaved his way around the world and back again. Where better to begin, if you were Irish, than in England, right next door? And once you were in England, why not go to London, with half of its four million people in need of a shave?

London, where barbers practiced surgery, aside from scraping whiskers off and cutting hair.

London, where Jack the Ripper killed and mutilated working girls during the grim autumn of 1888.

Five years ago.

Were they the killer's first? Slade couldn't guess and didn't have the time or resources at hand to make a global search of newspapers. He didn't know the normal age when barbers started practicing their trade, much less the "normal" age when maniacs began to kill.

He'd pegged Connor MacGowan's age somewhere in the vicinity of thirty-four to thirty-six. Certainly old enough to ply a razor—or a scalpel—in the streets of London's slums when Red Jack was at large. If Slade could find a way to track him backward, would he find girls dead in Ireland, or in other parts of England? Coming forward, would a trail of blood and butchered bodies stretch around the world, from Britain all the way to Jubilee?

Slade didn't want to think about that, now. He couldn't dwell on the mistakes of others that had left the madman free to cross his path today, in this specific place.

At the moment, Slade was focused on Emmeline Johansson's plight and hoping that he wouldn't be too late.

Wherever he was going.

Come alone, MacGowan had demanded, but that didn't tell Slade *where* he was supposed to come. First thought, of course, the spotless barber's shop where he'd first seen MacGowan's smiling, freckled face and listened to his blarney while a razor slid across his throat.

The Ripper could have killed him then, but would've had to bolt immediately, couldn't claim it was an accidental slip or twitch. As satisfying as it might have been, it would have spoiled MacGowan's game.

Whatever *that* was.

Slade had spent hours pondering the killer's motive. Did he hate all women? And, if so, why target only prostitutes? Simply because they were available? Was he a victim of venereal disease, infected by a working girl, or had he known and loved someone who was? The wilder speculation on Red Jack had run to Devil worshipers, mad doctors, and the like.

Was he a sodomite, as some had claimed of London's Jack? That theory, although fairly popular, rang hollow in Slade's mind. Since pinning on a badge, he'd seen that killers driven by a sex urge generally targeted their objects of desire. A lunatic who lusted after females preyed on girls or women, and the same should be true in reverse.

Guess I'll just have to ask him, Slade thought, as he neared the barber's shop. Across the street, he knew, Vandiver would be watching from his office with a Winchester in hand, prepared to put his two cents in if things went sour. Still, he wouldn't show himself unless he knew for sure that Slade was down and out. Untimely intervention could spell death for Emmeline Johansson.

Unless she was already dead.

It would simplify things for MacGowan, but Slade clung to hope that he'd find the mayor's wife still alive, in one piece. There'd been no blood where she was taken, and he figured that MacGowan still had chloroform to spare. It was an oddity that no one on the street had seen the two of them together, much less managed to observe the barber carrying a woman in his arms, but that was life, as any lawman could've said.

Never a witness handy when you needed one.

Slade found the barber's shop unlocked, went in with one hand on his holstered Colt, and checked the rooms from front to back.

Nothing.

Which left the home address that Vandiver had offered for MacGowan. He would try it, next. And if he didn't find the killer with his hostage there, what options would remain?

Slade didn't want to think about that at the moment.

Not until he had no other choice.

"He'll be here soon," Connor MacGowan told his guest. "No cause for worry in the least, marm."

Well, there *was* good cause for worry, if the truth be told.

It simply wouldn't do her any good.

Emmeline Johansson lay spread-eagle on an oval oaken table, ropes securing her wrists and ankles to the table's legs below her. She was nude, but covered with a sheet in temporary deference to modesty.

Hers or his own? MacGowan wasn't sure and frankly didn't give a tinker's damn.

She was an object to MacGowan—say a tool—no more or less important than the others he had ranged beside her on the table. Glinting steel, those were, and razor-edged. The perfect items for transforming tender flesh.

Of course, the secret he had sought for so long was not hidden in the good wife's loins. She didn't qualify for clinical dissection in the huntsman's quest. But she would serve a role today, entirely unexpected when she'd gotten up that morning and begun to putter through her basic, mediocre life.

Slade might have reached the shop by now and maybe finished searching it. The timetable was flexible. Its start depended on the mayor, when he got finished reassuring troubled citizens and ambled home again. Give him a bit of time to notice that his wife was gone, then find the message in the kitchen. Hail the constable or Slade, whichever was more readily available—and add more time if it was Mills Vandiver, since he'd have to turn around and look for Slade, to share the shocking news.

Say thirty minutes to an hour, then, from when Roland Johansson crossed his own threshold until the search began. Jack Slade would recognize and understand the clue—the signature—MacGowan had provided for him at the mayor's house. After that . . . well, it was all downhill.

MacGowan knew his man. Slade wouldn't dawdle, wouldn't pause to speculate—and wouldn't hesitate to kill him, given half a chance. The mayor's lady was his insurance, or a major part of it. MacGowan had some other tricks left, up his sleeve.

He didn't plan to die today—or any day at all, in Jubilee. The present exercise was one part cleaning house, one part a personal farewell, and one part a diversion for his getaway. MacGowan had a good, fast horse outside, all saddled up and ready to leave Jubilee and its survivors in a cloud of dust.

For dust thou art, and unto dust shalt thou return.

God's disappointed words to his original creations, after the first whore lured Adam into carnal sin.

Eve knew the secret, and MacGowan wished that he could meet her. Introduce himself and delve into her mystery. Too late for that, of course, so he made due with pallid imitations of the first deceiver.

Was that a quiet footstep on the walk, outside? MacGowan held his breath, to listen better, but that only amplified the pulse beat in his ears. A long, tense moment later, he heard yet another footfall and was sure.

Then came the solid, eager knocking on his door.

"Come in!" he called out, smiling now. "You're right on time. Let's have a word together, Jack to Jack."

"You'll want to leave your weapons by the door," MacGowan ordered, from another room, as Slade entered his modest home. "No nasty tricks, now, or the lady pays for 'em."

Slade thought about it for a moment, pictured striding through the small house with his Peacemaker in hand and firing as soon as he spotted the barber, but how could he know that there'd be a clear shot? It wouldn't take a heartbeat for MacGowan to slit Emmeline Johansson's throat, and even if Slade killed him in the next split second, it would be too late.

Unbuckling his gunbelt, Slade stooped down and set it on the floor. He considered keeping the Colt and tucking it under his belt at the back, but knew there'd be some kind of test to confirm that he'd followed orders. Feeling naked,

Slade followed the voice to find his quarry in a combination kitchen-dining room.

The meal, it seemed, would be Emmeline Johansson.

She was lying on a table, anchored to its legs by rope at her extremities and covered by a sheet—which MacGowan whipped aside as Slade entered the room. Slade grimaced, trying not to see the naked flesh displayed before him, but he registered that it was still unmarked by wounds.

"You look embarrassed, Jack," MacGowan said. "Why not relax? Enjoy it while you can."

"You've got me at a disadvantage," Slade replied. "What should I call you, now?"

"If 'Jack' confuses you too much, just stick with 'Connor.' Anyhow, what's in a name?"

"Can you even remember yours?" asked Slade.

"Vaguely. It doesn't matter, now."

Emmeline Johansson stirred and moaned, a mournful sound. Slade kept his eyes away from her, locked on the madman's face. Negotiating over hostages had never been his strong point, but he had to try. Relieve some of the tension first, if possible.

"So, that *was* you in London, then?" he asked.

"Indeed, old son. A modest effort, looking back, though I'll admit it caused a stir."

"We heard about it over here, of course," Slade said. "I guess folks read about it everywhere."

"Not my debut, but still," MacGowan said. "The papers ran away with it, of course. I only studied five harlots in Whitechapel, no matter what they're claiming now."

Studied? Slade let it go and framed another question.

"And the letters?"

"Most of 'em weren't mine. Reporters wrote their fair share, boosting circulation, and the loonies climbed aboard. They always do. They're still writing, from what I understand. Can't let it go."

"But you moved on," Slade said.

"Oh, my, yes. To the great U.S. of A., after some other ports of call. Someday, when the story's told at last . . . well . . . you won't be around to read it, Jack."

MacGowan chose some kind of carving knife from the array of cutlery before him. A wedge-shaped blade, at least ten inches long.

"You mentioned study, earlier," he said. "What's that about?"

"We don't have time for that, now, Jack," MacGowan said. "Can't leave Hizzoner and the constable on tenterhooks. It wouldn't be . . . humane."

"I've given thought to how you might come out of this alive," Slade said.

"That's mighty kind of you," MacGowan said. "It's also horse shite, I suspect."

Slade shrugged. "You want to hang, it's fine with me, but if you'd rather live . . ."

"And how would that work, Jack? I'm guessing it involves releasing sweet Emmeline, here, with her lovely skin intact."

"Step one, without a doubt," said Slade.

"And step two, let me guess, is where I throw myself upon some judge's tender mercy, eh?"

"No, mercy wouldn't work," Slade answered. "You would have to plead insanity."

MacGowan gaped at Slade, a flood of livid color rising in his face. The long knife trembled in his hand, above Emmeline Johansson's abdomen.

"*Insane*, is it? Just up and tell the world I'm crazy as a shit-house rat?"

"They have a hospital in Fort Smith, Arkansas," Slade said. "It's not a palace, but it's better than the gallows."

"Is it, now? You ever see the inside of a lunatic asylum, Jack? Ever submit yourself to such an institution's tender, loving care?"

Slade shook his head.

"I didn't think so. Still, it's kind of you to offer, on behalf of your employers, even though they'd laugh me out of court."

"How so?" asked Slade.

"A lawman ought to study law, Jack. I guess you never heard of Dan M'Naghten, eh?"

"Can't say I have," Slade answered.

"Danny boy was Scottish. Killed himself one of your lower British civil servants, fifty years ago. The court found him insane and made a list of rules for future cases, to be ready when they came along. The same rules used today in your great country, I should mention."

"So?"

"So, Jack, to escape the rope, you first need a diseased mind, meaning some disease that doctors recognize. Next comes an inability to comprehend the nature of an act. Let's say I open sweet Emmeline from bum to breadbasket, believing she's a watermelon, eh? And third, crazy or not, I'd have to prove I didn't know my acts were criminal. Strike three, as I believe your baseballers would say."

Slade edged closer to the table, saying, "I still think—"

"That's far enough, old son. You have a clear view of the operating table, as it is."

"You can't believe I'll just stand here and watch you do this," Slade replied.

"Indeed, not," said MacGowan, picking up a cleaver with his left hand, as a balance to the long knife in his right. "You're bound to stop me, I expect."

And with a smile, he rushed around the table, straight at Slade.

Slade hated knife fights and avoided them whenever possible. Of course, it wasn't always possible, and now he missed the knife sheathed on his gunbelt, lying far beyond his reach in Jack the Ripper's living room.

His first trick, dodging two blades as MacGowan charged him, thrusting with the knife and hacking with his cleaver. In a normal contest, both combatants would have knives, or there would only be one blade in play. The unarmed fighter could try different moves to pin, throw, or disarm his adversary.

Not this time.

If Slade tried clutching at MacGowan's knife arm, he'd be open to the cleaver that could split his skull, maybe decapitate him if MacGowan's swing was powerful enough. Go for the cleaver as it fell, and he'd be slashed or punctured by MacGowan's carving knife. A major wound would put him down, but any cuts at all would weaken Slade through loss of blood, maybe disable him by slicing muscle.

And the damned town didn't even have a doctor left to stitch him up.

The "good" news: they were fighting in a kitchen, with utensils on display. Aside from London Jack's remaining blades, laid out beside Emmeline, there was a heavy skillet on the stove, some hanging pots and pans, and who knew what else in the drawers.

Retreating from a bright whirlwind of steel, Slade tried his luck, reached out to snag a drawer and hurled it at MacGowan, spraying him with silverware. MacGowan slapped the forks and spoons aside, but caught the drawer itself high on his scalp and staggered back a step, blood showing from a smallish cut.

"Have to do better, I'm afraid," MacGowan goaded Slade.

"I'm working on it," Slade replied, already feeling short of breath.

He glanced off toward the knives arrayed beside Emmeline. MacGowan caught the look and said, "Think twice about that, Jackie boy. Try using any of my toys against me, and I'll slit her throat."

Slade took the madman at his word. Why *wouldn't* he retaliate against Johansson's wife for something Slade might do? She was another weapon in his arsenal, perhaps most dangerous of all because she was distracting Slade and limiting his options in the fight.

If at first you don't succeed . . .

Slade backpedaled, grabbed a second kitchen drawer and threw it. Cleaning rags this time, a wasted effort as MacGowan ducked the flying drawer completely. Still, during the second when he was distracted, Slade scooped up the skillet. Six or seven pounds of solid cast iron in his hand.

Not bad.

Slade stood his ground this time, swaying a little, when MacGowan came for him. His skillet blocked the falling cleaver with a *clang* that sent vibrations up his right arm, nearly to the shoulder. At the same time, Slade grabbed for MacGowan's right hand with his left and slashed a kick toward the Irishman's groin. Missed that with the pointed toe of his boot but struck MacGowan's thigh a solid blow.

The Ripper grunted, cursing, leaned into his knife thrust with a will, while drawing back his cleaver for another swing. Slade took a chance and rammed the skillet's edge into MacGowan's face, feeling his front teeth buckle inward.

Slade's second kick was better, found its mark precisely, and the killer's breath rushed out of him. He still had strength enough to lunge again, but Slade stepped well inside the probing knife hand, let the cleaver hurtle past him on his right, and brought the heavy skillet down atop MacGowan's head.

His man was falling, and he leaped clear, let MacGowan drop facedown. Another wheezing grunt came out of him, as Slade stepped on his left wrist, pried the cleaver free from spastic fingers, and hurled it toward the far side of the kitchen.

Looking for the knife, Slade only saw MacGowan's right arm tucked beneath him. Ready with the skillet drawn well back to land a crushing blow, he turned MacGowan over. Saw the ten-inch blade buried between its owner's ribs.

MacGowan blinked at Slade, blew crimson bubbles from his lips, trying to speak.

"Too bad . . . now neither . . . one of us . . . will ever . . ."

Ever what? Slade nearly asked him, as the light went out behind the Ripper's eyes. Then he decided that he didn't give a damn, too busy looking for the sheet to drape Emmeline Johansson's form and yet another of MacGowan's blades to cut her bonds.

The next morning, finally, Slade said good-bye to Jubilee. The mayor and constable were at the livery to see him off, Roland Johansson still wearing a vaguely dazed expression on his face, Vandiver simply looking weary from the whole ordeal.

"Your wife's all right this morning?" Slade inquired.

Johansson bobbed his head and shrugged at the same time, an awkward set of moves. "Embarrassed, mostly, to be seen . . . the way she was," he said.

"Nothing to be ashamed of, there," Slade said. And quickly added, "It was out of her control, I mean."

"Oh, sure." The mayor gazed off along Main Street and said, "I wonder if we'll ever be the same?"

Uncertain whether he meant Jubilee or his domestic situation, Slade replied, "I couldn't answer that. People survive. Towns, too. Sometimes they learn and grow."

"I hope so," said Johansson, sounding lost.

"So, what about them books?" Vandiver asked.

Searching MacGowan's house, Slade had discovered thirteen journals filled with rambling thoughts, discussion of so-called experiments, and diagrams that nearly put him off his final breakfast at MacDonald's restaurant. Hunger had won out in the end, but still . . .

"I'll show them to Judge Dennison," he said. "See what he wants to do about them."

"All crazy talk, I'm guessing."

"If it's not," Slade told him, "it'll do until some comes along."

"Some fella from the newspapers will likely pay a pretty penny for it, though," Vandiver said.

"Not my department," Slade replied.

The books, filled with MacGowan's spidery script, were tied behind Slade's saddle in the carpetbag their author kept them in. Slade thought it would be raining sleet in Hell before he opened them again.

"Whatever happens," said the mayor, returning to the here and now, "we're in your debt."

"Forget it," Slade advised. *God knows I'll try to.*

"Well."

Johansson and Vandiver had run out of things to say, and it was just as well. Slade wanted to be on his way, back home to Faith. Each mile he put behind him now would place him that much closer to normality.

Closer to Faith.

His roan seemed anxious, too, after the days and nights pent up inside the livery. She broke into a trot along Main Street, then pushed into a gallop as they reached the edge of town.

Jack Slade hung on and let her run.

20

"I do . . . I *do* . . . I *do* . . ."

Slade thought he nearly had it right, although his shirt was threatening to strangle him. His shoes, new black ones, pinched his feet, and there was something going on behind him, underneath his trousers, with his underwear. Altogether, he felt trussed and bound, a hundred miles away from anything resembling comfort.

And he'd never been happier.

This was the day he'd been anticipating since he had dredged up the nerve to propose. The image of it had sustained him on the long ride back from Jubilee, after his mare had tired of galloping and struck a normal walking pace to suit herself. Thinking of Faith had kept him from MacGowan's hellish journals on the night he'd spent camped out, beneath a sky that seemed latent with menace.

How could any person drift so far from common, everyday humanity? The outlaws Slade had known killed for basic reasons—money or revenge, sometimes for sheer excitement—that a normal mind could comprehend. Even

when he had faced the Benders, there had been a brutal
kind of logic to their crimes: they lived by killing others,
taking everything their victims had, like sea raiders or
Mongols from the olden times.

But with MacGowan, Red Jack, whatever his name was,
even sampling his demented ravings had made Slade's mind
feel unhinged. The words were plain enough, but might as
well have represented some exotic language from the Orient
or Africa, for all the sense they made.

And, God, the diagrams . . .

Slade had given the books to Judge Dennison, hoping
that he'd never see them again. Whether the judge burned
them, committed them to memory, or sent them to the Li-
brary of Congress, Slade wanted no more than to forget his
time in Jubilee as rapidly as possible.

But something told him that it wouldn't be that easy.

Doggedly, he gripped the mental reins and drew his stray
thoughts back to Faith. Though they'd visited over the past
two days, there'd been no sleeping over for him since he had
returned. Her notion of beginning fresh, and Slade knew
better than to argue. He had caught a glimpse of what appeared to be her wedding dress, but Faith had kept him from
it with a kiss and not-so-gentle shove, telling him bad luck
might result if he was nosy.

God forbid.

For years, Slade had believed he was a lucky man—at
cards, with the ladies, and the few times that he'd had to
fight in earnest for his life. But meeting Faith had made him
understand that he could ask for more than simply getting
by from day to day. He could be happy without drinking,
without raking in a poker pot or spending half an hour with
a whore.

That thought, in turn, reminded Slade of the girls who'd
died in Jubilee and those who had survived. He couldn't save
them from the lives they'd chosen; he wasn't a reformer or
evangelist. He couldn't travel back through time and find the

point where any one of them had gone astray, correct them in the past, and thereby help them to avoid their fate.

Fate, so close in sound to *Faith*, brought him back.

While Slade rehearsed his vows, he watched and waited for the Reverend Alton Frick, a Methodist from Enid who would marry any couple for a fee, whether they patronized his church or not. It seemed a fair arrangement, since a preacher had to eat, the same as anybody else.

No sign of Frick so far, but there was still an hour and something left before the ceremony was supposed to start. Slade reckoned he was on the way by now, had likely reached Faith's land and met one of her outriders, who'd guide him in.

All perfect, on a perfect day.

Faith Connover had nearly finished dressing, with some help from Eileen Drood, her closest neighbor to the west. They had been friends for six years, going on a lifetime, and Eileen had volunteered to help with any details that seemed likely to undo Faith's special day. There'd been no crises yet, thank heavens, but a helping hand was always welcome at such times.

Eileen had served another function, too. As Faith's de facto matron of honor, she'd volunteered her husband to stand up as Jack's best man. They barely knew each other, but it plugged a slot that Jack, as stubborn as he was, had deemed impossible to fill.

He wouldn't ask Judge Dennison because, he said, it wasn't right to have your boss as a best man. He wouldn't ask another deputy because they might be called away at any time, and picking one could put the others' noses out of joint. That had eliminated everyone he knew in town, beyond a casual "hello" in passing, and had left Jack visibly depressed for—as he put it—ruining the day.

Faith had been pleased to solve that problem, had enjoyed seeing the storm clouds lift from Jack's face when she told him. He had offered no objection, one more sign that he had reached his wit's end and was dangling. Not afraid of marriage, no. Faith knew that wasn't true, in both her mind and heart. Nor was he frightened by a thought of being tethered to the ranch, the soil, since no such thing had been discussed between them.

Change itself troubled a certain kind of man, but once committed to it and enlightened to its benefits, Jack was prepared to lead a new life and enjoy it to the fullest.

If only she could get him off the road, away from criminals, out from behind his badge.

There'd been no detailed talk of that, though Jack himself had raised the question once. Faith had admitted worrying about him, saw no reason she should lie, but told him honestly that she desired his happiness in all aspects of life. She didn't care how Jack earned money—or, indeed, if he held any job at all. If something happened in the law-enforcement line that took him from her, she would grieve.

What else was there to say?

At the same time, she knew that worrying about her attitude, her fear, could get him killed. If Jack was called to face a gunman, he could not afford distractions that might cloud his mind or slow his hand.

Strangely, she never thought of them as killer's hands. She knew that Jack had killed men, but she didn't have a number fixed in mind and knew that every time he pulled a trigger it was necessary. Jack was like a soldier sent to battle, with a job to do, and he performed as circumstances demanded. Her fondest hope—aside from children, naturally—was that Jack could find his peace and leave the war to someone else.

But as to when or whether that would happen, Faith had no idea.

And meanwhile, there was love. Enough to carry both of them through life . . . and possibly another one or two, to spare.

They hadn't talked about that, either, but Faith reckoned Jack could be persuaded, once she took the matter well in hand.

"Easy, you said."

Burch Thornton turned to face the man who'd spoken and replied, "It will be. Trust me."

"*Trust* you? I don't hardly *know* you, boy. You talk a lot, but talk's cheap. You say easy pickin's, but I'm lookin' at two riders packin' Winchesters and Colts."

"Two out of six or seven," Thornton said. "She can't afford no more'n that. It's half the men we got."

"You mean that *I* got," said the older man. "You've only rid with us a little while, and if this thing goes sour on us, you ain't ridin' anywhere no more."

Thornton was sick and tired of being bossed around and threatened by the older man, by all of them, but that was how things worked with gangs. He was the new guy, hadn't proved himself as yet, to earn respect.

That was about to change.

"Them two are nothin'," he assured the man in charge, while handing back the spyglass. "One with the black hat is Euliss Green—I'd call him 'Useless'—and the other one is Ed Murdoch."

A special anger churned in Thornton's gut at the sight of Murdoch, who had tattled to the boss lady and got him fired for nothing much at all. A little peek and borrowing some trifles from his bunkmates.

"Reckon you can take 'em?" asked the man in charge, a smirking kind of question.

"Sure I can," Thornton replied, before he had a chance to think about it. Wondering, almost before the words were out, if he could follow through. "Gimme the Sharps, and—"

"No. I mean ride down there like a man and *take* 'em."

Shit!

"I left on bad terms," Thornton said. "It could be they'll shoot me on sight."

"Only one way to know, eh?"

"I don't think—"

"That's right. I'm the thinker. You shut up and do like I tell ya."

Thornton looked around and saw the others sitting easy in their saddles, hands on pistols and a couple of them smiling at him. Nothing he could do but follow orders now and try to stay alive, keeping his eyes peeled down the road for any chance to get even.

Thornton drew his Smith & Wesson Model 3 revolver, cradling it in his lap to let the saddle horn conceal a bit of it. He clucked and spurred his piebald gelding, slumping forward in his saddle to reduce the size of the target he presented as he rode down the slope toward Green and Murdoch.

They were passing, might not even notice Thornton if his luck held, but his orders were to take them, not just watch them ride on by. If neither one of them should glance in his direction, he would have to hail them, take an even bigger risk to satisfy the old man and the others.

Joining up with them had seemed to be a good idea when Thornton did it, laying out his plan for easy money and a little sweet revenge. The old man liked it, seemed to have some kind of grudge against Judge Dennison in Enid, and the others went along because the old man ran the game. You didn't like it, you were out—and like as not, that meant that you were dead.

Too many secrets in the family to let one of its members wander off and carry tales.

Now Thornton was a member, and he had to pay his way. At least until he found a way to change the rules.

Murdoch was first to spot him, from a couple hundred

yards. He said something to Green and they reined in, waiting. Too far away to recognize him, Thornton knew, but he had to be ready when they did.

"Hey, fellas!" he called out to them, when he had halved the gap. "You miss me?"

Couldn't hear the talk between them, but he knew that neither one of them would spare him any compliments.

"What are you doin' here?" Green asked him. Fifty yards and closing.

"Thought I'd try'n get my old job back," said Thornton, laughing at himself to put the pair of them at ease. "Think she's forgiven me?"

"Thornton, you were warned—"

His first shot silenced any threat that Murdoch planned to make, punched through his upper chest, and pitched him over backward from his saddle as his horse shied. Green was slapping leather, but the odds were all against him now, as Thornton swung around and shot him in the face.

Not bad.

He turned back toward the ridge, could feel the old man watching through his spyglass. Thornton raised his six-gun, twirled it with his index finger through the trigger guard.

"Well?" he called back to them. "What are you waiting for?"

The minister made it on time, but only just. He was apologetic, talked about some problem back in town Slade didn't understand or care a thing about. By now, Slade's feelings were precisely split between anticipation and anxiety.

The good part was all Faith. Her smile and all the rest of her, soon to be his forever, giving Slade a sense of peace he'd never known before. Knowing that she would always be there, always loving him because she said so, and he didn't think she'd ever learned to tell a decent lie.

The bad side: Slade himself. Self-doubts that haunted

him relentlessly. There was a chance he'd let her down somehow, not even meaning to, and Slade thought it might kill him to see disappointment in her eyes. He'd never be unfaithful to her, wouldn't even think of it, but there were other ways to wound a woman, break her down by slow degrees until her love turned into loathing, and the stupid bastard who had caused it never even saw it coming.

Leaving her alone to hunt for thieves and killers might do that, Slade thought. Not right away, but maybe over time. He'd been a marshal when they met. She'd never known him any other way, but Faith might still be hoping for a different life. And soured hopes were just a step away from letting someone go.

Around the time that Reverend Frick arrived, Slade thought he heard gunshots, a pair of them, but far away. Most likely on Faith's property, considering its size, but there could be a dozen explanations that were no cause for alarm. A rattlesnake, an injured steer relieved of misery, maybe a couple of the hands signaling one another from a distance.

Anything.

The one thing that he absolutely *would not* do was ride out to investigate, just when the minister was getting ready to begin. If Slade did that, he knew he might as well keep going all the way to Mexico or California and be done with it.

Home weddings had their compensations. They cut down on costs and made it easier to limit guest lists without hurting anybody's tender feelings. They were more relaxed, in Slade's experience, than ceremonies carried out in church. But there were drawbacks, too. For instance, Faith had a piano, but she was the only person present who could play it, meaning that she couldn't hear the wedding march as she emerged to join the rest of them, a vision that appeared to float, rather than walking.

Slade was dumbstruck, absolutely stunned by the emotions

roiling up inside him. Nothing he had ever seen or felt before prepared him for the vision of his bride approaching, smiling bashfully, almost as if they'd never met before.

Another moment, and she stood beside him. Slade faced Pastor Frick, hoping that gravity would do its job and that he wouldn't simply drift away.

Another gunshot. Closer?

Never mind.

"Dearly beloved, we are gathered here today . . ."

Slade couldn't keep from smiling, thought his face would split wide-open any second now and spill whatever little brains he had.

". . . to join this man and woman in the bond of holy—"

"Riders!" someone cried out, forcing Slade to turn against his will and face the sound. He recognized the horseman who was rapidly approaching. Art Hanes, one of Faith's men, with his shirtfront crimson-stained.

"Riders!" Hanes gasped again, about to tumble from his saddle as he reached them. "Riders, coming fast!"

The rest, Slade would remember only vaguely, and long afterward. Trying to question Hanes before the man died or lost consciousness. Failing at that, and hearing Faith say, "There they are!" before Slade saw the horsemen charging from atop a ridge, maybe a thousand yards away.

It took another beat for Slade to register exactly what was happening. Shocked by the incongruity of it, the sense of violation, he recovered quickly, acting more on instinct than with any kind of plan in mind.

"Inside!" he shouted, steering Faith by her right arm, across the yard and up the two steps to her front porch, through the door and into shade.

"Stay here!" he ordered, moving toward the gun rack on the south wall, twenty feet away. There was no time to reach the bedroom and his gunbelt coiled atop a closet shelf. He